SOME

UNFINISHED

BUSINESS

SOME UNFINISHED BUSINESS

a novel by

ANTANAS SILEIKA

Piretei —
viso geriausio!

Antanas Sileika

Cormorant Books

The publisher gratefully acknowledges the support of the Canada Council
for the Arts and the Ontario Arts Council for its publishing program.
We acknowledge the financial support of the Government of Canada through
the Canada Book Fund (CBF) for our publishing activities, and the
Government of Ontario through Ontario Creates, an agency of the Ontario
Ministry of Culture, and the Ontario Book Publishing Tax Credit Program.

LIBRARY AND ARCHIVES CANADA CATALOGUING IN PUBLICATION

Title: Some unfinished business / a novel by Antanas Sileika.
Names: Sileika, Antanas, 1953– author.
Identifiers: Canadiana (print) 20220459746 | Canadiana (ebook) 20220459789 |
ISBN 9781770866737 (softcover) | ISBN 9781770866744 (HTML)
Classification: LCC PS8587.I2656 S66 2023 | DDC C813/.54—dc23

Cover image and design: Angel Guerra / Archetype
Interior text design: Tannice Goddard, tannicegdesigns.ca

Manufactured by Friesens in Altona, Manitoba in January, 2023.

This book is printed on 100% post-consumer waste recycled paper.

Printed and bound in Canada.

CORMORANT BOOKS INC.
260 ISHPADINAA (SPADINA) AVENUE, SUITE 502, TKARONTO (TORONTO), ON M5T 2E4
www.cormorantbooks.com

Dedicated to the residents of Lyn Lake (Lynežeris),
living and dead

1

PAŽAISLIS MONASTERY ASYLUM
SOVIET SOCIALIST REPUBLIC OF LITHUANIA, 1959

MARTIN GINGERLY SET HIS knapsack on the stone floor and winced at the clinking it made despite his care. He listened for a moment, but there was no other sound or movement in the gloom of the church. He looked up.

High in the cupola's frescoes, the Virgin Mary was being crowned and an orchestra of angels played lutes, harps, and cymbals. Other angels, from seraphim to cherubim, spilled across the heavens and the many martyrs displayed their wounds. But the light was poor and the heavens were very far above. It was hard to make out finer details.

This milling crowd of saints and sinners peering down from the frescoes in the dome of the church tended to frighten any patients who appeared below. Even a healthy mind might have trouble with this kind of divine display and scrutiny. If the uneasy souls below had demons in them, those devils became uneasy and began to squirm, precipitating tremors in some and shrieks of fear and rage in others.

Even simple depressives and neurotics could not resist looking and suffering the kind of moral vertigo an inexperienced alpinist suffered by looking down. As a result, none of the troubled internees could be allowed into the old baroque church of the former monastery. Far better to close that door and use the old church only for storage.

In any case, these days the heavenly hosts didn't pay much attention to what went on below. Those on the ground had to settle their own affairs now, to determine what was a sin and what was not, and to apportion reward or punishment on a scale with variable weights.

Martin had stumbled into the place while searching for a certain patient. Obviously, he wasn't in here. The rest of the former monastery complex was a useful sanatorium for its dozens of cells among several wings. The massive wooden doors and high walls contained the troubled and murmuring invalids, each assigned to a particular wing for those with a particular affliction.

Martin stood in the dim light of the church and surveyed the storage boxes, old beds, broken chairs, and stacks of manila folders bulging with histories of psychosis and tied up with black ribbons. Outside, it was a spring evening, and up at this northern latitude it would still be light for very long. Not inside the church, though. Here came only cycles of perpetual dusk followed by darkness.

Martin wore sturdy working men's clothes and a short-billed cap on his head because he had lost his hair in a fever in the gulag. He was only twenty-six. Some of the years had been difficult and made him look older, but he had borne a great deal and come out stronger for it. Others had broken, but he refused to break.

The Pažaislis Monastery was a convent no more, its nuns evicted and scattered in 1948. The Soviets went about their activities: closing the monasteries, confiscating the farms, taking away the businesses and shipping off streams of men, women, and children in a river of humanity to the far reaches of the massive prison state. The Komi Republic, Krasnoyarsk, Irkutsk, and other locations were very far away from the newly-annexed, formerly-independent state of Lithuania.

Now Pažaislis was a crumbling asylum near Kaunas, a place

where the mentally unstable were kept in the cells of former nuns who were making their precarious way as unmarried women in the Soviet world. Where once there was prayer, now there was madness. The grounds were walled to contain it, albeit imperfectly, and the madness pooled here and there and bled out everywhere, and after a while, it didn't even feel like madness any longer, just the way of life in this country.

Such an unhappy place in such an unlucky country! First came the Soviets in 1940, arresting and deporting and leaving a trail of murdered bodies as they fled before the Nazis in 1941. Then came the many tens of thousands of deaths, mostly of Jews, killed by the Germans and their local collaborators. In 1944, the Soviets returned. Those who could, those with a little education, fled west. Those caught behind had to adapt or resist. Resisters were doomed to die eventually, but those who chose to adapt were sometimes lucky. Many times not.

The asylum was not all that far from Vilnius, but it had taken Martin a day of hitching rides and then walking out to the countryside near Kaunas under light rain. He was wet, but as a former farm boy and prisoner was not greatly inconvenienced by a little bad weather. His backpack was heavy and its contents were fragile, but he had once returned across all of Russia with more weight than this.

It had not been easy to find the man he was looking for, but the gentle library director back in Vilnius seemed to know just about everything there was to know about everyone in the small country.

"No one likes to talk about Kostas much," said Director Stonkus, studying the spine of a Polish volume bound in leather. Many subjects were too risky to talk about. Silence was safest. The Lithuanians even had a saying, about the virtues of silence. *Tyla gera byla* — silence is the best defence. Maybe the idea was never to be noticed at all, to behave like a mouse and to lose the squeak.

It was a sign of the director's regard for Martin that he spoke at all about the private life of the esteemed Kostas.

"His drinking was completely out of hand. You saw him here that day when you were married, but that was nothing compared to what came later. He couldn't go out to children's events any more. He sat at the bar in the commissary in the basement of the Writers' Union all day long. Even his wife couldn't lure him home. His skin turned yellow. I expected his liver to explode at any moment. It still might, with what he put it through. And worst of all, he started to talk all sorts of nonsense after he'd been drinking for a while."

Director Stonkus stopped there like a man who decided he had said too much. Like Kostas, he had violated the rule of silence and now seemed to regret it. One must never talk too much in the Soviet Union, unless on certain subjects. Stonkus opened the book and began to read it silently, but Martin could not let it go at that.

"So Kostas is still down there at the Writers' Union Bar?"

Stonkus looked up at him, exasperated. "Mr. Kostas is recovering in a rest home near Kaunas and I am sure the whole nation wishes him quick recovery from his illness so he can return to his valuable work."

PAŽAISLIS WAS NOT AN ordinary drunk tank. A man of Kostas's stature received the best treatment, and the Pažaislis rehabilitation facility was intended for party members. But even the best rehab centre in the Soviet Union had only a mouldering former nun's cell where the man was locked in a room between injections and cleanings in order to shout, tremble, and weep his way through his withdrawal.

The asylum was imperfectly restricted territory. There were walls, but they were in poor repair and easily breached in several places. There was a doorman at the front gate, but he went for walks and napped right in his chair. It took a while for Martin to get his bearings once he was inside.

The night shift orderlies in the lunchroom didn't care who Martin was. They told him the cell doors were locked for the night.

These men were thuggish but corruptible, and one bottle of vodka was all it took to find out where Kostas was and that the windows on the ground floor of his wing were barred with hinges and clasps on the outside. After all, no expected anyone to break *into* one of those rooms.

"Lights out" was more an aspiration than a reality in this northern climate, where the summer sky was barely willing to darken at ten in the evening. Only a skeleton crew stayed behind for the evening and night, and part of that crew could be counted upon to be sitting at the night station with a bottle of vodka. Given Martin's donation, they now had a second one, and besides, it was Saturday night and no important administrators would be showing up the next morning. The orderlies saw no relationship between their own drinking and that of the recovering alcoholics in their cells.

The evening was still bright, but it didn't really matter because there were no guards patrolling the property. Martin made his way through the yard past broken farm machinery unused for a very long time, a rusted-out Studebaker truck, one of the many given to the Soviets by the Americans during the war.

He made his way across the unkempt yard and peered through the window into the cell. The walls had not been painted in a long time and what paint there was came flaking off. Kostas lay on his narrow cot with his eyes closed. He twitched like someone in a dream remembering a blow or an insult. Martin smeared a little grease to loosen the pin that held the bars shut and a little more on the hinges. The metal still squeaked as he opened the bars. He pushed open the window, set his heavy bag inside, and then climbed in.

Kostas had turned on his side, and his eyes were open as he watched Martin reach back outside to pull the bars shut. Kostas's greying hair had been cut short in the hospital, but the widow's peak was still there. His skin was a ghastly shade of yellow that showed the damage to his liver, and his eyes were watery. He wore a stained, grey smock over underclothes.

"Close the window too," said Kostas. "The place is drafty."

The room contained a chair and a small table with a pitcher of water on it and a glass. There were two buckets at the end of the bed, but thankfully, these were both empty.

"You don't seem surprised to see me," said Martin. "Do you know who I am?"

"I have no idea."

"But I remember you all too well," said Martin.

2

FROM THE TOWN OF RUDNIA TO
THE VILLAGE OF LYN LAKE, VARĖNA PROVINCE,
SOVIET SOCIALIST REPUBLIC OF LITHUANIA,
TWELVE YEARS EARLIER, 1947

"AH, HERE YOU ARE," said the principal to young Martin on the front steps of the high school. The principal was standing beside a tall man with long, wavy hair swept back from a widow's peak on a high forehead. Over his suit he wore a black raincoat that went down below his knees and he was carrying a battered suitcase in one hand and an overstuffed briefcase in the other. Martin was fourteen and had no idea of how a bohemian might look, but he sensed this man was not like anyone he had ever seen before.

"Take the suitcase," said the principal.

Almost a thousand people lived in Rudnia, and to Martin, it was practically a metropolis, with a big wooden church with its tin roof and a two-storey high school that attracted youths with ambitions. Ordinary children made do with the four grades offered in village schools.

"Mr. Kostas is the new elementary teacher for Lyn Lake. I want you to take him home with you and put him up at your father's house," said the principal.

Martin's family hadn't received any notice, but the mail didn't come through very often in 1947 because the forest was full of anti-Soviet partisans and government employees were fearful of travelling without escort.

"Take him by the road," said the principal.

Mr. Kostas saw the look on Martin's face.

"What's the fastest way?" Kostas asked.

"Through the forest. It saves you half an hour."

"Then let's go by the forest path."

The principal didn't like it. He ran his finger between his frayed shirt collar and his neck as if loosening a noose that was already there.

"I'm a simple man from a village too," said Mr. Kostas. "I'm sure we have nothing to fear. What's your name?"

"Martin."

"Come on, Martin. It gets dark early in the forest and we don't want to go tripping over tree roots or stones."

Martin knew the woods and he didn't trip in them by day or by night. His village was deep in the forest and the trees stretched for miles and miles in all directions, with other villages few and far between, all the way into Byelorussia not twenty kilometres away southeast, and on toward Poland, a hundred kilometres west. His father had once walked to Poland to visit his sister, even though the border was supposed to be closed.

For all the denseness of the forest, the armies kept sweeping through this part of the world as if it were a highway.

The earth was sandy in these parts, not much good for farming, and the locals were often short of bread by spring. There were some meadows where they kept cows and sheep on thin grass, but people lived mostly on buckwheat — poor man's porridge — and they were grateful their bellies weren't empty too often. Luckily, the forest was also full of berries and mushrooms and there were plenty of fish in the rivers.

The trees were familiar to Martin, tall and golden-barked, not too tightly spaced, like soldiers standing at arms. There were birches and alders closer to the rivers and lakes, and bushes grew here and there, but the undergrowth was low in most places and he could see some distance among the trees until they seemed to close ranks a little further on and make an impassable line. Yet the deeper he walked into the forest, the farther the line drew back, like warriors parting the way for an honoured visitor.

The forest was a friend and refuge to him and to the resisting partisans who flitted among the trees, waiting impatiently for the west to intervene against the Soviets, for the Americans to come to the rescue. But what was taking them so long?

To the new red authorities, the forest was a grim and threatening place; a wilderness peppered with the nests of wasps and vipers, to say nothing of the sucking bogs over which clouds of mosquitos waited for blood offerings.

Anybody who needed to disappear from the vicious occupying governments took to the forest. First, in 1939, came the occupying reds; then Jews fled there during Nazi times — the few that had escaped their mass slaughter. Red partisans terrorized the Nazis from there during the war.

Then the Soviets returned in 1944 in order to complete the task of erasing the independent country. Some men took to the forest to resist them and await the Americans who were sure to come soon in order to crush Stalin's tyranny. But by 1947, nobody had any idea of when "soon" was going to be.

If you fled to the forest now, you could never come out. The Soviet authorities would want to know where you'd been, and so there were many, many people in hiding, mostly men, and mostly armed. The sound of gunfire wasn't unusual in the forest, where villagers heard machine guns rattling on for some time as the reds engaged one or another group of partisans in battle. Rockets often flew into the sky, red markers by day or white phosphorus by night.

The reds displayed their trophies by dumping the bodies of partisans in the village squares as warnings to the locals to stay out of the forest. The shoes and socks had been taken off the dead partisans. Martin didn't know why, unless the boots of the reds were worse than those of the men they killed.

According to the authorities, people should stay out of the forests and register properly and wait their turns to be moved into collective farms, sent off by train to the north, or left alone until they were needed for some purpose, such as celebrating Mayday. Collaboration with the reds was a sort of limited protection. A man could join the Destroyer Platoons and avoid the draft into the red army, and live unpaid and under-armed as military auxiliary to the reds. But the partisans hated Destroyers even more than they hated the reds and would warn them to quit on first sighting and then kill them on second. One could give up any land or cattle he might own and join a communal farm. Communal farmers received no pay.

The forest was littered with the castoffs of soldiers in flight. Martin and his older brother had found three treasures there. The first was an abandoned motorcycle right after the Germans withdrew. His father towed it home with the horse, traded a bucket of moonshine for a bucket of gasoline, and figured out how to use it with the boys' help. The second was a Sturmgewehr 44, a light machine pistol. It was illegal to possess arms. His father threw that into the lake, and they waited a day before fishing it out and hiding it. Much later, after his brother was gone, Martin also found a small pistol, and he didn't show that to his father. The pistol held only empty casings, so Martin used them to make his own bullets from other ammunition he'd found. His bullets worked pretty well when they worked, which was not always. One of them could almost go through a half-inch board.

Townies were reputed to be weak and to tire easily, but Mr. Kostas kept up well with his long legs. Martin was afraid to say much, dressed as he was in rustic homespun clothes and unsure of what a proper subject for conversation might be with a man such as this. City people had the reputation of being superior and dismissive, making Martin wary of opening his mouth.

"Tell me about Lyn Lake," said Kostas once they were deep among the trees.

"It's just a village, sir."

Kostas stopped. Martin walked forward two steps before realizing what happened and he turned back to look at the man.

"Did you just call me *sir*? Young man, you can get away with that word out here in the countryside, but in the city it will mark you as a bourgeois. Very dangerous. There are no more *sirs* in this new Soviet society of ours. Just friends."

"Yes, sir."

The teacher laughed. "Don't worry. It takes time to lose a habit."

He stepped forward and they carried on their way.

"Now tell me again about your village. You need to give me a little more detail to add to what you've said."

"My father's the alderman and we counted the people. We have thirty-seven houses and fifty families."

"Much better. Stories need to be fleshed out with details. No church, no proper schoolhouse, and no store, right?"

"That's right."

"How many children between the ages of eight and twelve, do you guess?"

Martin thought about it for a bit. "Around forty."

Kostas sighed. "It's going to be a big class. Can any of them read and write already?"

"Some."

Mr. Kostas fell silent, musing on what Martin had told him, calculating how the older ones in the class might help teach the younger ones and lighten his load. Then he shook his head like a man awaking from a dream, not necessarily a pleasant one. "So, Martin, tell me a little bit about yourself."

Martin didn't know what to say. He had never been asked a question like this one. Kostas waited and then prodded him.

"What do you like?"

This new teacher was a curious person. It was a friendly sort of question, but not the sort of question adults posed. They were usually too busy or too tired and didn't care what he liked. They just cared about his chores and other obligations. He hesitated to say anything, but Kostas was looking at him and waiting for a response.

"I like making things, and I like reading."

"A good combination."

Encouraged by this unusual kindness, Martin blurted out a little more.

"My older brother and I taught my father how to use a motor-cycle."

"I'm astonished. Where could you have learned how to run a motorcycle?"

"My brother watched the German soldiers when they were here."

"But you must have been children then."

"Yes, but we liked motorcycles. My brother was older. I like machines. When my father got the motorcycle, I showed him how to start it."

"A remarkable facility for a boy your age. You must have some talent. Maybe you'll be a mechanical engineer one day."

Martin had never thought of that. He only vaguely knew what an engineer was, but the word sounded very fine. Martin warmed to Mr. Kostas, who had seemed so strange when he met him on the steps, the kind of man who usually made village people feel second-rate. Martin mused on the idea for a moment. Two villagers had gone on to great success as far as he knew. One was a bookbinder in Varėna and the other wrote a letter home to say he was a bus driver in Riga. It may even have been true.

"Don't you have to go to university to be an engineer?" Martin asked.

"Yes, or a technical school."

"No one from our village has ever been to one of those."

"Maybe you'll be the first."

Kostas said it so easily, so quickly, as if he knew everything there was to know in the world. Martin glowed in the light of his reflected knowledge and wished he could find out more.

As the afternoon gave way to early evening, the mosquitoes rose up and began to harass them. The pair stopped to break off leafy birch branches to fan the mosquitos away as they walked. Kostas also lit up his pipe, which he kept clenched between his teeth because he held his briefcase in one hand and the branch in the other. As they walked, he looked around himself with interest, pausing to admire the landscape wherever the path drew close to Lake Ula or skirted the river of the same name.

They left the lake behind them and were on the path among a dense growth of bushes when Pike stepped out just ahead of them. He was in partisan uniform with the tricolour patch on his shoulder and he held his rifle cradled in one arm. Neither he nor Martin acknowledged one another. A little deeper in the undergrowth and now visible, Pretty Boy had a rifle trained on Mr. Kostas.

"Who are you and what are you doing here?" asked Pike.

Kostas looked down to Martin, who shrugged his shoulders and set the suitcase on the path.

"I'm the new teacher for Lyn Lake. Now I can ask you the same question."

"Step away a little, boy," said Pike. Martin did as he was told and crouched aside on the ground, gently waving the leafy branch around his face to keep the mosquitos off.

"I need to see what you have in the suitcase and the briefcase. Set the one beside the other and go sit with the boy."

"Do you want to see my letter of assignment? I can pull it out for you."

"Just do as I say."

Pretty Boy kept his rifle trained on Kostas — who had the courtesy

not to sit too close to Martin — as Pike set down his rifle, opened
the suitcase, and began to pick his way carefully through it. There
were socks and underwear, a spare shirt but no spare trousers.
About a kilo of bread, a paper bag of tobacco and another of tea,
as well as hard sausage, and a small bottle of clear liquor.

"Have a sip if you like," said Kostas. "It's good store-bought
liquor."

"We don't drink."

"Then a bite of something to eat?"

"We're not thieves."

"Then what are you looking for?"

"Just making sure you are what you say you are." Pike replaced
the items in the suitcase roughly as they had been and snapped it
shut. He opened the briefcase and pulled out various manila enve-
lopes and folders that he flipped through, glancing from time to
time at the writing, both printed and hand-written.

"Want me to check?" asked Pretty Boy from a distance.

"No, I'm fine. Everything is in order."

But he had not been thorough. Martin had never thought about
it before, but it occurred to him now that Pike couldn't read.

"No weapons?" asked Pike.

"No."

"Then you won't mind if I check." He had Kostas stand and
he patted him down, pausing for a moment where he felt a wallet
in his breast pocket but not asking Kostas to take it out. Satisfied,
he stood back.

"Do you want to make a contribution to the cause?"

"You can take my money."

"I said we're not thieves. How much money do you have?"

"Eight roubles."

"Two would be plenty. Welcome to Lyn Lake. We'll do our best
to make sure you're safe from the communists here, and you should
do the same for us. Do you ever write letters?"

"I need to report to the ministry through the post office at Rudnia every month. I'll get my pay there."

"So don't write about us. Don't talk about us either. You too," he said, looking to Martin, but this was all for show. "Now walk on."

They walked silently for a distance before Kostas spoke out.

"Do the partisans show up like that often?"

"Not much."

"Did you know them?"

"No."

Pike came from outside the district, but Pretty Boy once had a regular name and lived in a nearby village with his grandmother. He'd lorded over the smaller children in the village school, and now he lorded over whoever he could. Martin knew these things. He did not like to lie to the man at his side, but everybody had secrets in these times.

"How do you think they knew where to find us?"

"Word spreads fast in these parts, or maybe they were just out on patrol."

"Well, let's not let that frighten us, shall we?"

"I'm not frightened."

"No, but I am a bit. Let's sing. Do you know the song about the horseman trying to rouse his beloved from her father's house?"

"I don't think so."

"I'll start and you can join in. It will forewarn any other partisans we meet, and it will keep the adders off our path."

"Singing frightens adders? I've never heard of that."

"Oh yes. Snakes are like trolls. They can't stand the sound of songs and rhymes."

Kostas was smiling as he said this, so Martin did not know whether it was a joke or if the teacher had some sort of expertise Martin had never heard of before. They sang together as they walked toward the village and the forest rang, and Martin found

himself happier than he had been in some time, without ever having
been aware he was unhappy before.

Half an hour later, the forest opened up suddenly to branching
roads in a meadow with wooden houses scattered among them.
Down a gentle slope to the left lay Lyn Lake, for which the village
was named.

Some houses stood along the road and others by the lake and
still more stood further off. There was no centre to the village
unless you considered the intersection of two roads that met at a
T at the cemetery. It was as if each house had been built wherever
the owner happened to be standing when he thought of it. All of
the houses were made of squared logs, and some were pretty, with
white gingerbread around the eaves. Others had mouldy thatched
roofs or overgrown yards because the men had died or been
deported and the women made do as well as they could.

The children came running toward them when they saw Martin
was bringing in a stranger. Kostas kept singing and children who
knew the words joined in, and those that did not danced along
beside them until they entered the village. Then little ones, who
didn't know any better, peppered Kostas with questions as he
strode along the dusty road with his long legs, laughing and speaking to some of them.

When Martin brought Kostas home, his flustered mother laid
out the best linen and his father opened a bottle of *naminė* — the
rye liquor they distilled whenever there was enough grain — and
they gave him their best room with two doors, one to the house
and the other leading outside, so Kostas could come in and go out
when he pleased without disturbing the others. The room had once
belonged to Martin's older brother, and it had sat unused all these
years until the singing teacher was installed there, eliminating the
lingering air of melancholy in that place.

It was troublesome and expensive to have a teacher boarding in
your house. Nobody paid rent and nobody paid for food, but on

the other hand it was an honour to be chosen, so his father swallowed his losses and mentioned the presence of the teacher as often as possible when he stood smoking and talking with other village men.

As for Martin, he loved Kostas already for the world he had just opened up to him. Martin had long thought it might be very good to be a mechanic because motors interested him, but engineer? He had never thought such a thing was possible because he barely knew such a position existed. It belonged somewhere in the wider world beyond the forest which he had inhabited all of his life, and the word made him hungry to seek that world out.

3

PAŽAISLIS MONASTERY ASYLUM, 1959

MARTIN SAT ON THE chair while Kostas lay calmly on his side with one hand under his head on the pillow. He seemed so much less agitated than when he had been asleep a moment ago. But for all his composure, his skin was yellow and his eyes seemed to have sunk deep into their sockets.

"You don't look well," said Martin.

"No. I have suffered, but I'm getting better. I'll get out of here. I could have done it on my own, but this state claims it knows what's best and they stuck me in this place as if I was some kind of child. My entire life I have been forced to do things that I didn't want to do."

He spoke fluidly enough for a man who looked so bad.

"This is the Soviet Union. A lot of us don't get to do what we want to do. Has your family visited?"

"Forbidden! Not that Aleksa would be in any rush after what I've put her through. Poor woman, I tested her patience more than once. And this is no place for children. But I've had a whole cavalcade of visitors, especially at the beginning. At least you have human shape. Others didn't. A badger, monstrously large insects, two fish, things barely human. And then dozens of people, living and dead have been coming in and out of here for a long time. You're just the latest. None of you surprises me."

"You're so calm. Did anyone else come through the window?"

"I have been under attack from all directions. Through the window, through the closed door, up from below the floorboards and down from the ceiling. I was afraid at first but not anymore. The humans are the worst. Each of you has a complaint of one kind or another and I have no choice but to lie here and listen to you. It's like hell, really, but it turns out you can get used to anything."

"You don't have to listen to me," said Martin. "I want to hear from you."

"No, no. Why should you be different from all my other visitors? You have some kind of complaint, so go ahead and spill it out. Look around you. What else do I have to pass the time? And anyway, the monsters only come one at a time. Unless they're insects. The insects are the worst. They swarm and they make awful clicking sounds, as if they're smacking their mandibles. Anyway, I have nothing to explain. I am a public person. My life is an open book."

"Maybe. But first, do you remember me now that I'm up close?"

Kostas sighed and sat up, an exhausted man given yet another boring task. Facing him, Martin could smell his breath, something sour and metallic, and resisted the urge to pull back as Kostas studied his face from nearby. Martin took off his hat and Kostas studied his bare head. After a few moments of concentration, Kostas waved his hand dismissively and lay back down. "I remember nobody. All of you keep telling me who you are, so why don't you tell me too?"

"Are you sure you don't remember me? Martin, one of the boys in the village of Lyn Lake when you were a teacher there right after the war."

"Miserable place, as I recall, full of half-starved children and gaunt men. I gave my best there, though. I tried to raise the morale of the children besides teaching them to read and write. The forest was full of bandits. But I had to do my duty and go there."

"You seemed happy there at first. The children loved you."

"Ah yes, children. They don't judge, do they? I mean, they do judge, but they are easy to please if you're willing to pay them a little attention. Amuse them and they will love you. Were you one of the children who loved me?"

Martin could not bring himself to admit it. "I wasn't quite that small at the time. You lived in my parents' house."

"Of course, good country people. They won't let you down."

"I thought you said it was a miserable place."

"Both are true! Misery and kindness were balanced there. Not that I was really the sort of person who could live in a village. But I could see how other people might live there and even be content with it. If not for the politics. That was the problem. You didn't need to go looking for trouble in that place. It came looking for you."

4

LYN LAKE, 1947

MARTIN'S GRANDMOTHER WORE A kerchief over her hair and the shapeless uniform of old women: a sweater even in the heat of the day; a long, dark dress; and wooden clogs on her feet. She seemed very old as she looked at him with her pale eyes. His parents were out in the fields.

"Why aren't you in school?" she asked.

"The teacher's sick. The boys told me about a lake a few kilometres away where the fish are jumping. I want to put in a line."

"Going fishing? That's very bad luck, Martin. Look where it got your brother."

"It wasn't the fishing that caused it."

"No, but it's still bad luck. You have to stay away from the places where bad luck might strike you down."

There was no use arguing with her. He let her speak her many fears, but he refused to back down. She shook her head but stopped arguing and only added what any grandmother would add.

"Take something to eat," she said, and she didn't seem to notice when he cut a very thick piece of fatty bacon off one of the sides hanging in the larder, as well as two big slices of dense black bread. He wrapped everything in a linen tea towel.

"Be very careful, but if you're determined to do it, at least bring home a lot of fish," she said, and she muttered a few words and waved her fingers at him. He wasn't sure if she had said a prayer or cast a spell. There didn't seem to be much difference between the two of them anyway.

Martin ran back to where Dovas waited for him and showed him what he had in the towel.

Dovas didn't speak or even swat at the fly on his ear. Dovas rarely said anything of interest and half the time you didn't know if he understood what you were saying, but he would defend you in a fight, so he was not much trouble to have around. He didn't go to the high school in Rudnia. He hadn't even finished four grades in the village school. He was almost as good as a dog, but he wouldn't fetch.

"Did you tell anyone what we're doing?" asked Martin.

"No."

"You're not afraid?"

Dovas shrugged.

"Let's go."

The train tracks ran past Marcikonys, a real town twelve kilometres away by road, but if they cut through the forest they could lose a couple of kilometres. They knew all the forest paths because villagers fanned out after rainfalls to gather mushrooms or to gather blueberries, lingonberries, or cranberries. In the past, they had sold what was found in the forest, but the post-war years were hungry and the farmers had to feed not only themselves but men who showed up day or night to demand food.

The boys made their way under the green canopy. They stepped across grey mosses that crunched under their feet and they sometimes stooped to pull off a few lingonberries hanging under the leathery leaves on low stems. They picked their way along. Shoes were expensive, bast slippers too fragile, and clogs unwieldy in the forest. They walked barefoot on hardened soles, but the youths still needed to be watchful of what they were stepping on.

A sharp, upturned branch could pierce their flesh and a bad cut was dangerous.

When they reached the train tracks, the rails were hot to the touch in the early afternoon sun. The bacon itself, mostly fat with very little lean, was sweating as hard as the boys, and it bled grease easily as the twosome worked along one hundred metres of rise, rubbing and rubbing the bacon on the hot rail. Then they stopped to look back. One rail now glistened more than the other, and so Dovas took over from Martin. He rubbed the other rail down to where they had begun with the first.

Not much of the bacon remained except for the thin layer of lean meat. They walked back fifty metres from the rail bed and found a place where the line was visible through a gap in the bushes. Then they sat in the shade and waited.

"When is the next train going to come?" asked Dovas.

Martin shrugged his shoulders. Badger hadn't told him much. The boys were supposed to leave once they had greased the rails, but Martin chose to stay and see what was going to happen. They watched and waited, and even from that distance they could see many flies had landed on the greased rails. Nothing happened for a long time, and although Martin listened hard, he couldn't hear anything but the chirping of birds and the rustle of leaves in the breeze. Others had to be nearby, but they had hidden themselves well and kept very quiet.

The sun swung right over the tracks and they glinted, bright and painful to look at.

Finally came the chugging of the locomotive from the south-west. The boys rose up on their haunches, two pairs of eyes above a mass of bushes, and they waited as the sound grew nearer. Soon the plume of smoke appeared above the tree line.

There were half a dozen boxcars pulled by an under-powered locomotive, moving slowly as the engine strained forward like a

weary horse with a heavy load. And like horses' hooves that struggled up a wet hill, the wheels of the engine began to slip as they
came upon the greased rails. The train slowed as the iron wheels
turned but failed to make it up the rise.

The cows in the cattle cars were troubled by the change and
they mooed uneasily. For a moment the train was still as the wheels
spun madly, and then the engineer disengaged the drive. The
wheels stopped turning, and the train slid back slowly to the level
earth.

Two dozen partisans in uniform swarmed from the forest with
weapons drawn, Pike leaping up to the cab where the fireman
doubled as a guard, but the fireman's rifle jammed and Pike shot
him and pushed his body out onto the ground beside the track. The
man landed with his rifle in his hands and his finger on the trigger.
The weapon fired once on impact, as if in mockery of the dead
man's failed defence. Pike pushed the engineer down onto the floor
and made him sit with his hands on his head and then looked out
and signalled that the engine was secure.

The two red guards in the rear car were protected by light
armour, but from the swarm of bullets fired upon them, some made
it through the viewfinders. Once the guards stopped returning fire,
Pretty Boy pulled himself up to the narrow opening and tossed a
hand grenade inside the rear car, before dropping back down to the
earth. He covered his ears for the blast that splintered the boards
behind him, and then he went to join the others without looking
back. The cows were lowing in panic and when the first boxcar was
opened, a frightened cow jumped and broke its leg before the ramp
came down. A partisan stepped up to shoot it and soon the other
cars were opened and ramps dropped and the men led the cows
out. When Martin saw Badger, he rose and ran out to him by the
locomotive.

"Good job, Martin, but you should have left as soon as you
greased the rails."

"I wanted to see it happen."

"I know you did, but the first rule is to follow all orders, and you haven't followed yours."

Badger looked to the engine. Pike was watching them, and the engineer had dropped his hands and was studying Martin and Dovas.

Badger's mood sharpened immediately. "You haven't obeyed me, you understand?" said Badger. "You do what I tell you and nothing else. Now go. We have to lead the cows away and reds will be coming out of town soon enough."

Martin was stung by the reprimand from the man he admired so much. "What else can I do?"

"Nothing now. But later find us all the salt you can. We'll have to butcher these cows soon and there's enough meat on the hoof to last us to the new year if we can only preserve it. Go home, and run, don't walk. And this time, listen to what I say."

But Martin stopped with Dovas as soon as they were in the forest.

"He told us to go," said Dovas.

"Wait a minute."

Martin parted the branches of a tree so he could look back upon the train. There Badger approached the engine while talking angrily to Pike. The boys could not hear the words, but the tone from a distance was clear enough. Pike made the engineer stand and then pushed him out so he fell onto the ground. From his position above him, Pike shot him, and Badger took out his pistol and fired a second shot.

"Why did they kill him?" asked Dovas.

"Because he'd seen us."

The boys ran swiftly through the forest, like rabbits, zigzagging and keeping their heads low. Soon they were wet with sweat, and the mosquitos came out and descended on them as they ran. But still they flew, not looking where they put their feet, and soon they were bleeding from them. Martin was filled with panic raised by the running, as if a red soldier was right on his heels.

At the village, they separated and Martin waited in the shadow of a tree to let the sweat dry off his face. When he made it home, his parents and grandmother were sitting at the dinner table and Kostas was sitting with them.

"What, no fish?" his grandmother asked.

"Bad luck," said Martin, and he sat down to a bowl of beet soup and bread and butter. But he wasn't comfortable, somehow, and his foot hurt, and soon he felt himself sweating.

"You took a day off school to go fishing?" asked Kostas. "It doesn't sound like you. I thought you were very serious about your studies."

"Fishing, of all things," said his mother. Kostas looked at her as if expecting more, but she did not explain.

"I am serious about my studies, but sometimes temptation is too much."

"You're flushed," said Kostas. "Are you all right?"

How could he reveal himself in this way? He was embarrassed for showing himself a poor liar and he began to shake.

"I think I hurt my foot."

He had barely thought about it until he said it. His mother made him hobble over toward the door where the light was better. His left foot was swollen and beginning to discolour. She made him wash his feet and sit and hold his sole up to the light until she found a double pin-prick.

"He's been bitten by an adder," she said.

His mother laid him in a cot in the kitchen and his grandmother prayed over him while his father went to get water over which the village healer had said restorative words. With this special water, his mother washed his foot again and then used some of it to wash the sweat from his brow. He shook and he vomited. His father permitted the lamp to burn all night, and in moments when he awoke, he saw his mother with the rosary in her hand and he wondered briefly if he was already dead. Kostas came to look at him once, patted him on the shoulder and told him to be brave. His grandmother made him drink twice from a massive spoon, practically a ladle, of black currant wine.

"This wine has special qualities," she said as she stood over him, and no sooner had he drunk the wine than he fell into sleep.

That afternoon, a Studebaker truck that the Americans had supplied to the Soviets during the war drove into the village. Eight soldiers came down from the back and along with the driver from the cab came a civilian communist activist from Marcinkonys to accompany the interrogating lieutenant. Not all the people spoke Russian yet, practically a scandal to the authorities when the Lithuanians had been "liberated" by them three years earlier. The activist would translate.

The men spread across the village to search for suspicious cows. Local ones demonstrated their origin by showing their ribs through their sides because the grass was so poor that year. Still, the farmers had to prove their close relationship to their cows by calling their names for the lieutenant and his translator to see if the cows would respond to them. The soldiers looked for caches of fresh beef and stuck bayonets into haystacks in case partisans were hiding inside. They prodded the earth with heavy iron rods to search for underground partisan bunkers in the yards of the houses and out by the barns. The damned peasants were born liars and would deny knowledge of anything unless they were beaten very hard, and even then, it was not clear if the beatings produced truth or lies.

How could a herd of cows disappear so thoroughly, the bosses in Vilnius wanted to know, especially when Moscow was breathing down their necks to quash the so-called banditry in the countryside? It was an embarrassment that the peasants were not enthusiastic about the new regime. It was an embarrassment that so many men were hiding in the forest all these years after the war and they melted away when tracked only to reappear in ambushes.

Anger had worked its way down the lines from Moscow to Vilnius to the eight men and their lieutenant and translator. The ordinary soldiers paid the price for the errors of their superiors and so these men and their lieutenant needed to get results. Moscow and Vilnius might be angry, but they were not at risk from ambushes, so the soldiers had to contend with demanding superiors and danger in the forest. This made them jumpy and irritated.

The translator was a member called a *stribas* by the locals, based on the Russian word *istrebiteli*, or "Destroyer," a designation created for local communist activist collaborators. They had been renamed "Defenders of the Folk" by the government, but the name did not stick. The translating *stribas* was under pressure to produce before his lieutenant, a lean and hungry careerist who needed his assistant but despised him because the coward took the job to avoid service in the army. They went together with a guarding soldier from house to house, asking after cows and partisans, cajoling where it seemed productive, threatening when results did not come out. They showed a little pity in Martin's house because the boy was clearly too sick to answer questions but they reprimanded Kostas harshly for not keeping his eyes open for potential bandits.

The lieutenant's rage increased as the day went on, another blistering farm day when the villagers should have been out in the fields, but they were forbidden to go until the search was over. And then the lieutenant came upon a thread which he hoped might take him to his prize.

Dovas's father had a cowhide curing in salt in his shed, and since the animal to whom the skin had belonged could not respond to his owner's calls, the cowhide was suspicious, and the beating began. It did no good to say the hide had come from a sick cow and besides, any tanner could see it was already a few weeks into the process. The soldiers beat him out of frustration, and when Dovas could not bear to see it any more he tried to intervene and a soldier hit him hard across the face and his head hit a fencepost before he fell to the ground.

The reds finally quit in frustration, and left the battered man and his son where they lay and packed themselves into their truck to go to the next village to continue their interrogations. Dovas's father was badly beaten; his wife bandaged him and put him to bed. Dovas complained of a ringing in his ears and a headache, but these were the least of her worries. Still, she let him go to bed too, and considered herself lucky that neither father nor son had been killed or imprisoned.

That night, Dovas's mother heard the lowing of their one living cow in the barn. With all the trouble of the day, the animal had not been milked, so she took a lantern and went out to do it herself. But the reds had left behind a pair of men in hiding, just in case the partisans came that night to find out what had happened. The two soldiers were terrified that they were not enough because the partisan often travelled in groups of four or more. Frightened they might be outnumbered unless they shot first, the men fired at her, killed her, and fled. Through great good fortune, the lantern fell on a cow pie and did not burn down the barn, but no one went out to investigate the shooting because it was dark and dangerous and the villagers only found her body in the morning.

As to her husband, he was barely able to understand what had happened in his pain, but when he finally did, he also learned that Dovas's blow to the head had somehow blinded the boy. So he was left without wife or son to help him on the farm and who knew when he would be well enough to bring in the hay or harvest his buckwheat and potatoes. Someone would need to take care of Dovas, so he couldn't even hang himself and be rid of his earthly troubles.

"It's too bad they didn't have any black currant wine," said his grandmother.

"How would that have helped?"

"It cures everything. The soldiers would have been kinder if they had some, and it might have done the boy some good."

5

PAŽAISLIS MONASTERY ASYLUM, 1959

KOSTAS SAT UP AGAIN.

"I wonder what you have in this large bag you have brought into the room."

"Why do you ask?"

"I heard a sound when you set it down."

"Yes. A clinking sound."

"So familiar to me from times past. So welcome. Like the sound of bells on a horse pulling a sled in the winter time, or of running water over stones in a brook on a hot summer's day."

"I was going to surprise you."

"No surprise. My nose as well as my ears let me know what you have."

"Your nose? I don't smell anything at all."

"Oh, but I do. My wife hated to waste things, so even though she disapproved of alcohol she would not throw it out. She would try to hide a bottle somewhere in the flat, behind the cooking oil or among the winter shoes on the floor at the back of the closet. But in addition to my talent for shaping lines of poetry, I have a talent for sniffing out mysteries. I must have inherited Gogol's nose."

"Do you think I'm carrying a mystery?"

"Most certainly. I know you are, or you wouldn't be here. But

I don't care about that. I care about the mystery of what you have in your backpack.

"You seemed so unwell a few moments ago. Now you're sprightly." But he looked fragile too, although Martin did not want to say it. Kostas's arms and legs were thin, but his belly was bloated.

"In anticipation," said Kostas. "Tell me what you have."

"I do have something I brought along to ease our conversation, and I'm feeling more than a little guilty about it. You shouldn't be drinking. You were supposed to dry out here, right?"

Kostas blinked and paused, assessing the information slowly. He finally smiled.

"I can handle my liquor. It's been my companion my entire life, often my inspiration. Philosophers must smoke to find their ideas in the clouds of tobacco, and a writer must drink to silence the imps in his head that keep telling him his work is unworthy. That he would be better off enjoying the depth of blue in the sky or the smell of fresh-cut hay. But one can drink too much. First you get inspiration and then you get oblivion. The philosophers tell us to aim for the golden mean, but that is a very narrow line, practically a tightrope. I just got carried away a couple of times in the recent past and tipped over. It's all about moderation and remembering to eat something. Do you have anything to eat?"

"Not really."

"Then we'll have to rely on moderation. So, are you going to pour something out or are you just going to talk about it?"

"I will pour us a drink, but very, very little. I want to talk. I have a story to tell and so do you, so don't expect a big piss-up or anything."

"I am a cultured person. I find that comment more than a little insulting."

"Let's speak frankly. I have seen you on the streets, staggering. You were even an uninvited guest at my wedding. Do you remember that?"

"I remember almost nothing. But that has to do with age, not alcohol."

"Come on. You're not much over forty. A bit early for senility to be coming on."

"Why are you provoking me? You have something to drink, don't you?"

"I know alcohol is troublesome for you. You get only a little."

Martin opened up the pack and took out one of his bottles of vodka.

He poured out a single shot for each of them. Kostas sat up, reached out, took the tin cup and drank down the contents in a single gulp.

"One more, please," he said.

"What happened to moderation?"

"Moderation begins after the second drink. You have to prime the pump first."

Martin did as Kostas asked, and the man did as before and set down his glass and looked at Martin expectantly.

"Now moderation begins," said Martin.

"You're not drinking?"

"I'll take a sip."

Sitting on the edge of the bed, Kostas crossed his legs and put his cupped hands on the upper knee. Martin almost laughed to see the man take that youthful pose, as if he were at home and talking to a friend.

"So now that I have a little medicine in my system, I can see that you are a real human being and not one of my ghosts. How is it that you ever found me?"

"I found you two years ago."

"You did? I don't remember you from my recent past."

"No. I followed you from a distance."

"Followed me? You mean you were stalking me?"

"Not exactly. I needed to understand you and I was intimidated by your fame. You've come a long way. But I was a peasant boy, if you remember, one who never had much of a chance to improve himself. I meant to get to you sooner, but then I fell in love and that slowed me down."

"A complicated relationship?"

"A little."

"I'm all ears."

6

A PALE RECTANGLE LOOMED on the wall above the woman's head where a portrait of Stalin had once hung. Martin could hear someone bickering in the hall in Russian, but the words were indistinct — just "I'm sorry" repeated again and again by a woman, and a man's muffled but obviously unsympathetic words.

Martin's pardon lay on top of the documents in the folder, but the woman flipped past it to look at the other papers. She wore a grey suit the colour of the wall behind her, and her colourless hair was pulled back tightly. Her face was broad and her skin pasty, the complexion of an office worker who rarely got outside. Her lips moved as she was reading.

After Stalin's death in 1953, the food rations had improved in the camp, and now, three years later in 1956, Martin was released from the gulag after some bureaucrat with a conscience realized he'd been imprisoned illegally at age fifteen in 1948.

The grim woman across the desk from him looked up above her reading glasses, slapped the folder shut, and pushed it across the desk in front of her.

"Request denied. You may not register to reside in the Soviet Socialist Republic of Lithuania."

Stalin was gone, but his ghost lingered.

"I was born here in Lithuania and I have a pardon."

"Issued by Moscow. This is Vilnius. The law states returning deportees must settle elsewhere."

"So you're saying local decrees overrule the law in Moscow?"

Most officials were susceptible to bribes and the weaker ones could be bullied, but he didn't have much money and fifteen minutes of attempted bullying got him escorted out to the street by two men who seemed accustomed to their work by the way they held his wrists tightly on either side of his body as they led him out.

He was gathering his wits on the sidewalk when a legless man rolled himself up on a low cart and seized Martin's pant leg above the knee as if he were going to take possession of the leg itself.

"Help a war vet." The man wore a crushed cap and a ribbon of some kind on his chest. His hands and fingers were filthy from dragging himself along through the city on his cart.

It was not a request. The vet who had helped drive out the Nazis in 1944 also brought in the Soviets who deported Martin and many tens of thousands of others. The irony of giving money to this "liberator" was not lost on Martin, but the man had no legs, after all, and so he gave the vet a few kopeks. Martin expected no thanks and he got none. The man bumped away on his cart, in danger of tipping over on Vilnius's notoriously bad and broken cobbles.

The horrible woman had only been following orders, an excuse that was perfectly acceptable in the Soviet Union. The local collaborators hoped the deportees they had sent north after the war would die, or at least have the good sense to stay away. What good was deporting a hundred and thirty thousand, if Moscow let the survivors come back? The returning former prisoners might cause trouble when they discovered their homes and property had been confiscated. Besides, it would be uncomfortable to run into someone on the street you'd sent to the gulag, or, worse, in an alley.

Dressed in a worn canvas jacket and pants, with a cap on his wispy hair and a backpack on one shoulder, Martin considered his options. No residency meant no possibility of employment, and unemployed people were vagrants who could be arrested and shipped back to the gulag.

Martin was free, but he wouldn't stay that way for long unless he could legalize himself somehow. To do that he needed to find a job and a place to live. For eight years, he'd thought of not much else except his home village of Lyn Lake. No more. His father was dead and his mother was still in the gulag. Their farm had been expropriated. There was no longer a home for him in his village. He wanted to stay in Vilnius, but it wasn't going to be easy.

The fauna of the country had changed since Martin had lived here.

If presently Soviet Lithuania was a sea, the bureaucrats floated in it like almost invisible jellyfish. The bureaucracy was made up of soft but slippery and resilient enemies, impossible to harm with fists or bullets. But they in turn had powerful stings. And if the sting was not enough, the matter reached the police, whose name had been changed to the "militia" because there was no need for "bourgeois police" in the new socialist paradise they were building.

Resistance after the war had been strong at first, but then Stalin opted for a tactic that had worked well in the thirties in Russia. He instituted a new terror. In 1948 and 1949, seventy thousand Lithuanians were shipped off. Some had been shipped off before and more would be shipped off later. The farms were folded into collectives run by the reds, and soon collaborating party members sat in control of residency permits, employment records, and all associations from chess clubs to women's choirs, from artists' unions to children's summer camps. How to fight when the enemy was everywhere and therefore nowhere in particular?

Some people broke under the more traditional tyranny in the

gulag prison camps, and some people drowned in the sea of bureaucracy if they made it back home. Martin was damned if he'd survived prison only to go down now.

ASIDE FROM MOSCOW, WHERE Martin had only changed trains, he had never really spent much time in cities; he was inclined to think he would like them better than living in the countryside. Cities provided more anonymity and he had no desire to return to the village where his parents had probably been denounced by some neighbour. He'd forever be wondering about each person he greeted on the road or on the other side of a fenced yard. And he had intended to leave his village anyway, if not exactly the way he did. There was no going back.

In his home village of Lyn Lake, there had been hardly more than a crossroads, but here in the old city of Vilnius, the medieval streets twisted and turned and contained alleys and passageways impossible for newcomers to navigate. They might wander like animals in a maze uncertain where to find their reward or even be sure one existed in the first place.

Vilnius had many baroque churches, still very beautiful, but decrepit and sad too, aristocrats fallen on hard times, repurposed, with their stucco crumbling, their frescoes painted over and their pews removed to make room for storage of industrial machinery.

The ancient Lithuanian capital had declined into provincial obscurity before regaining its status after the war. Most of its former inhabitants — Jews, Poles, and Byelorussians — had been killed or deported. There were many ghosts, but they were barely audible in the din of everyday life. Vilnius was full of newcomers from the provinces to work in the infernal mills of socialism, scraping the bran of capitalism from the kernel of the Soviet New Man.

Some of the neighbourhoods remained in ruins over a decade after the war, when the buildings had been liberated from the Germans one at a time. For all its tribulations, Vilnius bustled in its modest way. The streets were full. People went about the business of living their lives — hard for them with line-ups for bread and eggs, but not as hard as where Martin had come from.

He hadn't been beaten down like some of the older prisoners in the gulag. Tired and sick, nostalgic and broken, they dreamt not so much of going home as returning to the past they remembered from their youth. Some died in the winter forests and some lay ill and hopeless in bunks as they awaited their end. The children in their unsupervised barracks played with fleas while waiting for their mothers to return from the day's work and bring them frozen potatoes to cook on the woodstove. The children wept if their mothers died — Martin didn't know what happened to the orphans.

Martin was glad to be among the people on the streets now, ones living their ordinary lives, no matter what their worries might be. All he wanted was an ordinary life of his own and he was going to make the world let him have it. He wandered out along German Street, a boulevard by the bombed-out former Jewish ghetto. The street was flanked on one side by empty lots with salvaged bricks piled up in them where the old synagogue had been demolished. The Polish Home Army fought the Germans house-by-house along the street in 1944. For their sacrifice, the Polish survivors were sent to the gulag by the reds. Martin had worked with one of them back in the Siberian forest, and as far as Martin knew, the Pole was still there for committing the crime of being a Pole.

The man had an ironic view of history — he'd told Martin that the Jews and the Poles were not the first to suffer in Vilnius — the ragged leftovers of Napoleon's Grande Armée were hacked to pieces on the very same street. Maybe Vilnius was an unlucky place. That's just how things were in eastern Europe, where the definition of happiness was different from the version in the west. In western Europe and especially in America, people expected not only to survive but to flourish in some way, perhaps even to be happy.

Yet this particular day was beautiful and warm just after a brief downpour. The air smelled fresh and, if not for the ruins, it would have been a pleasant setting. Martin was trying to focus on the now, and at present he was free on a sunny street, with a piece of smoked sausage and a heel of bread in his backpack. The worries of tomorrow could wait until tomorrow, and he didn't want to carry the burden of the past if he could help it.

He was thinking about where he was going to spend the night. Most likely this partially ruined neighbourhood was a place where he could look for a hidey-hole to tuck himself into until he started his siege of the government offices again the next day. He saw a green space on the other side of a rubble-filled lot where about fifty children gathered in a half-circle on the grass in some kind of miniature park. A couple of teachers stood watch as a man was sitting on a bench and reading to them. With nothing much better to do, Martin picked his way across the expanse of broken bricks and went up to the low fence behind which the children were sitting.

Martin couldn't get enough of the sun. He set down his knapsack and leaned on the fence with his forearms and ignored the dirty glance from one of the young teachers, a blonde around his age. He was used to those sorts of expressions. He looked like a tramp or worse, and she was protective of her children. But he just wanted to hear what the man was reading.

If not for the voice, Martin wouldn't have known it was Skylark. He looked different, filled out and with his black hair so much shorter. He had a drinker's nose now, but he was still very expressive, making big gestures with his free hand while holding his book in the other. He was reading a rhyming story about building a farm and the various animals that would live there. The children were all rapt, eight- and nine-year-olds with chins on their fists, except when they sat up to laugh and clap at the more clever rhymes. And they really were clever. Skylark's words rolled out easily and sweetly, like the sound of water running over stones in a stream, and the story held not only the children but the adults as well. Martin found himself deep into the story in spite of himself, and once or twice he laughed right along with the children. Skylark was a kind of magician of words, making the simple sentences sound both delightful and spellbinding. One awoke from them as if from a happy dream.

Having finished his story, Skylark looked at the children, and then the teachers, and then he looked over at Martin. But Skylark didn't recognize him. Martin didn't at all resemble the youth Skylark had last seen eight years before. Martin had worked in the forest at first, all during the most brutal weather, and he'd lost most of his hair in a fever, to say nothing of the naïve freshness he wore when he was only fourteen. The hair never came back. To people on the sidewalk, Martin was just another scruffy street person with nothing better to do than listen to a children's poet reading in a park.

So much for putting the past behind him, so much for living in the moment. Some ghosts spoke more loudly than others.

What was Skylark doing here?

MARTIN STEPPED BACK FROM the fence where he had watched Skylark reading to the children. The poet accepted flowers from the teachers who then herded the children away, and he walked toward the car whose chunky driver in an undersized suit and sweater-vest butted a cigarette and got behind the wheel as the poet got in the back. But the car would not start. The engine barely turned over a few times and backfired once with a puff of black smoke. The driver got out and exchanged a few words with Skylark, who shook his irritated head and marched off into the city.

Martin walked over to the driver in his tight suit and stubble on his chin.

"Won't start?" asked Martin.

"This piece of trash is unreliable, but it's the only car the Writers'

Union has, on loan from the Book Depository. They're going to be angry."

"Not your fault."

"No, but they'll blame me. I'm a driver, not a mechanic."

"Mind if I look under the hood?"

"What's it to you?"

"I know machines a bit, and I've got nothing else going on. Maybe I can help."

There were not many cars in Vilnius and this was the only one parked on the street; as soon as the driver opened the hood, three boys and a girl appeared to watch them. Children gathered at the slightest hint of something interesting going on. One of the boys was around twelve years old, and he leaned in to peer at the engine along with the two men.

Martin looked down at the engine and put his hand on the end of one of the cables to the spark plugs.

"Cable's wet. I can help you push the car into the sun. If you have tools in the boot, undo the cables and let them sit in the sun for an hour or two to dry out."

The driver agreed and opened his door to put one hand on the steering wheel as he pushed and the older boy who had been watching them stepped forward.

"Want me to watch your backpack while you push?" he asked.

"Nice try, my friend. Why don't I just rest it on the seat inside and you can help to push the car as well?"

"You don't trust me?" the boy asked.

"No, of course not. What are you doing here anyway? Shouldn't you be in school?"

"I don't go to school."

"What do your parents say about that?"

"They're gone."

He didn't say any more and Martin looked him over. They boy wore a coat too big for him with the sleeves rolled back, revealing

thin wrists and dirty hands. His thick hair had been cut by someone not too experienced, and his face was not exactly clean but
not exactly dirty. A street boy, likely an occasional thief when he
needed to get by.

In the later deportations, husbands and wives were seized. What
happened to the children left behind wasn't the arresting party's
concern. There had once been gangs of children after the earlier
waves of deportations — self-sufficient thieves — but most were
rounded up and put into orphanages. Some who didn't end up
there managed to survive on their own.

"What's the last time you saw your parents?" Martin asked. The
boy looked at him oddly. Even he knew one did not ask questions
like that.

"Four years ago."

"Are you expecting them back?"

"Eventually."

That was all he needed to know. He made the boy join him to
help push the car into sunlight. When they had put the car into
place and set the cables out on the dashboard where the sun was
very warm through the windshield, Martin reached into his pocket
and took out fifty kopeks to hand to the boy.

"What's your name?" asked Martin.

"Tomas." He looked at the coins for a moment and then pock-
eted them.

"Where do you live?"

"Around the old city gate. If you ever need more help from me,
just ask. Kids in this neighbourhood know me."

The driver watched this exchange with some interest.

"What did you pay him for?"

"He looked like he needed it."

"What kind of man walks around helping drivers and street
children?"

"I don't know. I'm new around here. Just leave the car out in the sun for a couple of hours. Do you think you can reconnect the cables yourself?"

"I could, but I won't. You'll do it for me. Come on. I can watch the car on the street from the window of this tavern. We'll drink a few beers in the meantime."

Peter was a former farm boy as well, one who had learned how to change gears, but he hadn't learned much else. He liked this job because half the time he just stood around waiting for his passenger and didn't have to do anything. The alternative was shovelling manure back on the collective farm. He made it all sound straightforward during the first couple of beers, but after the third and then the fourth, he explained how he had never become used to life in the city where nobody greeted one another on the street and no one lent a helping hand. He had seen an echo of his country self in Martin's friendliness.

After the sixth beer, Peter called Martin his brother and offered him help with getting a job.

They were both drunk when they came out three hours later, but the cables had indeed dried and the engine turned over and ran without stalling.

The driver left the engine running, stepped out of the car and embraced him. "Come see my boss tomorrow," and he gave an address. "I'm not as stupid as I look. I know who and what you are, and I know where you've been. But it's all right. I know someone who can help."

The boy who called himself Tomas nudged him just after dawn the next morning. There was a hag sweeping the courtyard where he'd spent the night. She was one of those old ladies dressed in scarves and shapeless coats all year round, a soldier in the army of grandmothers who patrolled the streets. She seemed neither friendly nor unfriendly, more like a raven than a human for her emotionless eyes. But her message was clear. It was time for him to go before the rest of the building awoke for the day.

"How did you find me?" Martin asked Tomas.

"I get around. In the morning, just after first light, you can find coins people have dropped the night before. Once I even found a wallet."

"And if I hadn't been sleeping with my hand wrapped around the strap of my pack?"

"I would have found that too. Do you have anything you want me to do? Any job?"

"Nothing now. I'm looking for work myself. But when I need you, I'll come searching for you."

"Anything to eat?"

Martin gave him the knob of sausage he had in his pack, and the boy disappeared.

Martin washed his face at an outdoor tap and drank some water. There was no place to buy bread at that time of the morning unless up at the train station, but he did not like to be around that sort of public place too much while his residency papers were not in order. He might attract the attention of an officious policeman with nothing better to do.

Martin asked the sweeper for directions, and then walked across town toward the address where the driver had told him to go. He went along a narrow street that had shabby, three-storey buildings on each side. Once they had been rather fine with their stucco ornaments around the doors and windows, but that was some time ago, when Vilnius had been a respectable provincial town rather than a ruined new capital of a Soviet Socialist Republic.

The fighting had gone from building to building at the end of the war, and reconstruction was slow. The Red Army, tired and frightened, had found it easier to torch some buildings with flame-throwers rather than go from room to room and risk German booby traps. Most of the German soldiers had fled across the river, and some of them were picked off there; but, still, who was going to give up his life to save some real estate? That was back in 1944, yet the neighbourhood still showed its wounds. The city was like a Chopin Mazurka played on a bad piano by a performer with a hangover.

Martin came to a T-intersection and crossed the main street, Lenin Prospect, at the bottom of which stood the white neoclassical cathedral, long-since closed and converted into a picture gallery. The city was awaiting the cold eyes of Soviet city planners, who thought the baroque churches might need to come down for an expressway through town even though there were hardly any cars.

Martin went across and down more deeply into the city along cobbled streets to a rather fine two-storey building with a cast iron and glass awning above a heavy wooden door whose brass plate said it was the home of the Lithuanian Soviet Socialist Republic's Writers' Union. He backed off as soon as he read the inscription, knowing that although it was terribly early in the morning for a writer, Martin did not want to be seen up close in case Skylark was around.

A little farther up the street and around a bend were a few steps that led up to a stone porch and a door between bas-relief columns in a high wall. No bell, no knocker, no plate on the door. There were niches on either side of the door, empty now, and he wondered what was missing from them. This was where the driver had told him to go. Martin walked up the steps and tried the door handle, fully expecting it to be locked, but it was open. He went through.

He found himself in the small park of an old Carmelite monastery, with residency rooms down two sides of the U and the church of St. George-the-Martyr at the far end of the garden. The yard was not well kept, with all the unripe apples already stolen from its orchard, and one of the concrete benches turned over, but the garden felt benign somehow, like the space between the outstretched arms of a grandmother. Sparrows massed in one of the apple trees and a pair of grey and black crows watched him from their perch on the broken bench. St. George's was a baroque church, with its curly ornamental front, and like many of the others in Vilnius, it was a little down on its luck. Martin tried the front door, and to his surprise, he found this one open too.

The only illumination came from windows high at the groined ceiling of the church. He looked up and saw dirty frescoes, among them a St. George slaying the dragon, and a bird flying too high for him to tell what it was beyond its slight size. Not a dove, perhaps a titmouse. The nave had no pews, just row upon row of impossibly tall, tall bookcases that reached almost as high as the upper windows. How the books on those high shelves were reached, he did not know.

Martin was so accustomed to being chased out of buildings by doormen and guards that he half-expected someone to call out or to seize him by the shoulder. But there was no one about. The church was silent, except for the sound of the occasional bird in flight on high or the rustle of a mouse on low, moving among some leaves that had blown inside. He walked past dozens of shelves on toward the fine altar, and there on the left the vestry door was open and weak lamp light bled out against the growing competition of the strengthening morning sun. Someone was in the vestry. Martin stopped.

"I can hear you out there. Come inside and show yourself."

Martin did as he was told and walked into a room heaped with books stacked on several desks pushed against the walls. There were many cabinets where vestments must once have been stored, but now some of the doors were open and on shelves inside, books were stacked high and in a couple of other places manuscripts were stacked as well, some tied with string and others in folders and others just heaped up and in danger of spilling onto the floor.

Standing behind what must have been his own desk was a man in a suit, mostly balding and wearing a moustache and studying the spine of a book over the top of his eyeglasses.

"Do you read Hebrew?" the man asked after raising his head to look through his lenses at Martin.

"No."

"Yiddish?"

"No."

"Pity. We must have some rare Jewish books here, but the Jews are mostly dead and buried in the pits at Ponary. The few that survived emigrated as soon as they could. Who is going to be able to tell if these books contain treasures?"

"I don't know."

"No. Of course not." The man set down the book on his desk and studied Martin more carefully. "Did you come looking for bread? People show up all the time, thinking this is still a church and we can help out with meals. I have a few of yesterday's rolls in my drawer."

"No, I came looking for work. Peter the driver told me I should come here today."

"You're the one who fixed the car and sent him home drunk?"

"The beer was part of the repair."

"Are you a mechanic?"

"Not really, but I know engines. I grew up on a farm and we did everything there. I know machines all right, but I'm mostly a carpenter."

"Well that's good news, actually. We share that car with the Writers' Union and we have a dilapidated truck that we send out to bring in books from across the country, but those two are hardly enough to employ a mechanic. However, we always need new shelves and sometimes the old ones need to be rebuilt. Are you afraid of heights?"

"No."

"Good. So we can use you. Welcome aboard."

"Excuse me, but just like that?"

"Did you want to hear about your pay? It will be terrible, but you won't starve on it."

"You don't even know my name."

"Right. What is it?"

"Martin Averka."

"My name is Antanas Stonkus. I'm the director of the Book Depository."

"The director? What are you doing here so early?"

"Oh, right. Is it light outside already?"

"Quite some time ago, actually."

He sighed. "So many books. I've let the night get away with me. My wife will be furious. Listen, come back during office hours and speak to Kristina, our bookkeeper. She'll set you up. And one more thing."

"Yes?"

"We are great believers in privacy here, and although we're not a library, we do tend to keep quiet most of the time out of respect for the books. Do you understand?"

Stonkus had been looking at Martin's knapsack. So he had divined who Marin was, and yet he had hired him on the spot.

Martin walked back through the bookshelves and stood out in the yard. There were some very hard years behind him, and they had looked like they were going to continue right up to yesterday morning. But now he was getting lucky, and he was so unused to it that when his battered heart softened, he had to struggle to keep from weeping.

7

LYN LAKE, 1947

THE NEW TEACHER SAT with his notebook under a very broad oak tree overlooking Lyn Lake with the village behind him. Legend had it that the oak was planted during the time when the village belonged to the king's manor lands, but that was so long ago that no one could be sure it was true. How was it possible to tell what was true anyway? People just believed what they believed.

Deep in these forests there had always been stories, some of devils who walked the paths during Sunday mass in order to seize atheists and take them down to hell, the only place available since they did not believe in heaven. But devils were much rarer now that the forests were full of human dangers. What need was there for demons when you might come upon a group of Soviet collaborators with their Red Army helpers, poking the earth with iron rods, looking for underground bunkers? As soon as you were seen, you were under suspicion, and if you were suspicious, your well-being was at risk. They might take you and beat you to find out if you were on the way to a partisan underground bunker. And if they did not beat you, someone with eyes for the partisans might report you were talking to the collaborators and might well be one yourself. Then the partisans might come to your house by night to have a few words.

In any case, it might be safer to shoot the unwary wanderer and be free of the risk. Misplaced kindness cost lives in this place, and better the lives should be lost by someone else. And through all this, life went on, with planting and harvesting, births and deaths, and children needing to be taught to read and write. The village pupils loved Kostas for the easiness of his ways. In his classroom he was interested in the children, who were used to being ignored at home in case they died young and broke their parents' hearts. He was undemanding and could usually be counted upon to amuse them with his stories and verses. He never tried to beat knowledge into the older blockheads, but left them alone to dream their simple thoughts as others moved on from addition and subtraction to multiplication and division.

Kostas was genial in town unless he was working in his notebook. They learned to leave him alone when he was writing. Then he became another man altogether, distant and cool, irritated if a child persisted in trying to talk to him.

The villagers were a little frightened of him, not only because he was sent to them by impossibly remote authorities, but also because he let them know he was a poet and real published poets did not have to behave like everyone else. They imagined he must be wise and only wore his easy manner to disguise his insights. He visited the parents systematically, like a parish priest making the rounds, but the villagers did not unburden themselves to him because he was, after all, a stranger and not a priest. They soon discovered he would not say no to a drink, and so he was often treated to glass of *naminė*, a beverage more precious than food because there was hardly enough rye to feed people, yet some of it was needed to distil the strong homebrew.

One village elder consulted him on how to behave with the red soldiers when they came through and they took Kostas's advice on just how much bacon to hand over to the aggressive troops, and how many shots of *naminė* to pour for their officers.

Kostas was sitting with his back against the tree and a scribbler on his knees. A pipe and a half-bottle of *naminė* lay on the grass beside him; he sipped on it regularly throughout the late afternoon and early evening. He wrote lines tightly packed together because there was a shortage of paper and just about everything else after the war. But what was he writing on those pages?

"Poetry, Martin. I am a writer after all, aren't I?"

"Can I hear some of it?'

"Oh, it's not ready yet. I need to rewrite a lot of it."

"You do? I thought it just came to you all at once."

"Sometimes it does, but not often. Mostly poetry is hard work."

"As hard as mowing a field in the summer?"

Kostas looked at Martin sharply to see if the boy was being ironic, but he found no telltale half smile, just open-faced earnestness.

"I'm glad you're feeling better," said Kostas. "A snakebite is no joke. It's a shame about what happened to your friend. Do you think he knew something he wasn't telling the soldiers and that's why he was beaten so badly?"

"I think they just enjoy beating people."

Lyn Lake, as beautiful as a stage set, lay beyond Kostas, and he looked very much the poet with his long, curly hair and book and pencil and the still, dark water behind him. The villagers had rights to certain parts of the lake, where they set their nets for fish. *Lyn* was the local name for the most abundant fish, otherwise called *Tench* in English, cousin of the homely carp. Slippery as eels, they seemed to repopulate the lake for all the intensive fishing, so there was always hope of catching more of them.

"How are you finding life in our village?"

"The air is wonderfully fresh here and look at this bottle I have, will you? The people are generous with their food and liquor even though they don't have enough for themselves. What more could I possibly want?"

Martin wanted considerably more. Kostas had planted the seed of a dream within him, and once he had recovered from his snakebite, but still lay resting in bed, Martin thought of little else besides the steps he would need to take to become an engineer. At school in Rudnia, he had tried to find out everything he could about engineers, but there was little written about them and so he imagined himself in a lab coat like the one the science teacher wore, perhaps directing men in a factory or puzzling with them over some sort of difficult mechanical problem.

He was certain engineers worked in metropolises like Varėna, Kaunas, or even Riga, and so the lab coat would go on a hanger before he left work each day in order to walk out on a sidewalk and go home. And in that home, he would live as he had read others did in cities, without having to work from dawn to dusk. After that, his imagination grew vague. The sidewalk outside his workplace alone was already superior to the often-muddy paths he took in his own village or in Rudnia.

"I know someone who would like to see you."

Kostas looked down at his scribbler and began to sketch something. Martin could not see what it was.

"Does this someone have a name?" asked Kostas.

"He does, but he'd prefer to tell you his name himself. He's in the forest. It's important."

"In the forest. I see. All very mysterious, but I trust you, Martin. You're the one who led me here safely the first time I came here. So. Where and when am I to meet this unnamed person?"

"Right now would be the best time. I could take you to him."

"You mean at this moment?"

He did. The less warning the better, for security's sake. Kostas placed the pencil and notebook in the breast pocket of his jacket and swept up the bottle and put it in the pocket of his raincoat. His collar was frayed and the tie that held it together was old and stained, but these were unremarkable attributes for a country teacher who needed to maintain his self-respect despite his low income.

"Tell me about your parents," said Kostas as they walked along.

"There's not much to tell that you don't know already. They're country people, like my grandmother and even me."

"But they seem a little, oh, I don't know, quiet? Subdued? Maybe that's the word. When we're eating, sometimes I see your mother stop and stare into the distance."

"Watch her lips then. She's praying for my brother."

"I didn't know you had a brother."

"Well, I don't anymore. He was older than me and he died two years ago, just after we were liberated."

"I'm sorry to hear that. What was it, an illness or an accident?"

"An accident, I guess. The red soldiers hadn't been here long. They were hungry all the time and we didn't have all that much to give them. A red army soldier had this idea that he could drop a grenade in the water at a bend in the Ula River, and the dead fish would float up to the top, so he asked Linas to take him to a spot where the fish schooled. But the soldier dropped the grenade. He'd been drinking. Linas tried to run away, but a piece of metal caught him in the head."

"And the soldier?"

"He knew enough to drop to the ground to avoid the shrapnel. He said he was sorry."

They walked for a while before Kostas spoke again.

"Do you miss your brother?"

"I'm getting used to it. He was older. He was a kind of teacher. Now I have to figure things out for myself."

"But your father must teach you too. He needs you on the farm."

"He's pretty quiet. He says I'd be better off somewhere else."

THEY WALKED FROM THE lake up a path that led up a slight rise to the main dusty street. It was the time after supper when the day's work was done, and so the villagers were about, two old men smoking pipes on a bench on the sunny side of their houses and the children playing games in the yards. A woman deadheading her roses. Everyone within hailing distance greeted the teacher and he nodded back at them. For all the normality of the village, a mood hung over the scene. The recent tragedy could mean that bad luck was over for now, or it could mean that the death of Dovas's mother would just be the first in a forthcoming string of more unfortunate events.

They came up to the crossroads where the cemetery lay inside a low picket fence, and there they passed a middle-aged woman who knelt in prayer at a grave. She wore a Turkish scarf over her hair and her upturned soles were bare and black from walking the road.

"Who is that woman?" asked Kostas.

"I don't really know. They say she's from Zervynos."

"How far is that?"

"Eight kilometres. She comes here to pray at her uncle's grave."

"Who was he?"

Martin shrugged. Strangers were few in the village because it was on the way to nowhere. The nearest town of any account was Marcinkonys, right on the railway line, the place where the police took people who were to be sent north. Martin led Kostas a distance on the forest road out of town, and then he cut in among the trees for a hundred metres.

Pretty Boy was leaning with his back against a tree and his rifle held loosely in the crook of his left arm. He did not greet them, and he looked away when Martin tried to say hello. Pretty Boy admired himself for sacrificing his future by fighting against the occupiers of his nation, and he did not speak much to Martin, whom he considered a boy, although Martin was only four years younger. A little farther on they came to a clearing where a couple of fallen birches made opposing benches. Between them stood Badger with his arms crossed. Beyond him, out of earshot, Pike stood as sentry, looking the other way.

Badger was lean like so many of the perpetually hungry forest partisans. Those who lived in richer parts of the country could eat far better, but they were easier to catch in the fields of wheat and rye and barley. There they could die with full bellies. Here in the forests, where the farmers were poor, the partisans needed to risk their lives for cows on passing trains.

Badger had dark, backswept hair, except for the white streak just above his right temple. He had a slightly pointed nose, which he was sensitive about and which he covered with his hand whenever he was thinking. His StG 44 was leaning against the tree trunk beside him; the rifle Martin had pulled out of the lake. Badger said it had saved his life more than once and Martin was glad he had been useful. Even now, when Badger reached for the rifle, he sometimes looked to Martin with a slight nod to acknowledge his ongoing gratitude.

Badger walked up and studied Kostas, looking deeply into his eyes. Kostas did not move.

"That woman is back at the cemetery in town," said Martin.

"Tell Pretty Boy about her," said Badger, without looking away from Kostas. They were very close, and Badger stared as if trying to read deeply into the teacher's mind, far past what the eyes could show. Kostas remained very still until Badger took half a step back.

"All right. I need you to answer some questions."

"Not much of an introduction from a stranger who wants to see me on short notice," said Kostas, his shoulders falling slightly as he relaxed after Badger lessened the intensity of his gaze. "Don't you know the answers already? Your man down the way there met me when I was first coming into town. And I grew up in a village like this myself. News travels, so I'll bet you know everything about me there is to know already. And if you don't, and if you were one of my pupils, I'd tell you to do your homework."

Badger slapped him across the cheek and Kostas reeled back. Pike dropped his rifle from the crook of his arm and pointed it.

"Say the word," said Pike.

Badger shook his head. "He's harmless."

Kostas rubbed his cheek. "If I'm so harmless, what was that for?"

"For a very clever response from a man in a fashionable coat. Your wit might have carried the day in some smart café in Vilnius, but it's worthless currency in this place. They hunt us by day and by night. I lose good men all the time and I won't have this sacrifice diminished by some townie with a lack of respect."

Kostas rubbed his face. "It's not respect you'll get with your violence. The whole country is afraid enough as it is."

"Then it needs to stiffen its backbone."

"And now you've slapped the village teacher in front of one of the village boys. Just think how you've diminished my authority in front of Martin. Am I some sort of lackey you can push around?"

"For all I know, a spy was on your heels and the reds will be here at any moment."

"The only person on my heels was Martin, and if you don't trust him, who do you trust?"

Badger breathed deeply and looked to Pike, who put the rifle back up in the crook of his arm.

"We don't know who to trust any more. The ones who helped us before now betray us. I see accommodation and weakness all around me. I see cowardice masquerading as pragmatism."

"Well, you shouldn't judge who to trust based on the cut of his coat. This thing cost me three weeks' of my miserable teacher's salary and I bought it second-hand from a widow and I still owe her half the sum."

"All right, all right. Sit down, then."

"I'll stand, thank you."

"You'll sit as I told you."

They settled upon the logs after Kostas undid the buttons and lifted the coat so he sat on his pants instead of the tails.

"Let's begin again," said Badger. "Look, you sounded cocky, but you're in the woods with armed men. Shouldn't you be a little bit afraid?"

"Afraid of what? If you were the red army, I might tremble a bit. I've seen what they've done. But I've committed no crimes and I'm a patriot, so people like you are supposed to be defending my rights against the occupation. Instead, you slap me around like you're some kind of local tough. You ask me questions, but who are you anyway?"

"Call me Badger. I'm the leader of the partisan southwestern region."

"That's rather grand, isn't it? How big is this so-called southwestern region? Am I looking at the combined forces right now, you and your two, what shall I call them, *associates*?"

Badger made to stand but restrained himself.

"Where did you get this sarcastic mouth? I'm surprised you aren't dead or behind bars already. Why would you want to know how many of us there are? Do you want to tell someone something?"

"Calm down. You bring me into the woods to meet three armed men. I'm not sure I would have come at all if it wasn't for Martin. I can trust him, so I suppose I can trust you. And what kind of name is that you have anyway?"

"We use code names, you fool."

"But you have a white streak through your hair. What kind of a secret is your code name if the colour of your hair gives you away?"

"Very observant. You could be working for the security apparatus with attention to detail like that."

"Or I could be a writer. Writers notice things, the kind of detail everyone else ignores in their egocentricity."

"My, aren't you a confident fellow. Why?"

"And you are unnecessarily aggressive."

"Maybe. But answer my question."

"I'm confident because I have nothing to lose. I came from a godforsaken village and now I'm a village teacher. What could possibly be taken away from me?"

"A lot. You have no idea what suffering can be. You could lose your life, for example, but even worse, you could be sent off north to freeze and starve. Four to six weeks to get there. A certain number don't arrive. Or you could be tortured by those sadists in the red prisons. The loss of a single thumbnail would show you how much you have to lose."

"Yes, yes. I know that. Who doesn't know that? Look, we're living in terror. But I feel I have an obligation to keep up my spirits and the spirits of others too, especially the children. Otherwise, everything is too depressing. We're being crushed by the reds here, so we have to maintain morale just to piss them off."

"They say you're a poet."

"That's right.

"What is a poet doing in a village in the middle of nowhere at Lyn Lake?"

"Believe me, there are other places I would rather be. I got in trouble with the authorities. I'm out of the way here, and I thought I was safe until you slapped me across the face."

Kostas took a pipe out of his pocket, but Badger waved it off; the smell of smoke carried and could give them away.

"No place is safe anymore," said Badger. "The red clerks with their lists are scouring the country and eventually they'll come to scrape us up as well. So what did you do to get in their bad books?"

"Poetry bought me my ticket to this paradise. During Nazi occupation, I published a poem called *The Caterpillar*."

"So?"

"In my verses, the crawling thing was actually the pet Stalin kept under his nose because he couldn't grow a moustache. It crawled off his face and slept beside him on his pillow at night."

Badger snorted.

"Funny to you," said Kostas, "but not so funny to the *politruk* who found out once the Soviets came back in. Suddenly I'm some kind of Nazi collaborator."

"Where did you publish this poem?"

"It was in a mimeographed newsletter of the Catholic Students' League. Such a modest beginning, with a print run that must not have exceeded fifty copies. I hoped that people would notice, and when someone finally did, it was the wrong person at the wrong time in the wrong place."

"Betrayal. Again and again, it's the same story." Badger clenched and unclenched the fists resting on his knees. "We need solidarity, but our people keep giving in. We encourage them and encourage them, but sometimes you need to frighten them into good behaviour. If you know who did it, maybe I can help out."

"I think I do know who it was, but I'd rather leave him with his guilty conscience."

"What a romantic. Guilty conscience? Do you think he'll be some kind of Raskolnikov and lose sleep over it? The betrayers have no morality."

"You've read Dostoevsky?"

"Yes, so what?

"Unusual for a partisan, isn't it? All you rough and tumble soldiers would have been more likely to read Karl May."

"Oh please, cowboys and Indians and *Old Shatterhand*. I know May, but that's work for children."

"And do you and your men talk about books?"

"Again, the sarcasm. The winters are long and there is nothing to do then. If we go out in the snow, we leave footprints and they hunt us like rabbits. But no, the others do not read Dostoevsky or anything else very much past the newspapers."

"So you're an intellectual."

"Never mind about me. I am a soldier first. I need to know more about you."

"All right. I'm a little nobody from nowhere. I don't know who my father was and my mother wouldn't tell me. She was a hired girl who finally got someone to marry her after I was born. My stepfather was a drunk who meant well but never made much money. I was a barefoot shepherd by the time I was eight years old, but I was good at school and the teachers smiled at my rhymes. I also had a great memory. Even then, I could recite the main parts of the Latin mass without understanding a word of what I was saying. The priests liked that too and I became a scholarship boy in high school.

"I worked my way up, you see. I studied at the university in Vilnius until the Germans closed the place. And then when the reds came again it reopened and suddenly everyone loved me because I could write and I could talk and most of the older writers were dead or had fled west. I was even president of the Young Writers' Association until some scheming busybody denounced me."

"You got off easy for now, but watch out," said Badger.

"I know. I just hope if I keep my head down here, the storm will pass. In a few years, my sins will be forgotten."

"Not likely. The reds keep a ledger with a list of everything everyone has ever done, and once they've finished writing the list, they go back to the top and start meting out serious punishment. They haven't come to you yet, but they will. I hate to be the bearer of bad news, but your trials aren't over yet. Keep a bag with warm clothes and food nearby because they'll come for you one night and they might not give you time to pack."

Kostas took out his pipe and started to fill it, but remembered not to light it.

"So have I passed muster?" Kostas asked.

"You look harmless enough. Now you can tell me how you can contribute to the cause."

"I gave two roubles to your friend over there when he first saw me, and I only have two left."

"Not money. Listen, we put out a newspaper. The press here is full of lies, but we have someone listen to the radio from the west and then we print up the truth. But everything is hard to get. Now I have no paper to print the news. You're a writer. Get me some paper."

"How much do you need?"

"As much as you can find. Try for five hundred sheets."

"I can barely get scribblers to write on. I'll have to go back to Vilnius to find that much, and it's dangerous for me there."

"What do you think the last weeks have been like for us with the reds crawling all over the forest, looking for cows?"

Kostas laughed, but Badger did not join him.

"All right, all right. I agree. I have some *naminė* with me," Kostas said, drawing the bottle from his pocket. "We can drink on the deal."

"I don't make deals and I don't drink. My men are forbidden to drink. Put that away and think of your country. And anyway, we're not done yet."

Badger asked him many questions about where he was from and people they might know in common. Often, he came back to the same question in a different way. Martin heard it all and was glad he'd been allowed to listen.

ON THE SHORT WALK out of the forest with Martin, Kostas stopped to light his pipe. "That is quite a friend you have."

"He's a soldier, so he acts like one. But he's smart too. He's always reading books, and his men said he can sew up a wound."

"What kind of books?"

"Anything I can lay my hands on. I can barely keep up."

"So there's more to Badger than meets the eye. And by the looks of it, more to you too."

AS BADGER RETURNED TO his bunker with his men, he had a flash of sadness. These moments were coming over him more and more now that they were into their third year of resistance. He must not show his trouble to his men. They were mostly farm boys, as well as two leftover German wounded left behind to heal after their army's retreat, and then stranded. The men were unsure of their lives now that the Americans had not come to save them. They looked to him for solace and leadership. Badger did know how to sew up a wound and he had some military training so he knew when to attack and when to retreat; and, above all, he was lucky, and this was enough for the men.

But all of it was not quite enough for him. This poet, this Kostas, was probably doomed in the long run too, but for the time being he was lucky to be living a normal life, out among people.

The talk with Kostas had quickened Badger's mind somehow. He liked that, so he wasn't through with Kostas yet.

8

"WHY SHOULD I GO with you?"

The woman had been taken by surprise and stepped back from Martin, and then saw he was just a youth and became irritated by him.

"Because they're asking for you. If you don't go, they'll think you have something to hide and come looking for you."

"How do I know it's safe?"

"I know them. They never hurt our people."

Martin had been waiting for her on the forest road outside the village. She wore the headscarf of a married woman, but she did not look very old. Life would age her soon enough. She was wearing a linen shirt with an everyday woollen vest over it. She carried a small basket with a red ribbon tied to the handle and her feet were in clogs.

"I was going to pray at the cemetery."

"You can do that later."

"Where do they want me to go?"

"Just a little ways into the forest for a meeting."

He could see that she was not afraid of him, but she was concerned by what might happen if she did not do what he asked. Everything was dangerous in that time and place, but it was difficult to distinguish where the threats lay. Walk down a country road with a basket of bread and you might be accused of feeding the partisans and end up being shipped to a prison camp by the reds. Your whole family could be sent along to keep you company, and if one of the children wasn't home when they came for you, well, the lucky girl could learn how to survive on her own or go to an orphanage. Give simple directions to a group of reds and you might be misidentified by the partisans as a collaborator. It was best to do nothing, to say nothing, to keep your eyes on the ground and your mouth shut. But even so, mischievous fortune as personified by the reds or the partisans might come looking for you. And, so, she took off her clogs and held them in one hand and followed some distance behind in order to give herself a head start if she needed to run.

"Who do you pray for in the cemetery?" Martin asked over his shoulder.

"My uncle."

"What's his name?"

"Kinka."

"I've never heard of him."

"No. He died a long time ago."

"So why do you pray for him?"

"I don't pray *for* him. I pray *to* him. His children moved to America, but we lost touch with them. I want him to intercede with them from heaven, to send them a message so they think of us again. We're practically starving and could use some help." She was quiet for a bit before speaking up again from behind him. "I've seen you around. Do you go to school in Rudnia?"

"I do. How do you know?"

"I've seen you there."

Pretty Boy and Pike were waiting for them at the appointed place in the forest.

"Finally," said Pretty Boy. He was much younger than Pike, but much bolder, a talker accustomed to taking centre stage. Before he joined the partisans, Pike had been a ploughman and never learned to say much while looking at the rear end of a horse most of his days. But he knew right from wrong, and he hated the reds because they had arrested his father during the first occupation before the war. His unfortunate father. There were no real bourgeois in the villages of the region because it was so poor, but the enemies of the people needed to be punished by the reds whether they existed or not, and his father was one of them.

"Badger's not here?" asked Martin. If she was going to be interrogated, neither one of these men would know how to get answers out of her.

"No. Thanks for bringing her. There's one more thing I want you to do, though. Take this note to the girl. You know the one I mean."

The woman Martin had brought to the partisans stood uncertainly, not knowing what to do, feeling too little threat to run and too little certainty the men would leave her alone.

Martin thought of the girl Pretty Boy was talking about.

She lived in the village of Krokšlys, a good hour away. Martin did not mind being the runner for Badger, but Pretty Boy was another matter. The very code name Pretty Boy had chosen for himself was grating to Martin, to say nothing of the manner in which he carried himself. Now Martin was to leave this woman behind without ever learning her name and take a message to Pretty Boy's girlfriend, Raminta. The only reason he did not protest was Raminta herself. He didn't mind seeing her.

Raminta was a bit older, pretty, and took Martin seriously, unlike some of the haughtier girls who looked down on younger boys. Girls had recently become a mystery to Martin, especially girls a little older than he was. They were already like women, whereas so many of his friends were still boys with quite some distance to go before they became men. There was a girl in his school called Ona, and he found himself often looking at her without quite knowing why. But Raminta was different. She was older and her power of attraction so much stronger.

He left behind Pretty Boy and Pike along with the woman he had brought for interrogation.

Back he went on the forest paths, trying to stay off the main roads as much as possible. The village he was heading to was very much like Lyn Lake, a couple of hundred people huddled at a crossroads in the forest, with occasional fields scattered where there was a thin covering of arable earth. But beneath good earth lay sand. Let a hungry cow walk too often across the same spot in a field, and up came the sand to steal any hope of planting. There were also many bogs and marshes, which presented their own dangers, but mostly it was sand that lay beneath the surface of things, waiting to swallow up hope.

The village of Krokšlys was too small to have a church, but it was not so small as to be so unnaturally quiet as Martin approached it, with no children or old people about. In the bright sun at the village crossroads there lay a man in the dust. So odd to have a man lying there in the middle of the day, as if drunk and passed out after a night of swilling homebrew. Then came the buzz of flies and Martin knew what this inert man was and he forced himself to keep a measured step because the reds would be watching from somewhere.

The corpse had bare feet with the big toe of its left foot twisted to one side as if had tried to escape the foot it belonged to. The uniform was covered in blood that attracted the flies, but the partisan tricolour was clear enough on the shoulder patch. Half the face was blown away. It was impossible to look and it was impossible not to look.

If they stopped Martin and searched him, they would find the note he was carrying for Pretty Boy. He went to Raminta's house as he had planned, and knocked on the door. She opened it herself, a dark-haired beauty in homespun clothes.

"Come in, quickly."

Raminta was a seventeen-year-old orphan who lived with her brother, and her looks had attracted many young men, but she was in love with only one of them.

"I have a note for you. Read it quickly and then burn it. They saw me coming and they might come at any moment."

She took the folded piece of paper and stood by the open door of the brick oven where embers were still glowing from the morning's baking. Martin stayed by the window so he could watch the front door. Even in the dimness by the oven, she looked very attractive to him. How could someone as exceptional as Raminta love a man like Pretty Boy, a loathsome and arrogant village cock? Women were unreadable, unknowable, yet desirable in a strange, unfocussed way.

Raminta looked long at the few words on the paper and then dropped it onto the embers where it took a moment to catch flame. The proof was gone now, and they were a little safer.

"When did they drop the body outside?"

"Early this morning. Four of them are in the house across the way, waiting to see who comes to claim it."

"Do you know who it is?"

"No."

"You should be all right then."

"Maybe. Two of them were in to talk to me, and they acted like they knew something."

"What could they know?"

"I'm not sure. They gave me this bottle, and they told me not to tell anyone about it. Look." She held out a small blue bottle with an eyedropper lid. It contained a very strong sleeping drug that she was to put into milk or tea and give to any partisan who might come to visit her. The reds had told her not to speak of the bottle, but she had told him, so she trusted him and this made him glad.

"Do you think they know about Pretty Boy?"

"They must. Look at the body outside. They put it out for me, so I'd see what will happen if I don't do what they want. And for all I know, it might even be the right thing to use the drug on him. They say partisans aren't being shot any more if they give themselves up. They go to jail or they get sent to the north, but at least they have a chance of survival. I'm in love with Pretty Boy, and there's nothing I can do about that. I want him to live, you understand? All the partisans who don't give up will die. Nothing is going to change here, ever, and I want to have a child who has some hope of meeting his father in the future. Anything would be better than having him dead."

"What are you saying?"

She came to him and took his hands in hers. "Oh Martin, you're still a little young but you'll understand it all soon enough."

He liked the touch of her hands, but he resented her words. He had feelings like a man, but everyone except Kostas and Badger treated him like he was still a boy. She took his hands and placed them on her belly and he felt the slight roundness there and understood.

He pulled his hands away.

If he had disliked Pretty Boy before, now he hated him. Martin knew unwed women became pregnant, but he was young enough to be taken aback by the reality and all the more because he had thought, barely thought, that Raminta would come to her senses and give up Pretty Boy eventually. Now she was pregnant.

"My brother is going to be very angry," said Raminta. "I can't confide in him at all. But you're the one I can talk to. You're the little brother I never had, the one I can rely on."

If he had been shocked by the news of her pregnancy, he was stung by this comparison. A little brother indeed; a harmless boy, not much better than a puppy. He needed to prove himself.

"I can't tell you what to do," said Martin. "But the reds are liars. You might be able to save Pretty Boy and you might not, but you have to save yourself. Maybe I can help."

"What could you do?"

"I have a small pistol. It's very light. Do you think you'd be able to use it if you needed to defend yourself?"

"I'm not afraid of men. I can kill a man who wants to do me harm."

"Then I'll bring you the pistol. But you'll have to hide it very well, and I'll have to come some time when I know I won't be stopped and searched."

She looked at him and nodded, grateful in a way, but a pistol would do nothing to help her with her problem.

The two of them looked out the window at the body at the crossroads. It was terrible to leave a body out that way, disgraceful and disgusting, with flies hovering in the air above it. They looked away.

A pair of red collaborators did stop him on the way out of the village. They were a rough couple, also in homespun clothes, but even they could see he was a youth hopelessly charmed by the young woman he had visited, and they sent him off with only one cuff to the head and laughter at his foolishness.

9

LYN LAKE, 1947

"WHAT IS IT YOU'RE making with that chisel of yours, Martin?"

"A dugout."

"Do you mean a boat?"

"Yes."

"Good God, Martin, hacking the wood out of a log will take you days. Even in my poor village they made boats out of boards. It's much faster work, and the boat's less tippy."

"But there's no mill here to make boards, and cutting them by hand takes two people."

There had been two of them once, but Martin was too young at the time to help with a saw and instead he sat beside Linas as his older brother chipped away at the log to make them a dugout. It was taking a long time because Linas needed to help their father with the farm work, but in stolen moments with Martin at his side, he would work on the log, slowly hollowing it out. Not that Martin was much good at that young age at anything but sweeping away the wood flakes and peppering his brother with questions. But Linas had been patient. The dugout was almost finished.

"We'll catch a lot of fish because there are more of them out in the centre of the lake where we can't reach them with a line from shore."

"I never have any luck catching fish."

"I'll show you. There are a couple of tricks to baiting the hook and then working it on the bottom of the lake."

Martin had waited for the lesson, but the next thing he knew his brother was dead and some villager dragged away the half-finished dugout and used it for firewood.

Martin wasn't even sure what had come over him now to start work again. There really wasn't time to make a new dugout, with his homework and running errands for Badger. He didn't know the tricks his older brother had intended to show him, but still.

The thick morning mist was just rising off Lyn Lake, and somewhere nearby a large fish splashed and teacher and boy looked into the obscurity, but saw nothing until the ripples reached them at the edge of the grassy shore.

Although they lived in the same house, Kostas appeared only at meals, when he came to the table with stories of what the children had done in school. He sometimes brought out verses to read and asked what his parents thought of them.

Martin's father could not afford to hire a hand. His first son was dead and his second son was going to be educated and would therefore leave the farm. There was a lot of work to be done and his father was always sleepy around meals, but he did like having the teacher there, if only to listen to. As for Martin's grandmother and mother, they hung on Kostas's every word. Martin might have felt a little jealous for the attention if not for the delight that he took in having Kostas in the house. People behaved better with a guest in their home, everyone was just a little jollier. Kostas even asked him about his lessons from time to time.

Because Kostas's room had two doors, he could leave without going through the house. His door would fly open at mealtimes or when he wanted to get a cup of tea. The interior door squeaked on its hinges, but the exterior door swung smoothly and silently, and so Martin had not heard Kostas come upon him as he was working near the lake beyond the yard.

"I have the paper Badger wanted, Martin, so maybe you can take it to him."

Martin set down his mallet and chisel and stood up and brushed off his pants.

"Badger asked me to set up a meeting with you once you had the paper."

"All right, but I was trying to be discreet. I've heard there are spies just about everywhere. Some neighbour staring out the window might want to inform on me."

"Hard to believe in this town, sir. We all know each other."

"And do you all love one another?"

"No. There are some nasty people here too."

"Yes, there are always some malcontents. I've heard there are men and women who lie in ditches for the sake of spying on partisans and bring in news of them for a reward. Imagine? Lying in a ditch on the chance you could betray someone for twenty roubles?"

"Are you worried about meeting Badger?"

"No, not really, but I have nervous moments sometimes and no amount of drink settles me down. I'm a poet, not a soldier, like your *resolute* Badger. You admire him, don't you?"

"I do. Maybe I'll be a partisan when I'm old enough."

"So you won't be an engineer after all?"

Martin felt his cheeks turn red. He wasn't sure himself just what he would do. He did want to be an engineer, but he wanted everything and could not sort out in his mind what he wanted most. "I'll be fifteen next year and I only need to decide when I turn sixteen."

"How did you get involved with these men in the first place?"

"Most of them are from around here or from some place nearby. And when the reds started to steal from us toward the end of the

war, the partisans protected us, as much as they could. We have to
defend ourselves. Everybody in the countryside helps out any way
they can."

"You'll find me in my room when you want to get me."

THEY STEPPED INTO THE woods and walked for a hundred metres
and then stopped suddenly to listen for footsteps behind them. He
heard nothing but the gentle swishing of the branches of the trees
as the morning breezes finally picked up.

Martin regretted having told the teacher that he might join the
underground. Kostas was the man who had opened up his imagination to another life and he was hungry for more information about
this potential existence, this dream life. It was as if Kostas stood at
a doorway and could tell Martin what lay outside, while Martin
stood too far back to see anything and needed to hear Kostas
describe what he saw.

The forest was unvarying to the untrained eye, just an infinite
stretch of well-spaced trees with patches of underbrush and
mounds and hillocks. The reds feared the forests because how was
one, after all, to find one's bearings in such a place where bands
of partisans sometimes sprang up from hiding places beneath tall
ferns? But those who lived by the forest knew each place as well as
they knew the faces of the villagers they lived with.

Martin took Kostas to the lee of a hill where the moss was
dry and the men could sit on the ground to talk. Badger's bunker
was some distance off but not visible to Kostas from where they
sat.

"Three hundred and sixty pages! And very fine as well, by the
feel of them," said Badger. It was a warm day and he had taken off
his hat and set it beside him. He untied the ribbon that held the
pages together, careful not to bump the corners. Paper was very
valuable and always in short supply since the war. Kostas sat beside
him, his long coat folded and placed on the moss beside him.

"Are you pleased?" asked Kostas.

"It's very good paper, unlike the trash we usually have to work with. Where did you get it?"

"In Rudnia. The high school principal there helped me out."

Badger took a sheet of paper and held it up to where a bolt of sunlight shone through the trees in the forest. He sighed.

"Thank you for your efforts, Kostas. It's beautiful paper, but I can't use it."

"Why not?"

"It has a watermark on it and can be traced. See?"

He held the paper up to the sunlight and Kostas brought his head close to see the design.

"I'm sorry," said Kostas, "and to think of all the trouble I went to. Does it matter? Paper can be stolen from anywhere, so why do you care if your newspaper comes out on these pages?"

"We can't leave any hints for the enemy. I should have explained myself better," said Badger. "There's more you need to know. There's a KGB substation in Rudnia and the place is full of nosy people with watchful eyes. Try to stay out of Rudnia. Keep the paper and make sure you use it up in your class. I need ordinary paper, unmarked paper."

Neither Kostas nor Badger had asked Martin to step away. He was of two minds about this — happy to be recognized as an adult and therefore part of the conversation, but anxious that they might still consider him a boy who was harmless and therefore irrelevant.

Kostas took the sheaf of paper and put it back in his briefcase, but he kept out one sheet, peering at it again. He felt it between his fingers lovingly.

"Oh well, and such fine stuff too." There was a moment of silence as he looked at his surroundings, trying to situate himself among the trees. "How long have you been in this forest?" he asked Badger.

"From the first, but not always in this one. I was in officer school when the Soviets came the first time and I was slated to be arrested in 1941."

"How did you know that? Why you in particular?"

"I was in a whole category waiting to be arrested. Former policemen, high school principals, postmasters, government department heads. Anyone in military school. Stalin wanted to cut the head off the society so the dumb body could be made into some kind of golem to help build socialism. But a friend of mine let me know I should hide in the countryside. In those days, the red authorities were determined to arrest you, but if you weren't at home when they knocked the first or second time, you might escape. For a while, anyway. When the reds came back to defeat the Germans, I knew they'd finish the job and come looking for me again."

"You could have fled west with all of the others."

"I thought about it. Sometimes I wish I did, but my parents had me late and they were getting old. They wouldn't leave the country and I wouldn't leave without them."

"So where are they now?"

Badger laughed.

"They were arrested anyway because I was unaccounted for. I don't know where they are. I don't know if they're alive. Surprising, really. Usually, they don't touch the parents of suspects like me because their children might visit. And get snared that way. But someone was spiteful."

"So you were stuck."

"That's right. No exit. I could give myself up, but then I'd be forced help to hunt down the men I fought with. Not an option, is it? I didn't really choose to do this, but now that I'm fighting, I'll do it the best I can. And now I keep on doing this because I feel I owe it to the men who are still living and the ones who've died."

"Many?"

"Oh yes. There were so many when this all began. I started out in 1944 in a group of a hundred, a major formation, even though we only had light arms — what we wouldn't have given for tanks. But once the war with Germany ended, the reds could turn on us. Do you know about Kalniškės?"

"A big battle of some kind. There were songs about it."

"We were living in a fools' paradise, expecting the Americans to keep on moving east after Germany fell. You should have seen that camp of ours. We were on a hill, well-protected with machine gun emplacements and I thought we were on top of the world, invincible. But the reds swarmed us. We killed many, but even so, they overran us. Some managed to break out, maybe a dozen. A lot of hopes were destroyed that day. We became pragmatic. We settled in for the long fight, to wear them down. We learned to stay scattered in small groups."

"Maybe it was worth it. How many red soldiers did you kill that day?"

"It doesn't matter. The reds could always draft more. For us it was a pyrrhic victory."

Badger stopped at the word. "You know what I mean?"

"*Pyrrhic*. Oh yes, I do. But I'm a little surprised you do. There must be no one else in these villages who knows the meaning of the word."

"Yes, just the two of us." Badger glanced at Kostas for a moment, and then put his hand on his arm. "And what good does it do us?" He looked at Martin, who was sitting silently nearby. "It means a battle you win, but your losses are so high you lose the war," he said. Badger took his hand from Kostas's arm.

"See, now there are three of us who understand the word."

They laughed together

"A fancy expression, I guess. You must think I'm pretentious," said Badger.

"I think you're brilliant if you can both fight and have a decent vocabulary."

They shared a few moments of happy silence. The air was still and the forest remarkably quiet.

"You're sure I can't smoke?" asked Kostas.

"Oh, go ahead. We're pretty deep among the trees so we should be all right."

Kostas took out his pipe and filled it. He lit it with a match, sucking repeatedly on the stem to ignite the tobacco properly, and then he shook the match and pinched the dead end between his fingers to make sure it was not hot. He put it in his pocket. The tobacco smoke did not rise very high, but pooled near the earth as if it were thin mist.

10

LYN LAKE, 1947

BADGER WATCHED THE POOLED smoke and then bent down a little and inhaled deeply.

"What are you doing?" asked Kostas.

"Funny, isn't it? You'd think the taste for tobacco would go away, but your smoke still smells good to me. Where did you get the tobacco?"

"One of the villagers grows it in his yard at home. It's not too bad. Do you want a pull on the pipe?"

"No, I shouldn't. It will only make me want to start smoking again."

But Badger had a look on him.

"Sure?" asked Kostas.

"All right."

Badger took the pipe and pulled on it, and then let the smoke out of his mouth in a puff.

"You didn't inhale."

"No. I haven't smoked for a long time. If I inhaled, I'd just cough. I can't say the taste is as good as I remember."

"It's rough tobacco. But the nicotine helps you to think. It sharpens the mind."

Badger gave back the pipe, and the two were silent for a while.

"There is one thing I don't understand," said Kostas. "You

sound so rough sometimes. Why did you slap me that time when we first met?"

"I'm sorry about that."

"Don't concern yourself about it. But you seemed too irritable then, so explosive. I felt that if I said the wrong thing, you might kill me."

"No, no. We're not cruel like that. But we are hunted all the time. The pressure never ends, you know? Sometimes I act in a way I regret later."

Kostas nodded and looked at a sheet of paper that still lay on his lap. "I'm not going to waste all of this beautiful paper on my class. I'll make a few notebooks out of it. I've already been cramming my words into the margins of my sheets. I need a little white space to breathe in." He folded the single sheet twice and then placed it in his breast pocket.

"White space on a page gives you breathing room?" asked Badger.

"Yes. I don't want to be cramped all the time. The words need air."

Badger laughed a little. "We are coming from different perspectives. Imagine four men in a bunker underground in the winter for weeks at a time."

"You're talking about the physical world. I'm talking about aesthetic space."

"Really? And how is your aesthetic space right here, where we are sitting?"

"You're making fun of me."

"Sorry. A little. I'm just drawing your attention to the differences in our circumstances. What's it like to be a poet?"

Kostas looked up at him warily, ready to be mocked as poets so often were. "Well, everyone writes poems and songs. The villagers declaim their poems at parties. I see partisan poems in the underground press."

"But most people don't call themselves poets. Poetry is just something they dabble in when they're in love or the occasion calls for it. Sometimes when they're sad. There's nothing else to do when you're stuck in a bunker, so we scribble a bit. But we're soldiers. Our feelings are either too blunted by what we do, or sometimes they're too raw. Mostly we just write news we hear from the west on the radio. We write a little poetry to remind us we're not just lumps of flesh with guns in our hands."

Kostas saw that Badger was asking the question seriously, and so he decided to answer him seriously.

"Poetry is a tool that lets me see things better."

"What do you mean?"

"The world beyond the world we live in."

"Yes, of course. The spirit of things. The hand of God, for example," said Badger.

"Yes and no. There's a mystery to the world we inhabit all right. We see the surface and there may be something beyond that, but in poetry I try to see the thing itself even if there's nothing else behind it. The thing itself is sacred."

"I'm not following you. What is sacred?"

"All of creation. Our ancestors were animists who believed the world was sacred."

"Like what in particular?"

"Like the trees we're sitting among."

Badger looked around himself. "If I had to think about the particularity of every tree in the forest, I'd go crazy."

Kostas had finished smoking his pipe. He turned the bowl upside down and knocked the ash onto the earth and then ground it with his heel to make sure it was dead.

"I don't like to talk about poetry. Let's stop this. People laugh at me whenever I do. But I take it very seriously."

"And here I thought verses were all about looking for rhymes."

"It's that too. Especially when I write for children. They love rhymes, but obviously it's not just that. Poetry is something like philosophy put into a certain form, and you can't really separate the form from the philosophy."

Kostas fished a small bottle of liquor from his pocket and held it up as an offering, but Badger waved an admonishing finger. Kostas returned the bottle to his pocket.

"We don't get serious poets out here in the remoter provinces," said Badger. "And now Lyn Lake has a philosopher and literary giant in the woods."

"Giant?"

"My literature teacher once told me artists were egotists, so I was testing you."

"What your teacher said was unfair. Do you know what it's like to say you're a poet and have people shake their heads at you and smile? They think you're a dreamer at best or a fool at worst. And pretentious! You have to be a bit of an egotist just to survive the disdain, just to carry on."

"Such devotion to poetry! You keep insisting on it. Just how important is it to you?"

"Poetry is what helps me to understand the world I live in. It's like one of the senses, like sight or hearing. Maybe more like feeling because it touches the heart. Would you give up one of your senses? I knew a man who was blinded during the war and he killed himself because he couldn't live without the sight he'd lost. I couldn't live without my poetry."

"Now you're making metaphors."

"I'm not. I mean it. My poetry is so important I risked death for it."

"People risk death for love, for their children, for their countries," said Badger.

"I almost died for poetry. Listen, I was in Vilnius in July of '44 when the reds finally ended the siege by storming the city. Most of the German soldiers were dead and some tried to retreat, but others were holding out. It wasn't just reds on the attack. There were Jewish partisans and Polish Home Army too. The Germans dropped a hundred paratroopers to help out at the airport, but they were all killed as soon as they hit the ground. Pure chaos. Some of the defenders and some of the attackers ended up killing their own sides in the confusion."

"Why were you still there in the first place?"

"A smarter man would have fled to the countryside. But I loved Vilnius and wouldn't leave it."

"With the reds right at the gates? And you an intellectual, just waiting for some half-starved red army soldier to do what, listen to some verses? You don't sound like someone who knows how to take care of his own skin. Didn't you hear what they did to intellectuals the first time? Think of the Rainiai Forest."

It was a place where the fleeing reds had taken the time to cut up their prisoners before executing them as they were fleeing before the German advance of 1941.

"Oh, I stayed behind hoping to take care of poetry," said Kostas. "I'd had a decent life in Vilnius and I didn't want to give it up. I had managed to find a few editors in that city who seemed to appreciate my writing. But the city was on fire all around me. The Soviets were firing shells, and the Germans were burning buildings for the sake of the masking smoke.

"I found myself right in the heart of it. I was in a bad location, out-of-doors in a tiny park between the railway station and the Dawn Gate, in a fragment of the city's old defensive wall. Any fool knew a railway station was sure to be strategic to an invading army, and so was a main entrance to the city. I'd put myself between a hammer and an anvil."

"And what for?"

"There was a place I was trying to get to. I couldn't get into a locked building and a locked room I'd once been loaned. I had a valise with my best poems in that room, and I wanted to get to it somehow."

"That was madness. If you couldn't get into the room, you should have hidden yourself somewhere."

"I'd spent a lot of happy months in that room, but I'd seen some terrible things happening right outside my window. Mostly Jewish prisoners on their way to the train station in order to be taken to the Ponary execution pits. But that's not my point. I'd worked hard and long in that room and I had three years of work in a valise there."

"Everything you're saying is so strange. The Jews get marched to their deaths and you sit in a room watching them and writing your poetry. I wonder what that means. And what happened to this treasure trove of yours?"

"The reds were afraid of booby traps. I risked my life only to see a couple of soldiers blow open the doors and then fire into the building with a flamethrower and the whole place went up. From the streets down below, I could see the windows of my room blowing out and then the flames waving to me."

"All for nothing?"

"Yes. All for nothing. But I would do it again if I thought there'd be a chance to save that work the next time around. There are values people live by and some are more important than others. For me, literature is the highest value of all."

"Come on. It sounds noble but strange too. You die for your country, your children, not for your verses."

"Yes, I know all about those values. But they aren't mine. To make good art takes great devotion. I haven't made great art yet. I'm still learning, and maybe one day I will do that. But it's so easy for some people to forget the dreams of their youth. Not me. I've bound myself to poetry. I devote myself to literature."

"Very dramatic."

"Does it sound that way? I don't care. There are so many distractions in life. I'm in a kind of mental monastery, but instead of praying, I work on my writing. Nothing else matters as much to me."

"And for all the good it did you to stay in Vilnius, you might as well have fled."

"Look, I had that chance before the reds returned. I could have joined the refugees. The roads were filled with them."

"So why didn't you go?"

"Because I am a poet."

"Back to that again. And poets can't travel?"

"They can't travel outside their language. If I'm mocked for being a poet here, what would I be out there? Can you imagine some café in London where I'd introduce myself as a Lithuanian poet? They'd laugh at me. A rhymer in a language nobody understands from a country most people can't find on a map. The Lithuanian language is my instrument. It's my gift. But it's also my prison. I have to stay within the Lithuanian language no matter how bad things are here. There is no other place for me but here."

"And just how do you think things are in this country of yours you've decided to stay in just now?"

"Well, obviously, they're shit. My language is no metaphorical prison that keeps me here. This whole country is a prison now. But even so, poetry is a solace."

"Yes. It's a consolation, but not a solution. It eases the misery but doesn't remove it. My men and I are trying to do that, and we suffer more so you can suffer less. Give some consideration to me and my men. We're trying to unmake that prison."

"I understand what you're up against, and I love you for it. You have more courage than I do. But can't you understand my needs too?"

"Do you know what it's like to sit out the winter underground because your footprints in the snow will give you away? I have sat in the freezing cold and the dripping wet, too frightened to do anything more than look out from under the lifted lid of my bunker. Even if you have enough to eat under those circumstances, your heart aches for human company, maybe a little colour or some song. And the only thing that's sustained me at times like that is reading. My good-hearted fellow soldier snores on in the damp bunk above me, or he tells endless stories about the farm animals and his mother and father until I can barely stand to listen to one more word. But if I open a book, I have a way into another world. And you're the writer of books, or, anyway, of poems. Maybe one day you will write a book and I'll see your name on the spine.

"Never mind that. I don't even know how we came to this subject. I'm unaccustomed to speaking with intellectuals. I have a practical need, a favour to ask. Write something light and amusing that I can publish in the underground news. Write something that will give people hope. The world is so very grey and depressing that we need people like you to save us from despair."

Martin listened to this exchange with amazement and a little alarm. He had never heard either of these men speak in this manner. Badger was always the bluff, upbeat leader of men, sometimes angry, but otherwise a simple and dedicated soldier. Kostas was a teacher who liked rhymes. Martin had an uncomfortable feeling that the categories he had thought in before were melting, becoming fluid. Neither man was just the labels Martin had attached to them, and Martin was sorry for what he now knew. It had been far simpler before, and he had the uneasy feeling that this brief insight into the complications of adult life was just the beginning. Part of him wanted to close the door upon this revelation, and to return to a simpler, more child-like understanding of these men and the world they inhabited. But how to go back? Kostas, and even Badger, appeared embarrassingly sincere to Martin. He had never seen either of the men in this state.

"I'll tell Martin to bring you to our bunker on Sunday. When you come, bring some poems or an essay. I'll find a way to get the text printed and into our next newspaper. And see if you can find me some unmarked paper."

Now Badger had permitted Kostas entry to the secret life of the partisans, but he had said it lightly, without drawing proper attention to it. Martin had to say something.

"If he's coming to a bunker, doesn't he need a code name?"

The two looked at him, registering his presence for the first time since they began to speak.

"I think we should call him Skylark," said Martin.

"Why is that?" asked Badger.

"The children in the schoolhouse say his poetry is very happy, very beautiful, like a skylark chirping in spring."

Kostas considered the name with a smile.

"That's very fine. I've been named by the village children. I guess they've captured my essence."

"A teacher who's all sweetness will have children walking all over him soon enough," said Badger.

"Oh, don't worry. I won't forget the rod, but I'll try to use it as sparingly as I can."

11

PAŽAISLIS MONASTERY ASYLUM, 1959

MARTIN STUDIED THE DEEPENING shade of yellow of Kostas's face. Was it only the effect of the evening sun outside doing something to the man's face? No. The sunlight did not reach into the room directly. The change in colour was coming from inside his body, from the liver. There was no doubt. And yet the behaviour of Kostas had become more measured and urbane after his second shot of vodka. He sat on the edge of his bed with one leg crossed over the other; the only thing in his manner that gave away his need was the hand that still held the empty shot glass on the table before him.

"Ah yes," said Kostas. "Village life. Some of it comes back to me now, but not all that much. I think I tried to erase Lyn Lake from my mind because it reminded me so much of the place where I grew up. To work in that village school was like going backwards in my life. Old people talk fondly of their childhoods, but childhood and youth are the times when you stage your adult life before setting off on it. Imagine now having to go back to the school desk you shared with some childhood schoolmate who's done nothing with his life! It would be an abomination. The remembered past is golden and the imagined future has a certain glow to it as well, but to return to your own past as an adult is a nightmare.

"In the hamlet where I grew up, I wore a man's coat with the sleeves folded up twice so the sleeves at my childish wrists were like muffs, but heavy and hard and streaked with mud and dried snot because my nose was always running. The coat was so long on me it was practically a dress. The farmer sent me out into the fields unshod while the earth was still cold, practically frozen, and I had to stick my poor feet under a cow sometimes to warm them in her urine. Can you imagine?"

"A lot of us were shepherds for a while when we were kids. We're country people. It's what we had to do," said Martin.

"But some are made more miserable by it than others. Listen, what saved me was the rhymes. They ran in my head to distract me when the wind was so cold it reached right down below my upturned collar to pinch at my ears. And the other shepherds would come out to hear me recite the lines I made up in my head. They brought reed pipes when the weather became a little warmer and we put our words to country melodies.

"And if the weather warmed just a little, we set off on adventures. I myself sailed off on a spring-flooded river in an empty crate and the current carried me downstream, turning the box in the waters as I tried to steer with a stick. The crate went over and I fell into the water with that gigantic coat. If there hadn't been a teenager around to pull me out, I would have drowned.

"But most of all I remember the cold, the very, very cold. I shiver to think of it even now."

With this he lifted the shot glass slightly and then tapped it twice on the table.

"I get your point," said Martin, "but I don't want to give you any more to drink just now."

"You must. My throat is dry and I have nothing more to say unless you help me prime the pump."

"You still don't remember me?"

"Not at all."

"I'll tell you a little more about my life in Vilnius and then back in Lyn Lake."

Kostas sighed. "I'll listen only if I can have a drink later on. It's as exhausting to listen as it is to talk.

12

VILNIUS, 1956

THE VIEW FROM MARTIN'S basement room was of Soviet shoes and boots on the sidewalk outside. Heavy boots signalled country people, and military shoes were self-explanatory. Some of the feet were shod in poorly-repaired leather or canvas. Fine shoes were rare.

He lived in a ramshackle commercial row house that still showed bullet holes and traces of soot from the liberation. Martin's room was just across a busy corner from the high-roofed market, a yellow-brick building with many second-floor windows. Inside, with its high ceiling and iron beams, it was much like an old train station, with enough room for the smoke of a fantasy locomotive to billow up and away.

The official business of the market could not be contained within the walls, and spilled out to the adjoining pavements. There were always old women in headscarves on the sidewalk nearby. One might be standing with a hand outstretched for alms, another might hold a tiny bouquet of dill weed grown to supplement a meagre pension, a third a pair of knitted socks for sale. Communal farm workers received little pay, not much, but they had garden plots and sold whatever they had grown: potatoes from early summer right into spring, mountains of bright-yellow forest chanterelles gathered by their children, massive loaves of black, country rye baked with stolen grain, sold in pieces the size of bricks and weighing not much less. Flowers were sold privately in all seasons, grown who knew where. In that country, every guest arrived with a flower, so blooms were always in need. Clothing of all kinds was draped on tables or hung from improvised racks, much of it used and some of it very worn. There were rusty old locks with keys the size of small soup ladles and antique books in Polish, Russian, Lithuanian, and languages no one knew, sold by literary merchants hunched over, squatting by small rugs on which their wares were laid out.

The train station was not all that far off, and sometimes merchants showed up from as far away as Ukraine or Georgia, having come to offer oranges from within a sack. Most of the merchants were women, but there were also men about, invariably in caps, often standing in niches smoking cigarettes, neither offering anything nor asking for anything. One had to know their business, but one could never ask.

Through all this mass of goods flowed many people, both men and women, old and young, searching for what they could afford, or for some item available in no store — good coffee beans or chickens, shoe polish or ribbons. The sellers in their turn might be offering unlikely products no one would buy for weeks and weeks until a customer luckily showed up, wanting a large hasp, door hinges, a framed mirror. Occasionally one could catch sight of a bottle of liquor, but the glimpse was often fleeting; it was illegal to sell liquor in this way.

It was after just such a bottle that Martin was searching one early morning when he felt a tug on his pocket and reached quickly to seize the wrist of what he assumed was a pickpocket. He held tight to the wrist and looked into the eyes of a familiar boy with very short hair and a very big coat.

"What are you looking for?" asked the boy, as calmly as if his wrist naturally belonged in Martin's grip.

Martin did not let go.

"I wasn't looking for anything in my pocket where I found your hand. What was it doing there?"

"Come on," said the boy. "If what I wanted was inside your pocket, I would have taken it and been gone, and you wouldn't notice it until lunch time. I helped you once and you paid me. Maybe I can help you again."

"Tomas?" asked Martin.

"Tomas," the boy confirmed, and Martin released his wrist, half-expecting him to flee, but the boy stood his ground.

"What makes you think I need your help?" asked Martin.

"If you want anything, you need my help. I can get it for you at a good price."

"Even after your commission?"

"Sure."

The boy was cocky in the manner of street youths, and Martin was skeptical, but it wouldn't hurt to try. "I am looking for a half bottle of liquor."

Without even a blink. "Come with me."

Tomas led him up to an alley and told him to wait. He was gone no more than three minutes when he returned with what looked like a medicine bottle of the kind that might hold cough syrup. He gave it to Martin and named a price. Martin opened the bottle, sniffed it, and smelled the very strong odour of rye bread, which revealed that the liquor was homebrew of good quality.

"You amaze me," said Martin. "How did you come up with this?"

"It's a trade secret. I can get plenty of things you won't find anywhere else. I can help you. I know the right people."

"How old are you?"

"Twelve."

"What people do you know?"

"Street kids, like me."

"Do you work for a gang of adults?"

"You want to know too much. If you ever need anything, look for me around here or up by the Dawn Gate where I live."

"I don't have a lot of money to buy much from you."

"I just made enough from you for a cup of tea and a roll to carry me to lunch. That's enough for me for now."

"I have to get to work."

And the boy was gone.

MARTIN ARRIVED AT THE Book Depository a little earlier than most of the others, but Kristina was already in her place at the accountant's desk in a side chapel off the vast church nave. She was working the columns in her ledger. Behind her stood one of the minor altars of the former church and above her the painted saints and angels watched as she added and subtracted her sums on paper so fragile she had to be very careful in order not to tear the page when she erased her errors.

"Good morning, Martin," she said, without looking up from her ledger.

"Something for the cold," Martin said, and set the small bottle beside her tea cup.

She nodded, twisted open the bottle, and poured a measure into the waiting cup, and then she put the bottle in her drawer. The cost of this occasional gift was high, eating into his measly wages; she knew this and appreciated it. He, in turn, was grateful. She was good to him, this raven-haired woman with the mournful almond eyes. She was also very young, not more than twenty-one. How could a woman of that age be so hurt? And how was it that Stonkus had bestowed some authority on her? It didn't bear considering. Sometimes Kristina returned his favour with gifts of food, a small basket of apples, or a piece of the local sausage that was more water and gristle than meat. She had no family he knew of, so where the food came from was a mystery. He never saw her tremble with alcoholic withdrawal, but she never refused a drink. People coped however they could.

More often than food, his reward was her talk. She'd grown up in the city and knew it well. Nobody in the country said much about their pasts to colleagues and acquaintances. Although Stalin was dead and denunciations weren't common any more, the aura of danger still lingered. Opprobrium landed on anyone who had been in the gulag, or who had relatives still there. In a group, one never said where one had been or where one was going. Let the informer — and there was frequently an informer in the group — do his work and figure it out for himself.

But who were the informers in the Book Depository? There had to be some, or at least one, but if that were so, many of the workers should have been denounced. The Byelorussian specialist was a former nun, perhaps a secret nun even now although she wore no habit. She talked freely about God's will. Among the clerks were men who had odd small pieces of finery — good belts or soft hats that belonged to their families when they had been members of the bourgeoisie before the war. Had they returned from the gulag in some way similar to Martin, or had they never been deported at all and if not, how had they managed that?

All of them were lucky to be in the refuge of the Book Depository, but how long could luck last? Stonkus's health was a major concern to them all, so if he stayed home with a cold, and this was very rare, talk turned to acquaintances struck down young and families left without support. Stonkus was their shield. Long may he live.

"Stonkus protects us all because he was a communist even before the war and he retreated with the Russians when the Nazis invaded in 1941. When he returned, he saw what a hellhole this place was and so he's trying to save what he can of the past. We are relatively safe, you understand? He is a communist in good standing and we are all his children, protected from the harsh red rains beneath his vast umbrella."

"He told you this?"

"Oh, please. What do you think? I had to figure it out. Why else would someone like you be employed here?"

"How can you know anything about me?"

"It doesn't take a genius to understand what you are. A young man appears from out of nowhere — no talk of visiting his family in the countryside on the weekends, no friends, asks elementary questions about the city — so he must be a newcomer, likely from you-know-where."

No one spoke like this. He was a little frightened to hear her say those words, yet they felt liberating.

"So now I've heard more about him than I have about you," said Martin.

Martin didn't know many young alcoholics like Kristina, and the ones he had seen tended to have been brought low by tragedy and bad luck. Kristina drank moderately and steadily like a middle-aged woman in a bad marriage.

"Let's just say I live my life in books," she said.

"But they're not quite enough." Martin gestured toward the tea cup.

"No. I require a little help. Now listen, you'll need to drive today. Peter's sick and Stonkus wants you to go out on a collection with him. Do you have enough gasoline in the truck?"

"It depends how far we have to go."

"Around fifty kilometres each way, and just the two of you."

"The director is coming with me on an errand?"

"Oh yes. He doesn't shirk any job, and besides, he has the best knowledge of books. He'll know what to take and what to leave behind."

THE TRUCK WAS AN old lend-lease Studebaker the Americans had gifted to Stalin to help him fight the Nazis. After that, he got to keep the cars and trucks to help him transport the farmers resisting collectivization to the train stations, where they were ferried to the north. Martin had been taken on just such a truck eight years earlier, and, for all he knew, he or his parents had been hauled away in this very same vehicle.

But now Stalin was dead and the trucks were worn down and half-useless, so they could be parcelled out to people like Stonkus, working in niches no one paid attention to. The Depository had to maintain the vehicle, and so Martin was always scrounging for parts. He had re-stitched the canvas covering on the back of the truck because Stonkus was determined the books stay dry and suffer no more than they already had before he found them.

The roads became progressively worse the farther they drove out from Vilnius, and the truck rocked and rolled. Stonkus braced himself in his suit and tie by holding one hand on the dashboard and the other on the door handle at his side. With his slightly furry moustache and receding hair, Stonkus was the very image of an intellectual out of his element, and yet he was imperturbable, letting go of his bracing on a flat stretch to remove his eyeglasses and wipe the dust from them with his tie.

"Can I ask you something?" Martin shouted, and when he received a nod, "What are we about anyway? What are all those old books for?"

Stonkus smiled. "The books contain knowledge, of course."

"Yes, I know that. But why are all of them being kept in the church?"

"The Depository is a kind of cairn, a place to store things until we need them in the future. There has been so much war here for so long that the country is like a person in shock, and a person in shock doesn't read. He just tries to get by. We pull together everything we can find and protect it and wait until the country gets over its trauma and has the time and peace of mind to contemplate things again. But not yet. First it's time to rebuild, to feed ourselves. Just look at the miserable state of the city. Still so much rubble!"

Across the countryside, chimney smoke rose from farmstead houses here and there, but many of them were empty or in ruins. Since collectivization, the authorities were forcing people to move into collective farm villages where they would be closer to their work, and not coincidentally, easier to keep track of. In the past, the resistance partisans had been fed from the farmsteads, but now both the farmsteads and the partisans were pretty much gone, the men and women dead or shipped off to the north. No one was giving them early releases. None of the men from Badger's group were alive, as far as Martin knew, but he didn't know much. The country they had tried to save was becoming unrecognizable as the fences and cottages were torn down and the anonymous fields extended so the massive tractors of the collective farms could roll along unhindered.

Stonkus had him stop the truck twice to ask for directions, and finally they drove off from the collective farm director's house down a particularly muddy track and came upon the remains of a grand house with four columns out front, all within a yard fenced with wattle sticks. The windows were broken and doors were gone and a sow and half a dozen piglets made their way out of the former manor to croak and sniff at them as they came upon the gate. Stonkus reached into his satchel and threw out a few apples after which the sow chased and the piglets followed.

"Come on," he said.

Stonkus led Martin across the stinking muddy yard and through the doorway where the pigs lived inside. The staircase had a crude, low fence across it to prevent the pigs from going upstairs, and the men stepped over it and went up to the second storey.

In the long corridor above, the plaster had fallen off the walls in large patches, revealing the lathe below, and most of the

ornamental mouldings had been stripped from the door frames
except for one where a fire had left the carbonized wood like a
gateway into hell. Not the faintest whiff of grandeur remained,
and in what had once been the library, someone had stripped the
shelves for the sake of the boards and left several low mounds of
books.

"We're very lucky," said Stonkus. "The books are far from the
windows and so the rain hasn't got to them."

Martin had brought burlap sacks. Stonkus instructed him to
pack the books as carefully as he could and to keep loose pages in a
separate sack so they could be put back in their rightful places back
at the Depository.

For all his attempts to be rational and methodical, Stonkus was
a lover of books and he could not resist looking inside some of
them and when he did so, he fell into a kind of reverie, from which
he would shake himself to continue with the job, only to fall into
one again when he found something interesting.

"I can't believe it!" Stonkus said. He was holding a volume from
which the front and back leather covers had been cut.

"Do you know what this is?"

Martin shook his head.

"This is a *Silva Rerum*. Some of the manor houses kept journals
across the centuries, recording births and other events. They are
like diaries of the landscape, historical chronicles in a land that's
been wasted so many times there's hardly any history left. I understand the Germans burned all the *Silva Rerums* they could find
in order to destroy the memory of a state, but fragments remain.
It's incredible. We have no other book like this in the Depository.
I've heard of these, but it's the first one I've ever held in my hands.
The Destroyers try to annihilate everything, but no one succeeds.
Fragments always remain and we can use them to rebuild the past."

Martin had never seen the man like this. Stonkus was in ecstasy
and could not look away from the book. This enthusiasm reminded

Martin of his younger self, when he had become interested in engineering thanks to Kostas. Stonkus was an older man, yet he retained
his curiosity and Martin liked that. It was good to see a man alive
to his enthusiasms unlike so many of the living dead he had seen in
the camps. It was good to take delight in the world, whatever part
of it was available. It was good to put misery aside, whenever that
was possible.

Martin took it upon himself to bag the rest of the books and
loose sheets, and to carry the heavy sacks back down to the truck
while Stonkus stood by the open window in the fading light, turning the pages one by one.

13

VILNIUS, 1956

THE BOILED MEAT DUMPLINGS, *koldūnai*, came with a large dollop of sour cream. Martin added two heaping teaspoons of sugar to his black tea and stood at a counter to eat. The floor underfoot was grimy. Two red army privates on leave wolfed their meal nearby, speaking some kind of language he did not know but guessed was Turkic. Martin knew what hunger had once been, and when eating now, he tried to enjoy how well the food filled his belly.

He stepped out onto the street and pulled the backpack onto his shoulders, feeling the weight and wishing it was heavier. It contained a package he was going to post, a side of bacon wrapped in many layers of butcher paper, sugar and coffee, as well as stockings, two metres of wool cloth and some underclothing, which she had asked for in particular. He had had to borrow money to pay for all this and Tomas had helped him to get good prices.

Martin hoped his mother was doing all right. His grandmother had died during transport in 1948, and his father in a prison accident in the forest. His mother was still alive in a fishing prison camp in Yakutia, and wrote letters asking for wool cloth and meat. He sent packages when he could.

On his way to the post office, passing by the train station, he thought he saw a familiar woman at a distance, but he no longer tried to hurry up and see who such a person might be. His parents and village friends and teachers sometimes seemed to appear on Vilnius streets, and he had embarrassed himself by chasing after them. When he caught up, he found they were strangers who bore slight resemblances to people he knew, sometimes to the dead, as if ghosts were on the streets. Once he did actually find a classmate from his high school days in Rudnia, but the man was so frightened by this appearance of a former deportee that Martin felt like a leper and did not want to chance repeating the unhappy experience.

The past was over, wasn't it? He should make a new life for himself. Yet the past kept reappearing.

He had some time and was in no rush to go home. But there was an unpleasant cold mist in the air that made him want to go inside somewhere, and he found a bookstore in his rambling through the back streets of Vilnius. He had hardly any money left so he wasn't planning to buy, but looking at books was a form of entertainment. Multiple copies of analyses of Marx and Lenin were displayed in the shop window. He looked inside to see two middle-aged women talking to one another as they sat on stools behind a counter. He opened the squeaky door and went inside.

One of the women had hair dyed an atrocious shade of red, and she glared at him and told him to leave his backpack at the counter if he intended to look around. He did so and then went to the book-shelves along one wall and began to scan the titles. Half the books there were copies of ones he had already seen in the window. Some books were new and some were used. Then came annual reports of various kinds, having to do with the production of flax in Lithua-nia, improvements in pig breeding, and principles of field drainage for wetlands. Terrible novels written in the time of Stalin, poetry that sang the leader's praises, and memoirs of suffering under the so-called pre-war bourgeois regime.

Who would bother to steal this sort of trash? He did not have much hope, but he had nothing else to do, so he crouched down to study a bottom shelf, and there he found another report in paperback: a summary of the annual minutes of the Writers' Union from 1945 to the present.

There was no chair in the bookstore and no free wall against which to lean, so he stooped where he was and began to thumb through the book, scanning for the name. When he came upon it, he stood up and went to pay thirty kopeks before tucking the small book into his pocket. Back home, he sat under the narrow window with its passing feet on the sidewalk outside and he used a pencil to make small markings — dots, really that could be mistaken for stains, wherever material that he might want to find again lay in the pages.

Minutes of the Writers' Union of Soviet Socialist Lithuania

OCTOBER 29, 1945
Lithuanian Pravda announcement:

Writer K. Kostas will read from his children's work at a "Literary Monday" in Vilnius.

NOVEMBER 27, 1945
A group of young writers will meet to discuss the formation of the youth wing of the Writers' Union in order to help support their seniors in building a socialist foundation for literature in Lithuania: A. Bimba, K. Kostas, E. Mielželaitis, V. Mozuriūnas, and others.

FEB. 7, 1946
A Youth section of the Lithuanian Writers' Union has been established and the executive council will include A. Baltrūnas, K. Kostas, and A. Sprindis.

MARCH, 1946

K. *Kostas was awarded first prize in the youth poetry category
section for his poem, "The Dawn is Coming"*

MAY, 1946

The literary journal, Literature and Art, *has demanded in an
essay that K. Kostas and others be expelled from the Writers'
Union for conduct unbefitting a writer of the Lithuanian Soviet
Socialist Republic.*

1946

**Kazys Preikšas, Lithuanian Communist Party,
Secretary for Propaganda and Agitation**
*Friends! Bourgeois nationalism ruled our country for many
long years and the national spirit was further crushed by three
years of German and Lithuanian fascist ideology. We can feel
the results of their poison to this day. We are fighting a war
against the remains of this line of thought, and writers are at
the forefront of the battle. Comrade Stalin has called writers
"engineers of human souls."*

...

*Many of Lithuania's writers are still lost in bourgeois nation-
alism and even Balys Sruoga, who was captive in the Stutthof
concentration camp, writes his book about the experience without sufficient optimism ...*

*... The Writers' Union has paid insufficient attention to the
work of its members, bordering on dereliction of duty. Among
those young writers are persons such as K. Kostas who hid the
fact that in the past, during the fascist occupation, he spat out
filthy anti-Soviet nonsense and was permitted to publish it ....*

*J. Baltušis — Secretary of the Lithuanian Communist Writers'
Union*
*Friends, we have just heard some very bitter, yet truthful
words which have laid out the proper Bolshevik criticism of
our literature ...*

*... None of the leaders of the Writers' Union properly protested
against the membership of K. Kostas ...*

Balys Sruoga, writer
*Friends! Errare humanum est. Let me explain my regret for
the errors I made in interpreting my incarceration in the Nazi
Stutthof Concentration Camp ....*

V. Mozūriūnas — writer of Lithuania's Youth Pravda
*This Kostas, whom we raised to the leadership of the young
Writers' Union, turns out, wrote horrible things about the
Soviet Union during the fascist occupation. A young person,
one could say, might make an error, but to hide this past and
come to the Communist Writers' Union pretending to be a
Soviet writer was too much by far ....*

Jonas Šimkus —Assistant editor — Lithuanian Pravda
*... K. Kostas has stained the name of Lithuanian literature with
his pen and he has no authority whatsoever among the young
writers of this country ....*

They had really gone after him. So there it was, the story that
Kostas had told them all those years ago. Martin flipped forward,
but some of the pages had been cut out. He looked back to the front
of the book to see if he could identify the owner. Who would have
cut out pages like that?

Martin looked carefully, and found only one more entry about Kostas, one entered that very same year:

1956
M. Sluckis
... It's true that in the past we were a little hard on some of our young writers like K. Kostas, but at the time it seemed necessary ....

MARTIN WANTED TO FORGET and he wanted to remember. He wanted to see Kostas and yet, not to be seen by him, at least not up close. More than once he lingered at a cross street by the Writers' Union and determined that on most days, Kostas came in to his office late in the morning. He worked in a room up high beyond the grand slate staircase with the impressive balustrade installed by the last of the ladies of the ancient ruling class before she died just in time not to be dispossessed in 1945.

Kostas did most of his work at the Writers' Union. The building faced southeast and the Book Depository faced northwest, and so although they had nothing but a wall between them, each of these places looked in opposite directions. Martin and Kostas worked back to back. Kostas would not see him up close if Martin was careful about the way he came to work. Kostas had not recognized Martin the first time he put eyes on him, and he might not again, but Martin did not want to see him unexpectedly, just in case.

The Soviet Union loved the writers it could call its own and handed them fine offices, and designated special cafés and cafeterias so they would not need to line up with others on the grey and miserable streets. Once, Kostas came to his union office with a woman and a child, and by the way they carried themselves Martin saw they were a family. The woman had a harried sort of look to her, but the boy threw his arms around Kostas, who lifted him and kissed him and set him down before turning to go into the union office. He did not kiss the woman, who took the boy by his hand and walked away.

The Writers' Union had not only a cafeteria of its own but a bar in the basement as well. Sometimes if he had worked late, Martin would stand in the shadows and watch Kostas stagger out of the place. More than once, Martin saw the woman who must have been his wife go there to pull him away from the bar.

14

LYN LAKE, 1947

MARTIN SQUINTED IN THE poor light of the oil lamp, but he could not see properly and so his fingertips guided him to where the rough spots remained on the rifle stock he was sanding. The space in that bunker was tight as well. The walls were made of cedar posts and the leaky ceiling the same, and half the interior space was taken up with damp bunks for four men. He had offered to carve the new stock at home and be careful, but Badger did not want him working there on a part for a weapon for fear he might be seen. It was illegal to possess a weapon, and a rifle stock in hand was as good as a ticket to the gulag. Spies were everywhere, and not just collaborators. All across the country, people with grudges had found out how easy it was to denounce not only a suspicious man, but also a wealthier colleague, an irritating villager, or a neighbour whose dog barked too much.

"I can barely breathe in here," said Kostas.

Badger laughed. "You'll get used to it. Once there's not enough oxygen left, the lamp goes out. Even then you can survive for a while without opening the lid."

"Why don't you build air vents?"

"The steam coming off them in the winter would give us away. But if you're so starved for air, I'll have Martin open the lid and keep an eye out while he's at it."

Martin lifted the lid of the bunker halfway and made himself as comfortable as possible so he could better see what he was working on and still survey the approach to the hideaway from time to time. It was grim out there, grey and wet, but the light was pretty good for that time of year. Later, when the heavy rains came, the ceiling of the bunker would leak terribly and then when the snow arrived he'd have to brush away his footprints with a pine branch to disguise his trail.

"This is the book you've brought me," said Badger.

"Yes. It's infamous around here. Have you read it?"

"*In the Shadow of the Altar.* No. My parents wouldn't have let a book about a renegade priest into the house."

"It's a good book. It talks about the priest's conflicted feelings, how it's unnatural to have celibacy forced on humans."

"Are you trying to shock me? I'm not so easy to scandalize. It's hard to imagine a novel about priests in these 'religion-is-the-opium-of-the-people' days. Do you write stories and novels?"

"Not really. My talent is lyric, unfortunately."

"Why unfortunately?"

"Poets are the church mice of the writing world, pretty much invisible, slightly annoying. Sometimes mocked for what we do. But when someone dies, or a memorial day comes up, people call for us to read our lines. They want to be moved and helped to remember, to have eternity made comprehensible, and if that's impossible, to be consoled for all the blows and losses. We are wanted when needed, and at no other time, especially since priests aren't used much in public anymore. There's no money in poetry and we end up being teachers or clerks to make a living."

"Like you. How is it teaching in the village?"

"I'm used to it, but some of the children are always unteachable, slow or wild and sometimes worse, and most need just enough education to add and subtract and get by with a little reading."

"They make fine people. My partisans here are all country men, honest and straightforward."

"Maybe. Useful to help you fight or haul a load of hay, but you've been educated. That's a problem Badger, isn't it? It gives you the gift of an internal life, but that life needs to be fed."

Badger sighed. "I'm a soldier. I'm not sure I'm supposed to have an internal life."

"Everybody has an internal life; just some lives are richer than others."

"I wish I could afford to give myself that luxury."

"How can you afford not to? Every soul, in particular the souls of readers and thinkers, needs to be fed or it starves, the way you starve for oxygen unless you open the lid of your bunker."

"So how do you feed your soul?"

"By fighting for internal freedom. I carry my freedom with me. Look at where we are, at the edge of a country at the edge of a massive multinational state. Nobody from any important place knows about us, and never will. We are obscure, forgotten, but I can reach inside and write my poetry wherever I am and more-or-less whenever I want. I am the freest man in the world because I have this ability no matter where anyone puts me."

"Very impressive for you. If only I could say the same. When I was young, I wanted to be doctor. I wish sometimes that I could have fled with all the others who are living in Paris, or Rome, or New York."

"Not very patriotic, not from a partisan."

"Oh, I'd never admit to feelings like that in front of the men. What would be the use in demoralizing them? I was offered a mission to take documents out to the west through Poland once, and didn't take it. Others walked out that way and they made their way to France and America. But someone has to fight for his country and it looks like I'm one of them."

"You're a hero."

"Don't be ridiculous. I'm a victim of circumstance trying to do the best I can. There is no place for me anywhere but here, underground. Still, sometimes I feel, as you say, as if I can't breathe."

"Feed your soul."

"How am I supposed to do that?"

"By reading as you do, for one thing, and by talking about these things as well."

"This conversation we're having is a rare thing. I can't speak like this with my men."

"Then speak like this with me."

Badger seemed moved by these words. He was about to say something and stopped, and then started again.

"You aren't here that often. Maybe we could remedy that if you came underground."

"What? Just like that?"

"That's right. Choices get forced on us. Can searching for rhymes and the shape of truth behind the surface of things be the right thing to do now? We're under occupation. The reds are trying to annihilate us. I could use your talents."

"Very stirring, and honestly, I'm moved. I love my country as much as anybody else, but sometimes it seems to me that all those people who said the most pretty words about patriotism fled this country when the reds came back. Where are they now? On their way to America, I'll bet, ready to live in tall buildings while you and I are crouching underground here in the middle of a forest."

"Intellectuals don't really make the best soldiers. Country boys see things plainly and they aren't afraid. But country boys can't do everything."

"What do you need?"

"You're a writer and you've given me verses. Thank you. I need paper to get out the news, but I need more than that. I need someone to write it down for me. Yes, the more I think of it, the more

I believe it's necessary. I want you to commit. I want you to come into the forest with us."

Martin looked up at Badger and thought the man might be blushing.

"This is all so sudden. We hardly know one another, and I'm in enough trouble as it is. What you say would mean a death sentence for me and a one-way ticket to Irkutsk for my mother."

Emboldened by his idea, Badger pushed on.

"Nobody said sacrifice would be easy. But you don't have to step out all the way at first. You can just help in your free time. All I need you to do for now is to listen to the foreign news occasionally and to write summaries of what you hear. I have a radio here and you can come and absorb the material with me."

"First I'd have to know how to find you. I don't want to be led through the forest with a blindfold any more. Your bunkers are hidden better than Easter eggs."

"And rightly so. We move often and we don't tell anyone who doesn't need to know. I'll send Martin next Sunday before noon when the BBC broadcasts."

"All right."

"How often can I expect to see you?"

"I'll be a kind of reservist. I brought you this book and I'll bring you another when you've finished this one."

Badger had been leaning forward to make his case, and now he eased back. "How can you find novels in the village?"

"I do go away sometimes. We teachers have to appear in Vilnius occasionally to learn about the latest directives. I look for books. If I can, I'll find something for young Martin here, something about mechanics or engineering."

Martin looked up at them when Kostas said his name, and he nodded appreciatively, but the conversation was more of a shock to him than he showed on his face. It had never occurred to him that he might be one of the sort of men Badger had described, stalwart but a little simple.

And yet he wasn't simple. He was going to high school, one of the most gifted of the village children. He was different from the rest. As he listened to Badger, whom he had admired for so long, he saw what it might be like to be different from the others. Maybe not such a blessing after all.

"Don't expect too much of me," said Kostas. "I'll help you whenever I can, but I can't give up my legal life just now, and I can't give up my poetry."

15

VILNIUS, 1956

MARTIN HAD HIS LUMBER stacked beside him, his hammer and saw nearby, nails in his carpenter's apron. The two sawhorses stood ready. He had instructions to build tall bookcases directly in front of the chapel niche where Kristina did her bookkeeping work. She would become invisible to passers-by once the shelves were filled.

High above the side chapel where her desk was, the weak light came in through the stained-glass windows and the clear ones, with occasional flashes of shadow from birds flitting by. Not much of this light made it down from above to the dais upon which she worked at her desk, and even less light came from the nave where other tall book cases stood row on row. What little light there was would be further blocked, and Kristina's one lamp used an eccentric bulb whose replacement was hard to find. How could an accountant study the columns of numbers under these circumstances?

"Why do you want to block yourself off from the rest of us?" asked Martin.

"There will be no peace in this place unless I have books around me to muffle the sound, and they'll help to keep off the drafts. And anyway, what do you care? Stonkus told you to do it, so do it."

The vast Depository already seemed peaceful enough to Martin, who had worked in workshops with their buzzing saws and whining drills. A few dozen people worked in the repurposed church, but they were off in various niches of their own and the place was so massive it felt empty most of the time.

Kristina was not usually so short-tempered unless it was late in the day and her alcohol had run out, but now something was on her nerves. She bent down over her ledgers and worked her sums after pushing back a strand of hair that had fallen on the right side of her face. She kept her hair tied up most of the time, so Martin had never realized how long it was. Sometimes when the church was very cold, she wore a hat all day as well as a coat and gloves, disappearing into her clothes. And now, he felt as if he were entombing her.

Stonkus's instructions had been general, but Kristina had been very clear about what she wanted. Her chapel was to have two twelve-foot-high bookcases built in front of it, each covering three quarters of the opening and offset, so that anyone wanting to see Kristina would need to go around the front bookcase and back along a short corridor between the two stacks before coming into her sight.

"I've been sitting up here like an animal in a zoo," she said. "Everyone who walks by thinks he has to say something to me and I can't concentrate on my work. At least now I'll have a little privacy."

"You'll have less light."

"I'm like a cat. I can see in the dark."

And it was true she seemed to need less light than anyone else. Martin measured and marked his boards by moving them into the unpredictable shafts of light that came down in bolts from above, depending on the clarity of the sky and the season and the time of day. She worked on, unperturbed in the dimness.

She did not join him when he went to the common room for lunch, where they had a hot plate to boil water for tea and where there was a south-facing window that provided light and some warmth on sunny days. The walls of the church were thick as those of a fortress; they never warmed properly, a blessing in summer but not so much the rest of the year.

Stonkus appeared at lunch on Mondays and Fridays in order to oversee his family of book saviours — on the other days he ate lunch at home. On Fridays, he liked to remind his men and women to go for walks in order to get some sunlight on them and to breathe air not laden with dust, but he hardly ever took his own advice and often could be found after hours still in the Depository, as could some of the others he had encouraged to go out. The place was not warm, but it was dry and relatively safe, a kind of refuge when the cruel streets outside and the miserable apartments were too depressing to inhabit during time off. Martin wondered if some of his co-workers, bookbinders, translators, archivists, so silent and discreet, did not live in niches they had scraped out for themselves within the corridors and chambers, the crypts and the hidey-holes within the old church. He sometimes came upon a coat or a sweater on a windowsill or a shelf. Folded blankets sometimes lay among the books and even small pillows.

Midnight knocks on the door did not come often after Stalin died, but the memory of them remained vivid. Sometimes, it was better not to be found at home. Some of the old men and women worked in random places, whenever they could, rather than in their workshops and offices. Martin surmised that if someone came looking for them, these souls would be hard to find even at their workplace.

Not enough of them worked there to justify a commissary, but through channels Stonkus had in the communist party there would be unexpected gifts such as a loaf of bread each, bags of hard candies, or, memorably, a ticket which gave each of them the right to a boiling hen for Easter. The line-ups for the chickens were long, but at least the chicken itself was guaranteed to be there. This gift of fowls evolved into a sort of celebration when those without kitchens at home cooked the chickens in a large pot right in the immense lunch room itself. Seminarians had once sat at the worn wooden tables. One could imagine perhaps a few dozen young men eating there as one of their number read aloud from Aquinas.

There were moments of merriment, like the boiled chicken meal, spaced out rather thinly, but this was not to say that the times in between were grim. Whatever suffering the clerks and bookbinders, the labourers and librarians and archivists might endure in their private lives, they found a sort of refuge at work. They were moles labouring in the safety of their underground lives. Of course, this did not prevent sudden attacks of weeping among the older workers, trembling of hands after weekend benders, or prolonged silences while considering the fates of dead or deported relatives. These sorts of outbreaks were to be expected. The past decade and a half outside the walls of the Depository had witnessed all kinds of terrors. It was no wonder some of the pain bled inside.

News of the world seeped slowly into this sanctuary, and so the new liberalism after Stalin's death and Khrushchev's speech of 1956 could be discerned by a lessening of fear, but not its elimination. Those bureaucrats and communist party activists who had served Stalin so well were not gone. They still sat in judgment of current and historic infractions against communism and shady family histories that included uncles in America or religious inclinations. Disappearance might have been less frequent than before, but misery was not in short supply.

As for the post-war burst of suburban growth in America, the proliferation of refrigerators and automobiles, the men and women of the east had no knowledge of it except in an indirect way when the west was attacked in the Soviet press for unequal distribution of its wealth.

In Eastern Europe, history did not seem to move in the progressive way it did in the west, where freedom was a house to which new rooms were always being added for Jews or women or Blacks. Foolish hope sprang up in nearby Poland and Hungary in 1956, only to be crushed with a great outlay of blood, which the soil in those places seemed to call for.

All in all, it was best to be inside the walls of the former Church of St. George-the-Martyr and the Virgin Mary-of-the-Snows, now that it had been rechristened under the bland name of the Book Depository. Blandness was a great blanket under which safety could be found.

Kristina's need for a keep within the sanctuary was puzzling to Martin. They were all lucky to be where they were, safe as possible under the circumstances. So why did Kristina want yet another wall built around her?

16

RUDNIA, LYN LAKE,
KROKŠLYS, 1947

THE COLUMN OF MEN bearing the three caskets on their shoulders did not have very far to go. The distance from the front steps of the twin-spired wooden church in Rudnia to the cemetery on the other side of the front yard was no more than a hundred metres.

The red functionaries were waiting for the caskets just outside the church gates because it would not have been politic for the atheists to be on church ground. The chairman of the local red office would have preferred that the caskets not be carried into the church at all, but it took time to create the new Soviet man and the surviving relatives were adamant that a funeral was not a funeral without a funeral mass. Still, the authorities were not going to permit this moment to pass unremarked, and so three pairs of sawhorses were set out for three coffins between the gates of the church yard and the gates of the cemetery, and local communist agitators held up a banner which said, "Victims of Fascist Bandits."

The high school students were taken out of school to attend the funeral ceremonies, but only outside the church grounds, the better to learn all about the crimes of the forest bandits. The crowd swelled into the hundreds. The chairman of the communist party of the provincial capital in Varėna had come down with half a dozen soldiers as guards in order to give the speech, and he stood on a low riser prepared for him. The wind was strong and the red banner swelled and the church banner within the nearby gates of the church snapped in the wind again and again. Men held on to their hats and married women clutched the knots of the scarves tied below their chins. The chairman projected his words above the noise of the wind, but he would need honey tea for his throat once the day was over. It was a pity there were no lemons to be had.

Badger had instructed Martin to get as close to the open caskets as possible, but it was not easy because the red officials and the cousins and uncles of the deceased had rights of proximity. He managed to shoulder his way forward to look into the casket and confirm the woman was the one who had been praying at the cemetery in Lyn Lake, the one he had taken to Pretty Boy.

"Is that her husband?" Martin asked a weeping woman beside him.

"Of course, you fool. Weren't you at the mass?"

"The principal wouldn't let us go into the church. And the boy?"

"Her son. Just twelve, but he tried to protect them and look where it got him."

Martin's teacher took him by the shoulder and pulled him back into the ranks of the other high school students. The speeches began. Many people seemed to have something to say, but it was hard to catch their words because of the wind.

"HOW DO YOU THINK the people will support us if we treat them like this? We rely on them to protect and feed us. We're supposed to be defending them from the reds, not killing them ourselves."

"She was a traitor, remember? You're the one who gave the execution order."

A table had been set up in the field and a partisan secretary sat on a chair behind it, recording proceedings in a notebook. Two other bands of partisans had come for the trial, so a dozen men stood in their ranks as Badger interrogated Pretty Boy in the partisan field court martial.

"That is true, but I didn't tell you to kill her family."

"What could I do? She was fast and she slipped away from me on the way to the place where I was going to execute her. It never would've happened if I wasn't carrying a shovel to bury her with. It scared her, and at first, I didn't think to drop the shovel as I ran after her. She ran for miles, right into an open field where her husband and son were working. They came at me with a scythe and a pitchfork. What was I supposed to do?"

"Idiot. You could have let them be and finished the mission another time. Fear of a death sentence is almost as good as a death sentence and she would have been terrified and fled the province. Now they'll drop hundreds of soldiers on us. They will walk through these woods with their metal poles, plumbing every inch of earth to find our bunkers."

"She was a spy. She deserved what she got. Her husband must have known what she was doing."

"And the boy?"

"An accident. I never meant for this to happen."

"I am tempted to have you executed on the spot for unnecessary cruelty."

"You can't do that. I am your best man. You can't blame me for what happens in the heat of battle."

"Don't try to be familiar with me now. You're on trial. You've become a propaganda tool. They'll be writing about your cruelty all the way to Vilnius. But I will take into account your record so far."

"What does that mean?"

"It means you are forbidden to get out of the sight of any one of us and you are to be disarmed. I will leave your final sentence to The Hawk when the regional commander finds his way here again."

Pretty Boy paled. "It was an accident. I've already given up everything to fight for my country and now you want to make an enemy of me too. The reds kill us fast enough. Why do you have to help them? I can't give up my weapon. What if they come upon me unawares?"

"We'll be with you. And I warn you, don't try to run because the others will have orders to shoot you if you desert."

THERE WAS A GREAT deal to do then as the headquarters bunker needed to be abandoned because the locations of all bunkers, no matter how secret, somehow became known over time, and very soon the red army and their local collaborators would be upon them with their sounding rods. But even so, Badger gave Martin a few minutes.

"How did you find out she was a spy?" asked Martin.

"We interrogated her."

"What does that mean, exactly?"

"It means we asked her questions."

"And she answered them?"

"Yes."

"Just like that?"

"It's never that simple, Martin. But she gave herself away by lurking here and asking too many questions of her own. What business does a woman from Rudnia have coming here so often and asking questions and snooping around the village? She was either a communist or she was doing it for pay."

"Did you have to beat her to get her to talk?"

"Sadly, yes. She had to be frightened into telling the truth."

"But if she was so frightened, wouldn't she say anything to stop the beating?"

"We don't take it to that point. I have to consider her suspicious actions and what she says and then use my gut judgement. Look, this is terrible, but I have to do it to protect the others, the innocents. She could have harmed us all. I'm very sorry the way things turned out. You're young. You expect it all to be straightforward, but sometimes, even if you have the best of intentions, things end badly."

"Will The Hawk come for the sentencing?"

"He wrote to say he would. Nobody likes a court martial, but if anyone has the authority to carry out a sentence, he's the man."

"And how do you think it will end up for Pretty Boy?"

"I don't know."

"Do you mean he might actually be executed for cruelty?"

"It wouldn't be the first time. It's out of my hands now. We'll see how it turns out. Listen to me. I want you to disappear from my sight for a while. We're going to move the bunker, and I'm not telling you where the new one is. I'll let you know when I need you."

"You can trust me."

"I know I can, but the coming days are going to be hellish and the less you know the better. But you can be my eyes and ears in the village. I never would have known about the spy if you hadn't told me about her in the first place."

THE CEMETERY IN RUDNIA was just down the lane from Martin's high school. He didn't have to walk far to see the newly mounded earth above the graves of the family killed by Pretty Boy. And as to Pretty Boy, he was no longer the cocky young fighter the last time Martin saw him. Suddenly the very band that had protected him was turning on him, and there was no one left to admire him.

One morning, instead of going to school, Martin took a particularly long detour through the forest to the village of Krokšlys. He avoided not only roads, but major forest paths. He stopped often to look and listen, and he finally made his way to the home of Raminta. Martin waited until he saw her brother leave the house, and then he tapped on a side window. She looked out to see who it was and he asked her to open the window so he would not be seen going in through the door.

"Did you bring me another note?" she asked.

"Good morning to you too."

"Stop joking. You know how worried I am."

He looked to her belly, but she was wearing a baggy dress, and he could not see how much her pregnancy was showing.

"I came to bring you the pistol I told you about."

"Oh."

"You don't seem to understand about this pistol. If I'd been searched on my way here and someone found this on me, I'd be on a train to where the polar bears roam, or worse."

"Then why did you bring it to me?"

"For your protection. I told you before. But you have to hide it well, yet it has to be handy enough for you to defend yourself if you needed to."

"Yes, I'll figure that out later. If you don't have a letter from Pretty Boy, do you at least have news about him?"

"I do, but listen. This pistol has only six rounds in it. I hand-loaded them myself, so I'm not sure every bullet is going to fire or fire well. If you're in a tense situation, don't just pull the trigger and expect your problems to go away. You have to fire two or three times and then wait to see what damage you've done."

"Just tell me about Pretty Boy."

"I will, but keep listening. You need to be close for a pistol to have any effect at all. You can't just shoot at someone across a field, or even across a road unless your intention is to scare him off."

He could see that she was barely listening to him. He would repeat his instructions about the pistol before he left. All she wanted to know was about Pretty Boy. Martin told her about the deaths in Rudnia and then about Pretty Boy's impending court martial.

"They couldn't blame him for doing his duty, could they?"

"It wasn't his duty to kill the father and son."

"I'm sure he couldn't help it."

"That's what he says. But if The Hawk finds him guilty, he'll be executed by firing squad."

She shuddered. "By his own comrades?"

"That's how it's done. As a lesson to others."

"This can't be true. This is hell you're describing to me. Can you get a note to him?"

"It's too dangerous for me to carry a note. Anyway, I don't know where they're keeping him."

"I need to talk to him."

"I don't know if that's possible."

17

LYN LAKE, 1947

THE CLANG OF TRUCKS bouncing along the bad regional roads pealed throughout the countryside as red army soldiers poured in to find the men who had murdered a whole family in Rudnia. The despised collaborating Destroyers joined them, working like sniffing dogs for the red army, helping to beat suspects once they were caught.

Out of the backs of trucks they teemed into various suspicious villages, fields, and forests in order to thrust their iron sounding rods into the hard earth around houses and barns where they suspected the partisan bunkers might be concealed.

The villagers hid whatever goods might catch the fancy of these soldiers who were looking for men but took whatever items they liked. Bread was put out of sight, butter ladled into pots and buried in the earth, and bacon wrapped tightly before being concealed so it would not give itself away by its smell. Those who had hidden weapons thought nervously about the security of their hiding spots. Martin's father loved his motorcycle, but it was too big to hide, so he simply made sure there was very little gasoline in the tank so some rapacious officer couldn't get very far if he decided to sit upon it and try to ride away.

The region was vast and the bunkers were well-hidden, and the fruitless searches infuriated the officers whose job it was to get rid of the nationalist bandits once and for all. They took out their anger on the locals, who must have known something and who must have been hiding the criminals and therefore must have been guilty and deserving of beatings, which the reds and Destroyers parcelled out as mood and opportunity struck them. The less the reds found, the angrier they became. A sleeping shepherd was kicked until his jaw broke, Martin's father took a few blows from a stick, and Martin's high school teacher came to work with a black eye.

And yet these fearsome soldiers and Destroyers were a sort of blessing for Pretty Boy, who huddled inconsolably in a new, damp bunker with his guard occupying the bunk above him, waiting for the arrival of The Hawk, the partisan leader who would decide his sentence. No one would arrive while the reds were combing the countryside, thus his sentencing was delayed.

Pretty Boy was bitter; the deaths of the family he had killed were not his fault — just an unfortunate outcome of his trying to do his duty. And now for all he knew, he was going to be shot by some of the very people who had ordered him to take action. On top of all that, a raging red army soldier might come upon his bunker and thrust an iron rod through the ceiling of the secret chamber. Pretty Boy had plenty of time to think about this, and he imagined the pole going through the ceiling and then straight through the heart of his guard, who lay on the bunk above him. What would Pretty Boy do then? He could permit his own capture and lay the blame for the executed family on the dead man above him and take whatever prison sentence they doled out. Anything would be better than waiting for his partisan court martial.

He needed to get away and, luckily for him, the fool of a guard on this shift felt sorry for him. There were only two of them in the bunker once Badger had made them all scatter in anticipation of the red army sweep.

They had been together in the bunker intermittently for days, and proximity brought sympathy from Trout, the kind of man who had few friends and therefore went looking for them. "I'll need to show bruises," Trout had said after Pretty Boy convinced him of the injustice of his plight.

"I could shoot you with a flesh wound if you want to be more convincing," said Pretty Boy.

But Trout was not thoroughly a fool. "So convincing that I might die of blood poisoning? No thank you. A black eye will do it and I'll say I didn't have the heart to shoot you as you ran away after emptying the piss pot."

It was true the bucket was almost full and the stink in underground close quarters was nauseating. They did not go far from the bunker to execute their plan because the reds were still ranging across the countryside.

"I can't let you have a weapon though," said Trout.

"You know I'll need one."

"You'll be safer without. Find some clothes and dress in civvies and you'll be able to get by with forged papers if they stop you." And then Trout set down his rifle, steeled himself, and prepared to take the blow from Pretty Boy. When it came, it was much harder than he thought necessary, and before he had a chance to say anything Pretty Boy struck him again and he went down onto the field. Pretty Boy kicked him and then he felt nothing more as he slipped into unconsciousness.

Pretty Boy tied his hands and feet loosely, picked up the fallen rifle and dug in Trout's pockets for extra shells and money, and then made straight for the forest, trying to get as far away as possible. It crossed his mind that leaving Trout out like that, unconscious and in uniform, was dangerous to the man who had helped him escape, but he could not risk dragging the man back into his bunker in case he struggled and managed to escape his bonds. Pretty Boy needed to get away fast. At least all he had to fear was the reds because the other partisans were still squirrelled away in their various holes, waiting for the danger to pass.

Pretty Boy travelled only by night, dabbing the soles of his boots with lamp oil in case the reds were using sniffing dogs. By day he lay under thick bushes, jerking awake at times and then listening carefully because he had a reputation as a snorer and a snoring bush was sure to attract the attention of anyone walking by. And twice people did walk by, once a cowherd with his animals and another time a boy with a reed flute that he played as he walked. How unfair it was that he was now being hunted by partisans and reds alike, when all he had ever wanted was to serve his country. He had entered some kind of alternate world by joining the partisans, stepped through a looking-glass and now there was no way of stepping back out.

He was as careful as he could be, but he was also hungry and needed to get to Raminta's place to get some food. He risked travelling by late afternoon in order to arrive at her house in time to study the place and its surroundings over a few hours. If Raminta's house was being watched or if there were reds inside, they would give themselves away eventually.

And yet all was quiet.

Still, he waited and then waited some more throughout the night, ignoring both the pangs of hunger and the night-time cold. In the morning some of the nearby villagers went about their business and Raminta's brother left the house with his lunch in a linen bag as he went out to work a neighbour's fields.

Pretty Boy made his way to the window at the back of the house and tapped on it in a pattern. When Raminta's face showed, he was heartened by the sudden expression of joy on her face.

"Thank God you're alive," she said when she took him in her arms.

"Is it safe?"

"I haven't seen the reds since yesterday. They swept by, poking the ground around here, and then moved on."

"I'm in trouble. I'm going to need your help, but first I need to eat something."

She wondered that he did not notice her grown belly, but reasoned he had enough troubles of his own and forgave him. She put out bread and scrambled eggs. He explained between mouthfuls that he would need some of her brother's clothes.

"But where can you go?"

"Don't worry. I have a plan. I hold some documents under another name. I'll make my way to Klaipeda. With all the Germans driven out after the war, I hear they always need labour in port cities, so somebody will hire me to work in a factory or unload ships."

"I could go with you."

"Too dangerous, and besides, I can't get my hands on any documents for you."

"But we'd be more convincing together. A pregnant woman will seem less suspicious."

He winced at the mention of her pregnancy. "I'll be travelling rough, mostly by night. It's no way for a pregnant woman to travel."

She watched him wipe his plate with a piece of bread and then butter the bread on top of scraps of egg on the slice. He concentrated thoroughly on his plate. She knew he was hungry, poor man.

"What do you think will become of me? A pregnant, unmarried woman is as welcome in a village as a witch. As it is, my brother barely looks at me."

He popped the piece of bread into his mouth and looked at her thoughtfully. "I'll send for you once I've set myself up."

"How long will that take?"

"I don't know. But listen, it's the best chance we have. Who knows? Klaipėda is a port city. I've heard others have slipped away on ships through Gdansk. Maybe I could stow away on a ship and then I'd send for you from some place like Sweden, or America, or Canada. Think what our lives could be then."

"Please, you're letting your imagination carry you away. The only way you could get to places like that is on a magic carpet, and I have a feeling even a magic carpet would only have room for one."

"I know it's hard for you, but the first thing I have to think of is survival. Everybody wants to kill me now. I need to find some way out of here."

"The government declared an amnesty," she said.

"We've been forbidden to take the amnesty."

"Forbidden by the people who want to execute you for doing your duty. You don't owe them anything. You've paid enough."

"But what do you think would happen to me? Do you think I'd just give myself up and they'd congratulate me and let me go? I'd have to betray the partisans I've fought with all these years."

"They've betrayed you already. Why should you care? And anyway, they'll scatter once they know you've given yourself up. You've told me yourself no partisan stays in the same bunker for long. It's too dangerous. You can tell the reds everything you know and it won't matter."

"But then what? You keep talking as if it's like applying for a passport. Even if they didn't execute me, which I doubt, they'd beat me and still send me off to a prison camp."

"Maybe, but women follow their men up there. I could be useful. I'd get work in some nearby village and I could bring you packages of food."

"You're grasping at straws. It's too dangerous, and you're better off here for now. You have your brother and the village knows you. They may gossip, but so what? You'll know the truth. And it will just be for a while until I can get myself set up in Klaipeda."

"If you don't get yourself killed crossing the country first."

"There's a risk. I know it. But everything's risky."

"How did you get away in the first place?"

"I escaped when my guard fell asleep."

"Escaped?"

Clearly, she did not fully realize what he had done in Rudnia, but with any luck, neither did anyone but the partisans. As long as that execution couldn't be attributed to him, he might still survive even if he was caught. But he would take no voluntary amnesty. He knew better than that.

"Are you still hungry?" Raminta asked.

"Starving. Would you fry me some more eggs?"

"Of course. And I'll make you some more tea."

NEWS OF TROUT'S CAPTURE shot through the village telegraph and spread quickly through the region. The reds came upon him lying on the ground near an open bunker, like a gift to the local army commander who was under pressure to produce some results of success against the bandits. Martin did not know much because the rest of the partisans were still scattered out in new hiding places, but Martin did know that Trout had been guarding Pretty Boy, yet there was no word of Pretty Boy's capture.

Could Pretty Boy have always been a spy in the first place? But would a spy have killed a woman and her family for the sake of keeping his cover? He wished he could speak to Badger, who could parse these mysteries better than anyone.

Martin made his way carefully to Raminta's house late one afternoon. The curtains were all open wide, but the house was quiet. He did not dare to knock on the window, so he waited and once it became dark, he saw someone light a lamp inside, and then he knocked on the door and he was let in by Raminta's brother.

He had been sitting at a table with an open bottle of *naminė*. All the cupboard doors in the room were thrown open, the shelves were swept clean, and linens lay on the floor as well as shards of shattered crockery.

"Did they find anything?" asked Martin.

"Pretty Boy. He was sleeping at the table."

First Trout and now this.

"How is that possible?"

"I don't know. And they took Raminta too."

"Did she resist?"

"A pregnant woman? Please."

"Did they find anything?"

"I don't know. They tore the place apart."

"But they didn't take you."

"No. Not yet. But I think they will. Have you ever seen one family member taken and another left behind? When they sweep, they sweep up everyone."

"My mother keeps two bags made of knotted sheets. They sit inside the door day and night and we're forbidden to touch them. She has boots and coats in one of them. In the other she keeps bread and smoked meat. We eat three-day-old bread at home and she puts the fresh loaves into the knotted bag. If ever we're taken and put on the trains north, we'll carry the bags with us."

"You're a child. What do you know about all this?"

"I'm fourteen and in high school. I know more than you think. If I were you, I'd get a bag ready before I drank any more. If they do come for you, they might not give you any time."

"So young and so wise. Part of me wants to be taken."

"How could you want that?"

"They might put me in the same place as Pretty Boy. He's the one to blame for all of this. I'd love to let him know how I feel."

"I think Pretty Boy is going to have plenty of suffering to come as it is."

There were so many disappointments. All the plans turned to dust, but even within the disappointments there were mysteries. Martin wondered what had become of the pistol he gave to Raminta. He hated to lose it and it still might be hidden somewhere in the house. But he couldn't go looking for it. Either the reds had found it or it was so well hidden that he never would either.

Raminta had probably never used the pistol. Maybe she had never intended to use it. Among all the betrayals, he felt betrayed by her as well.

18

PAŽAISLIS MONASTERY ASYLUM, 1959

HEAVY FOOTSTEPS CAME ALONG outside Kostas's cell, and the two men froze and waited until they passed. A door closed somewhere at the end of the corridor.

"You could have called out to the orderly — said someone broke in," said Martin.

"What, and lose the opportunity to have a few drinks with you?"

"It doesn't make you anxious that I came in through the window?"

"Is that the way you came in? I'd forgotten."

"I've heard it said you have Korsakoff syndrome."

Martin had done a little reading on the condition that destroyed the minds of hard drinkers.

"I have nothing of the kind. My mind is fine. I could tell you the names of all the children I grew up with. I know the compass points, but I'm a little weak on what day this is because I have been in this cell for quite some time and there is nothing to distinguish one day from other. Do you know what's exhausting to a drinker?"

"Other people?"

"You're partially right. Certain kinds: The moralizers — the people who want to caution you about the error of your ways. Wives get hysterical and employers get angry and all I wish to do is have a little peace and relaxation in my spare time. I am still writing, for heaven's sakes. The children laugh and their mothers smile and why shouldn't

I have the freedom to take my ease as I choose? And besides, I have pain too, you know. I have suffered. I deserve a little understanding."

"Does your wife visit you here?"

"My wife has left me for another man."

"Really?"

"Yes. He is hanging on the cross and so he'll never bother her in bed with either his male parts or his snoring. Now listen, enough of my life. There is not much to the life of a writer anyway. He sits in a room and makes things up and then writes them down. I thought the idea was that we'd share a few drinks and you'd tell me about your life."

Kostas stopped talking. He had chatted like a café habitué among his friends, but now he was thinking, and it seemed as if he was doing it with some effort.

"I am running a little dry. I need a refill."

Martin poured out another shot and Kostas threw it back and then held the small glass in his cupped hands before looking up

"Should I be concerned about you?" asked Kostas.

"Oh yes. But let's catch up a little more."

19

VILNIUS, 1956

MANY OF THE SHELVES in the Book Depository sat empty, awaiting the delivery of more wounded and abandoned tomes from across the county. On the upper reaches of these empty shelves, birds found places for their nests. Birds and their chicks were bad for the books, but working on tall ladders, Martin did not have the heart to clear them away until the nestlings were gone.

Kristina managed to fill the two offset rows of book shelves in front of her alcove, and so she was out of sight unless Martin went looking for her. He regretted the loss of chance encounters, but he had no intention of missing her entirely. When he felt the need to see her, he stepped heavily on the way in toward her keep, and then knocked lightly on one shelf as he approached, all in order not to startle her. She was usually happy to see him, and the occasional smile from at least one person in Vilnius was like a blessing. But not this time. He took from his pocket the bottle Tomas had sold him that morning and set it on the table beside her cup of steaming tea.

"Go away," she said.

"I've come to ask you a favour."

"It's payday tomorrow. I'm busy preparing the sums. And by the way, stop this business with the bottle. I'm not so cheap, you know."

"You wish to stop drinking?"

"Yes. I do. What business is it of yours?"

"It's not my business at all."

"So what do you want?"

"I have a bit of a problem."

She set down her pencil, sighed, and looked up at him. Her face was very white and her hair very dark. Sometimes the contrast made her beautiful, but only if there was a little spark in her chocolate eyes. There was no spark just now.

"What do you want?"

"The director has asked me to take a book around to the Writers' Union because we have multiple copies and it might be something they could use."

"What is it?"

"A poetry book by Antanas Vincentas."

She snorted. "The darling of the regime. The Union might be offended that you're bringing this book over. Vincentas and his books deserve 'a place of honour in every library.' If we have two of them, we should consider ourselves twice as lucky."

"I wonder if you could take this over for me."

"What for? It's just around the corner. We're back to back with the Writers' Union. This would take you five minutes."

"I don't want to go over there, not inside."

"Why not?"

He hesitated. "I wouldn't fit in."

Martin could not explain to her that he did not wish to see or be seen by Kostas, who might be there. Not yet.

"You're a member of the working class. A real proletarian. This country belongs to you and you should feel no shame going anywhere."

"Stop it. I'm not in the mood."

"You didn't care so much what mood I was in. Why should I care about your mood?"

"Don't make such a big deal out of this. Help me, will you?"

She gave him an exasperated look and set down her pencil. "Give me the book."

He set it down. She put her hands on the desk and hunched over for a moment, as if gathering her strength to push herself up.

"Are you all right?"

She stood up and reached over to pull back a strand of hair and he saw her hand was trembling.

"Maybe you should take a drink before you go."

"Shut up."

"I may have asked too much."

"Stop talking. I'll take your damned book, but you'll owe me. Do you understand?" As she walked out of the chapel, she trailed her hand along the bookshelves to help balance herself.

Martin left the chapel and went to his workbench in an outbuilding where he was repairing chairs. He put his pot of horse hoof glue on the gas ring and sanded the ends of a spindle as he waited for the glue to melt. When the glue had melted and thinned in the heat, he painted the ends of the spindle with the glue and inserted it between the chair's legs and then tied a rope tourniquet to clamp the legs together and hold the spindles tight until the glue dried.

He turned off the gas and walked away to clear his head from the strong smell of the hoof glue. He went over to Kristina's chapel, but she was not there. She should have been back in ten minutes, but it was over an hour since he'd asked her to take the book. He walked outside to the yard and there he found her seated on a bench. She was hunched over and weeping.

"Are you all right?"

She raised her reddened face to him. "No, I am not. What are you, some messenger from hell that you sent me over there?"

"What happened?"

"You wouldn't understand. I was doing so well too. I thought I was near the end of drying out this time, but now you've ruined it all. Go back to my office and bring me the damned bottle, will you? And don't make a spectacle out of it. Pour some of the liquor on top of the tea and bring me the cup. Keep the rest of the bottle in your pocket."

When he returned, she took the cup and drank down half of it, and then looked around and had him add more liquor from the bottle.

"You should go home," said Martin. "I could walk you there."

"I don't want to go home. I wish I could just stay here."

"Then let's go inside somewhere. The crypt is private."

"Too cold and dark and frightening. There's a room off the bell tower. The doorman sleeps there, but if he's not around, I could bear to be there."

"I didn't know we even had a doorman. He's never at the door."

"No. I think he's a relative of some kind and Stonkus lets him work here in exchange for sweeping the floor and clearing the snow in the wintertime."

Although they could hear their colleagues stirring in parts of the church, and somewhere in the distance there was a muted conversation, they passed no one as they walked among the book cases to the room she had described. It had a table, two wide benches, and cigarette butts on the floor.

They sat across from one another at the table.

She set down her cup, wiped her cheeks with the palms of her hands, and then looked up. "I suppose you want some kind of explanation."

"Only if it will make you feel better."

"Nothing makes me feel better. I only feel bad or worse, you understand?"

"You need to drink less."

"I need to drink more."

"So what happened there?"

"There is a witch of a door lady who sits at a desk by the

entrance to the Writers' Union. I was going to ask her to deliver the book for me, but the woman told me she was no servant of mine and her knees were bothering her and I could take my book up to the library myself. So I went up the grand staircase. I haven't been there since I was a child. And there in the library was this lovely little display for a new book by Petras Vaitkus."

Martin looked at her blankly.

"The poet? I keep forgetting you've been away. You don't know who he was?"

"No."

"A writer who ran afoul of the regime. He's been blacklisted for years, but I guess he's been dead long enough for them to wipe out the past and publish him again."

"Who was he to you?"

"My stepfather. First they kill him, and then after a little time passes, they honour him. It makes me sick.

"He saved me at a terrible time. You don't know what it was like here after the occupation — a real wasteland right after the so-called liberation. The red army was fighting its way towards Berlin, and a lot of the city was still smoldering. I was just an orphan street girl in the ruins. And not the only one."

"What happened to your family?"

"I don't know. Never mind. Listen, will you? I was working my way through the Rasų cemetery. Do you know it?"

"No."

"The old cemetery on the other side of the train tracks, near the station. I was looking to see if there were any gravestones with names I recognized on them. I half-knew I wouldn't find any, but I believed that if I needed to know something badly enough, I'd find out. It had been a freezing cold day, and just after sunset I was going to have to look for a place to sleep.

"There was a bad accident nearby when a couple of trains collided. A long munitions train blew up right at the station. The blast knocked me down and I crawled behind a headstone as the other blasts went off, one after another. They happened not all at once, you understand. Just when I thought my ears might stop ringing and I could get up off the ground, other explosions happened and then something hit me. The next thing I knew it was morning and a man was bent over me, rubbing my hands. I couldn't even speak. I was half-dead from the cold. I could barely feel his hands on mine.

"He was one of the people who came out to look for the wounded after the explosion. Hundreds were hurt and many died, and some of the houses were blown right off the street. The survivors went out looking for the wounded. And that was how he found me."

"He kept you. How old were you?"

"I don't even know, really. Eight? Ten?"

"How can you not know your own age?"

"I don't know what I don't know, all right? Vaitkus took me to his home, rooms in a house not far from the cemetery. He lit a fire and made me tea. He asked me who my people were and where I had come from, but I could barely understand him through the ringing in my ears. I couldn't talk for days, and anyway, I didn't know. Auntie and Diana lived in the house too, and these women helped out with me. They became my family. Vaitkus went around to ask if anyone knew who I was. People were missing after the war. Sometimes someone would come in to look at my face, but nobody knew me. The police came too, but they didn't know any more than anyone else. A woman came to take me away to an orphanage, but I cried and Vaitkus and Auntie said they'd keep me. Who needed another wounded child in an institution anyway? The lady was happy to leave me where I was.

"I was tired and I was sick for a very long time. I could barely talk. I only started to speak a bit more as the weeks went by and here was this bachelor, this poet who didn't know what to do with me. He didn't have the heart to put me into an orphanage, and so he kept me and the neighbours helped. You understand? This man with nothing kept me and he fed me and the grandmothers in the neighbourhood got used to me. By spring, the children were playing with me. Auntie had had her own losses, but she took care of me when Vaitkus was away. Diana was an orphan too, but older than me, a teenager who was already working. She was like my older sister.

"In the fall, he sent me to school. I got a little stronger and clung to him when I was home. He must have been in his thirties, but he felt like an older brother instead of a father, or maybe an uncle. I don't know. And later, when he didn't know what to do with me, what a teenage girl needs, he would ask Auntie or Diana and they would tell him what to do or what to get for me.

"He disappeared for a while when I was in high school. Can you imagine? He was gone for over a year. I barely got by. He showed up again and begged me to forgive him. Forgive him! He'd been in jail for a stupid poem."

"He told you this?"

"Yes. He wrote a poem about a watch, a special watch that told the time even when the times were terrible, and, of course, the communists thought he meant communist times and they sentenced him to prison."

"But they let him go. That's strange."

"Yes, I know what you're thinking. They turned him into a spy for themselves. But that can't be true because of what happened later. He came back to me just for a while."

"What does that mean?"

"They never forgive. I was around fifteen by then, in 1952. I was going to be trained in typing and stenography as well as bookkeeping. Things were going to be all right. But he disappeared one night in the winter and they found him naked, frozen to death just a few blocks away from our house, right at the edge of town."

"What?"

"They took him out to the countryside."

"Who is *They*?"

"What are you, a child? *They* are *They*. The ones in the shadows, the ones who really run things in this country. *They* sent you to prison and *They* are watching us now. But not always. *They* don't know everything, even though *They* try hard.

"They beat him and they took his clothes because it was winter and they wanted to punish him. Maybe they didn't even plan to kill him. He must have run all the way back toward home to keep warm, but there are hardly any houses out in that direction and what houses there were wouldn't open their doors at night to a man shouting from outside. If they bothered to look from behind a curtain, they would have seen a naked man, and guessed he was crazy.

"He almost made it. But he died, you understand? The neighbours called me so I saw him before the police arrived to take away his body. I was mortified to see the corpse of my saviour, naked and cold, bruised, with bloody bare feet, cut by the ice.

"They killed him. This sweet, sweet man. The man who saved me more than once. And up at the library where I took your damned book, I saw they had his new collected poems on display. He's been rehabilitated, you see? His little poem about the watch is in that book. And it's as if they had never wronged him in the first place."

It was cold and damp in the room. The smell of stale cigarette butts on the floor was nauseating. Martin moved over to sit on her side of the bench and he took her in his arms and he held her a long time.

20

LYNN LAKE, 1947

WINTER CAME DOWN UPON the countryside, and for all the bite of the cold, at least the roads were no longer rivers of mud. The nights grew long, and in that darkness, a knock on the door alarmed everyone inside. It might only be a neighbour looking to pass the interminable evening hours, or a group of reds hunting for partisans, or partisans looking to evade them. Misunderstandings were bound to occur.

The partisans needed to learn to hibernate because footprints in the snow gave away the whereabouts of the summer bunkers, which were secreted in forests and swamps. During the winter it was better to have bunkers in well-travelled places. Some built their hideaways in shafts cut sideways into farm wells and others near barns where the passage of farmers and their animals compacted the snow in an unreadable manner.

But fresh snow froze partisans in their hiding places, locked them down until other footprints masked the ways to their hidey holes. In summer, the partisans owned the countryside where many farmers would feed them and sympathetic relatives lived among the villages. But in winter, the regime's trucks and sleds could make their way deep into the countryside, carrying loads of reds along with hounds to sniff out the dens of their enemies.

The losses of Pretty Boy and Trout had caused Badger to scatter his men yet again and to dig new bunkers before the winter hardened the earth; then to lower the numbers per bunker to two in order to minimize losses and to make it easier to get fed by locals who supported them. His men ate reasonably well in the countryside where poverty taught generosity to the locals. But Badger himself had to travel often among the bunkers with Pike, his right-hand man, a beefy cooper who was good with tools, insensitive to the gloom of winter, and reliable in a firefight. Pike was stalwart, but had little to say in the long hours, days, and weeks underground. His qualities in war had no counterpart in the peaceful times when they were not being hunted.

The partisan lines of communication kept being cut as one or another of their messengers was captured, often women or youths, often village teachers or the sisters of partisans. Did The Hawk know that he was no longer needed to rule in the case of Pretty Boy? Was The Hawk even alive? News came out so slowly and unreliably — one could never be sure of what was true. As to Pretty Boy and Trout, men taken alive would eventually betray everyone because nobody held up forever under torture. Word did eventually come that Trout had thrown himself from the third floor of the KGB building in Vilnius where he was being interrogated. He had managed to kill himself. But how much had he given away before he died?

As for Pretty Boy, he was likely singing and would continue to sing as long as he thought it would preserve his life. It was a shame they had been unable to execute him before he was taken because now he would have no residual sympathy for his comrades. Raminta's brother learned she had been given a light sentence of five years in a labour camp for supporting the partisans. Her assistance in the capture of Pretty Boy had been taken into consideration and so she did not receive the customary twenty-five-year sentence. Her baby would thus be born shortly after her arrival in the gulag. If it survived, it would be overseen by a deported grandmother too old to go out to the forest with the other women's work crews to fell trees in winter.

The snow did provide a convenient time for the partisan news to get written because what else was there to do in those long hours except to listen to the radio, its antenna laid out on the snow, and to make notes on what the Americans and the British said in their scratchy broadcasts? And what was taking them so long to act against the Soviet Union? The partisans had expected to hold out until American war with the Soviets liberated their country. They had even sent out emissaries on dangerous trips overland through Poland to bring fresh news to the west. The Americans were no longer friends with the Soviets and should have been fighting them by now. But they seemed to have lost their will after defeating the Germans.

Badger was sitting on a crate in a barn and bent over a typewriter on another crate in front of himself when Pike swung open the door to bring in Martin and Kostas.

"It's freezing in here," said Kostas. "How can you work like this?"

"You've lived too long in Vilnius, my friend," said Badger. "You've turned soft."

"Couldn't we at least meet in a bunker if not in some heated house?"

"Ah, no. The less you know about my whereabouts just now, the better for all of us. If some pack of reds came upon you on the way to my bunker and became suspicious, what would you say?"

"That I am going to the home of one of my pupils to speak to his parents."

"Very good. Plausible. And could you name the pupil and tell the reds where his parents' house is?"

Kostas hesitated.

"You hesitate. Next would come a beating, and if it was a bad one, you'd tell them where the bunker was and that would be the end of us. You see?"

"Is it right to be so suspicious?"

"I lost two of my men this fall and I'm not sure how it happened. It's not a question of being suspicious so much as cautious. Now, did you bring along some text for me to use in the press?"

"Yes. Some children's poems for the next issue of the newspaper. Something light, you know. You're always writing about resistance and the news from the west. Who can read that all the time without falling into depression? Especially this time of year. Listen to this."

He read some rhyming couplets with the usual animal characters — storks and frogs, owls and mice, set in the changing seasons.

"Very amusing," said Badger, after Kostas was done and looked up at him. "These are the sorts of lines that get you into the Writers' Union?"

"I read this to the children in the school last week and they asked me to repeat it to them every day. Obviously, it's not work for adults. But one of the mothers told me the children were saying these lines at the dinner table and some local genius put music to the words. Look around you. Isn't this just the worst of times when you know you'll hardly ever see the sun for the next few months? This little ditty gives the children hope in the natural cycle of things. Just as you asked for."

"I like it," said Pike from the place where he was standing guard by the barn door.

Badger looked at Pike in astonishment. "Those three words are the most he's spoken today. All right, we'll put it in the next bulletin, but you'll have to type the stencil yourself."

"I'm not really a typist, you know, but I'll be happy to do it, under better conditions. It will have to be in a warmer place. I'm sure the ink for the mimeograph won't flow when it's this cold."

"Not a typist, eh? Is it too menial a job for you?"

"I do what I have to, but if it was up to me, in a free world, I'd do nothing but write poetry. And what's gotten into you? Have I done something wrong? You ask for light verses and then criticize them. Next you want to waste my talent by turning me into a typist."

"We don't live in a free world."

"As if that were news of some kind. Maybe the winter has got you down, or maybe it's the loss of your friends. I don't know. But don't take it out on me. Anyway, we need to make niches of freedom, private freedoms, or freedoms of fellowship with only a few other people we trust. Like the freedom we have in this barn together, at this moment."

"True enough. But it's a very circumscribed freedom," said Badger. "Pike and I each have a price on our heads."

Pike looked at Badger briefly, and then returned his eyes to scan outside the door.

"You sound depressed. Something's certainly wrong. So finally the truth of your circumstances descends on you, like some sort of rain cloud that was always beyond the horizon in the past. You sound miserable to me," said Kostas.

Badger looked both to Martin and Pike, hesitating to reveal himself in the presence of an admiring boy and a comrade-in-arms. But sometimes the weight of the world was too much to keep hidden inside.

"Of course I'm miserable," he blurted. "What did you expect?"

"It's just that in front of others you're usually so direct and optimistic. You make jokes. The people in the village speak highly of you. They like it when you visit them. But here you are, telling me you feel melancholy. I'm touched, really, but confused."

"Confused by what?" he snapped. "The people of the village should never speak of me to anyone, and neither should you."

Kostas seemed unperturbed by Badger's irritation.

"It is a village, remember. Villages have no secrets inside them. But you're full of secrets, it seems, and I'm not talking military ones."

"Then what the hell are you talking about?"

"I'm talking about the secret feelings you keep wrapped up in your soul."

"Leave the care of my soul to the priest."

"I'm not talking about religion, really. More your spirit, then, the part of you that perks up when you hear a song you like."

"What about it? Everybody has that."

"They do, but you have more than most. You carry the burden of public optimism all the time. You keep up the morale of others, but it comes at a price. That's why you're feeling bad just now, I can see it in your face. You're actually more sensitive than others. The winter has you down. You read books. You've seen other countries. You probably have an imagination that could picture another life for yourself outside the confines of these four walls."

"What exactly are you about in this line of talk, Mr. Village Teacher? What lesson is it you're trying to get through to me?"

"My point is that to continue the fight that you're carrying on, you need to nourish not only the body, but the spirit. And not through confessions and long talks with priests. And to do that you need someone like me, someone on top of the literature of this country and abroad."

"What a strange conversation this is. Aren't I the one who recruited you in the first place? Are you not the one who is half-in and half-out? Lucky you, someone who can drop in and drop out of the resistance. You help me out with the press, but you're not willing to go entirely underground yourself. Why are you trying to ingratiate yourself now?"

"Ingratiate? Who said anything about ingratiating? You're in a terrible mood and you're taking it out on me. *Ingratiate*. That's a demeaning word. I don't want you to forget what I'm worth. You've been taking me for granted."

"Nonsense. Give me your texts. I'll type them up on the stencils myself. You behave as if you were in some Vilnius café. Keep in mind we're at war. Martin, take him away. Don't forget to walk back in your footprints when you come to the road."

"Wait," said Kostas.

"What for?"

"I've hurt you somehow. I'm sorry. You're under a lot of pressure, and I want to help you. I am with you, do you understand? You and the other two in this room, but you in particular. You're fighting a good fight. I know it, and I love you for it. But I am conflicted. Part of me wants to join you on some kind of raid, to do something real with you in the defence of my country. But I'm not made for that. Call me a coward, if you want, but I just can't be like you. I'm different, and I need to learn to live with who I am. I know I sound haughty sometimes, but it's only defence for my shame."

"Shame?"

"For not being more like you."

"The world has one like me already," said Badger. "It doesn't need another. Maybe it needs someone like you. Enough of this. I'm grateful for what you do, those lines of yours. Maybe there's something in them."

MARTIN TOOK KOSTAS BACK through the snow and, in his mind, Martin split the houseguest into three different men.

In the house, Kostas was a guest and treated as such, given the best portion of food and the best room. In the village, he was Mr. Kostas, the teacher, the one who earned the respect of the children and their parents. He could control a room containing both morons and bright girls who might go far under the right circumstances. He read them stories and he played games with them on holidays. Parents brought him gifts of food and drink. In the field, he was Skylark, a helper of the partisans, if not quite a partisan himself. He could be ironic at times, which was not the way of the armed underground that tended to be patriotic and firm in its ideals. But there was something attractive in his whiff of insolence. And yet, this insolent man had a heart as well, showing the kind of tenderness that one didn't often see among men at war, unless it was over a wounded comrade. And Badger was wounded, it turned out, but not with the sort of hurt that could be seen by any but a kind man.

And as to Badger, sitting in his bunker with the resolute but bland Pike, Skylark was the fresh air that rushed into a bunker when its lid had been opened after a very long time. Many of his colleagues had expressed care for him in the rough-and-ready way of the partisans. Badger could rely on them, and they could rely on him.

But when was the last time anyone had spoken to him about his spirit? Not even directly, because who did that, after all? But implicitly, say in listening to music together or talking about a book that had moved them both?

The Americans were not coming; the winter was upon them; Badger had lost two men in the autumn. Skylark was some sort of balm to these wounds. Not entirely, for what could be? But this impossible man, this children's poet whose poems were trivial in a dangerous time, somehow helped to make the underground life bearable, and yet he was an irritation in himself. He spoke as if they lived in a free world and all this insistence made the winter world seem all the worse for its distance from liberty.

21

VILNIUS, 1957

THE HEAT OF KRISTINA in the bed was a comfort, but they had lain together a long time and it was becoming too much. Martin stared at the pale rectangle of light behind the closed curtains and lifted the blanket from his chest. The sun had come around and now it was too warm under the covers.

"Let's go out and get a little fresh air for a change," said Martin.

"I'd rather stay here."

"We've been under the covers for hours. If I lie here any more, I won't be able to sleep tonight."

"I know what to do to keep you awake."

"We've done that already. I need to get some air."

He stepped out of bed, pulled back the curtains and blinked in the early afternoon light.

"Close the curtains."

"You're like a moth, aren't you?"

"I just want to get dressed if we have to go out and, anyway, you know my eyes are sensitive to the light."

Kristina often wore sunglasses, even on overcast days. She stayed indoors and kept her drapes closed most of the time, but Martin had grown up in the country and worked outside in the gulag; he longed for open space even though his life now belonged to the city. He stepped out into the small garden, where Auntie was sitting on a bench in the sun. She wore a Turkish scarf over her hair, a padded vest for warmth, a long woollen skirt, and in this case, even the felt boots of winter, although winter was still some distance away.

Auntie reminded him of his own grandmother, who died in transport to the gulag. His parents did not know the name of the station where her body was taken from the train. It was somewhere on the far side of the Urals. She had never travelled outside her own province during her life, except for this long voyage to some grave in an unknown place, where no one would honour her.

Old women like Auntie were everywhere — both in the city and in the countryside — but it was a mystery how they evolved. One day a woman was at work in an office or in the fields, and the next she appeared, as if from a cocoon, a fully formed old person who might be a street sweeper, or a beggar by church doors, or, in this case, a sort of collective grandmother to neighbourhood children.

"Are you taking her out?"

"Yes."

"Good. She needs the sun, but she's always avoided it."

He would have to buy this old woman some flowers on Mother's Day. Did old women like this really have pasts? He didn't know if she had children of her own. He had never seen any. Her only visitors were neighbourhood women like herself. She sometimes stood by the garden gate for long periods of time, looking up the road and waiting. Sooner or later, another grandmother of one kind or another would show up, but was that who Auntie was waiting for? For all he knew, it was somebody else.

The door opened and Martin thought it might be Kristina, but instead, a soldier stepped out; a lieutenant who adjusted his hat on his head, looked at them and nodded, and then walked off toward the city.

Auntie laughed. "Oh, you young people. Doing it day and night."

"Who was that?"

"Diana's lover. She still believes he will leave his wife, but I've heard that claim more than once."

Aunties knew secrets, but rarely divulged them, and hardly anyone thought to ask in the first place. They saw everything and had stories of their own, but like most old people, they were invisible in plain sight.

"Did you have lovers when you were young, Auntie?"

She laughed and then covered her mouth. "What a question!" She was pleased to have been asked.

"Where do you want to go?" Kristina asked when she came out.

"For a ramble."

Kristina lived outside the remains of the old city walls. The neighbourhood had dilapidated one- and two-storey houses built toward the end of the czarist period. They had once housed notaries and government department heads, but the houses later fell on hard times like so much of the city and were mostly broken up into one and two-room flats with shared kitchens. But they did have modest gardens where the apple trees and lilacs of happier times still bloomed in the spring.

Martin steered her into the Rasų cemetery on the other side of the railway tracks.

The cemetery rose up high on a hill and then fell down low into a valley. The steep sides of the hill, as well as the valley below, were filled with funeral monuments, some very old with decaying cherubs and leaning crosses. Enamelled photographs of the dead were countersunk into some of the monuments, fine women and gentlemen from other times, but many photographs were missing because the red army soldiers had come here to drink after the *liberation*, and they liked to take shots at the dead bourgeois in revenge for the squalid burials of their comrades during the war.

"Do you remember the monument you hid behind?"

"I'll show you."

She took him high up and then pointed to a worn grey stone monument whose names had worn away and whose low iron fence around the plot had long since crumbled to flakes.

"Does it bother you to look around here?"

"No. I come here once in a while. I was lucky. I'll bring you here one evening for All Souls when candles are burning on the graves and the place is full of people all night long, praying or singing hymns. It's like visiting a city of the dead. It's very beautiful."

"And where are your people?"

"What a question. You know I'm an orphan."

"But if you remember the explosion here in 1945, you must remember something from before that time."

"Not much. I've tried, believe me, but there's hardly anything there."

"You weren't exactly an infant before that."

"I guess not, but I don't even know my birth date. Vaitkus managed to get identity papers for me somehow, but he made up my name and he made up my birthdate."

"You don't remember even your first name from before then?"

"No."

Clouds drifted by overhead, casting them in light and then in shadow, and once when the light appeared she twitched slightly, enough that he could feel the movement in the arm she linked through his.

She showed him the grave of Antanas Basanavičius, the father of Lithuania, and then the grave of Marshall Pilsudski, who had seized the city back in the twenties and annexed it to Poland until the next war. The Lithuanians loved the one and the Poles loved the other and so the city was divided both in life and in death. There were no Jews in this cemetery. The long-dead were buried on the other side of town in a cemetery where bushes and long grass covered many of the stones. The wartime-murdered Jews lay in unmarked pits throughout the country.

They came out of the cemetery and hesitated, and then Martin led her toward the Dawn Gate in the only entranceway left in the otherwise demolished defensive walls of Vilnius. They were walking past a side street when Martin heard a shout and looked down the narrow way to see two young men on the road raining blows over a boy. It was mid-afternoon, but the road was already in shadow and the indifferent apartment windows that overlooked the scene were silent.

Martin let go of Kristina's hand and charged down the road with a roar. His footsteps alerted the men who turned to face him. One held on to the boy's collar and the other stepped away from the boy and squared to meet Martin's charge. The boy pulled his assailant's hand up, bent down with his mouth, and bit hard on the man's wrist. He howled and pulled his hand away. As soon as he did, the boy put two fingers in his mouth and let out a piercing whistle that he repeated twice more before Martin reached him.

The scruffy young man ready for him was a fighter, but Martin had been schooled in the gulag and knew how to take care of himself; he was a few years older and had more weight on him. Martin blocked the man's punch and used the force of his charge to push him back and then knock him to the road, where his head hit a cobble with a crack. Martin turned to face the other man who had let the boy go and was holding his bitten hand against his chest.

"What business is this of yours?" he asked, but before Martin could answer Kristina was on the man with a stick she had picked up and hit him across the shoulder. He seized the stick and threw it aside.

"The boy is a thief," he said, "and was only getting what he deserved."

"Liar."

The boy had a bloody nose, a bloody lip, and bruises that would soon come up on his face. It was Tomas, who had supplied Martin with the liquor he used to bring to Kristina.

"Tomas, are you all right?"

"Those two are worse off than I am." He turned to the man whose wrist he had bitten. "Stick around, why don't you? My friends will want to meet you."

Martin heard running steps, and from behind him in the distance he could see two boys Tomas's age coming towards them.

"Kids," the man spat.

"But it looks like there will be a lot of them," said Martin. "You should pick up your friend and get out of here."

Racing footsteps echoed from elsewhere. The man reached down for his groggy friend, held him under one arm, and led him away. "You'll be sorry," he called back.

"Stay out of this neighbourhood or you'll be the ones to be sorry," shouted Tomas, through a small rivulet of blood that was running down from his right eyebrow.

"What was that all about?" asked Martin

"Territory. Me and the boys sell *naminė* for Johnny in this neighbourhood. The only rule is we have to be fourteen or under because that makes it easier with the police. Those two belong to the territory next door where the boss uses older boys."

"Doesn't Johnny protect you?"

"He does when he can. We usually take care of ourselves. If I'd had a chance to whistle before they jumped me, I would've been all right."

The two boys whom Martin had seen approaching were joined by others within minutes and soon there were seven more, all versions of Tomas himself, in oversized coats, with badly cut hair and dirty faces. Martin guessed the youngest was ten and the oldest not much more than fourteen.

"What's your name, Miss?" Tomas asked Kristina. She answered him. "Both of you came to my rescue. Now I owe you. We all do. When you need help, call on us. There are more of us, you know. With a little notice, I can get twenty if you need a whole gang.

Johnny can get a couple of men if you have money to pay for them."

"You're beautiful," the smallest boy said, as he gazed up at Kristina "We'd all fight for you."

Kristina laughed. "You don't need to fight for me. I'm just glad to know we have some friends in this neighbourhood."

"You never know when you're going to need help. Nasty people come at you without warning and you have to be ready for them."

Two more boys appeared to swell the gang and Tomas introduced Martin and Kristina to all of them, instructing them to help when called upon.

"Tell me this, Mr. Martin," said Tomas. "Did you know it was me they were beating?"

"Not until I got up close. I just saw two men beating a smaller person."

"Most people don't jump out to help people in this town."

"You helped me push the car the first time I met you."

"Sure, and I was going to rob you, but then you gave me half a rouble."

"You could have robbed me anyway."

'No, that wouldn't have been right."

"You should see a doctor about that face," said Kristina.

"I've had worse. We know how to take care of ourselves."

Kristina looked around at the boys. "I wish I had enough money to buy each of you an ice cream," she said. "When I do, I'll owe you some."

"I'd prefer a cigarette," said a small boy, and she laughed.

As they walked away, Tomas remarked that Kristina seemed comfortable among the boys. Young toughs were usually unreliable because at that age, they didn't know how to control themselves beyond their immediate desires.

"Young teenagers in the gulag would go up against major criminals and get slapped down or worse. They thought they were invincible."

"Were you one of them?"

"No, I was just a bit older. I never belonged to a gang. But some of us formed alliances. We country boys didn't go looking for fights and no one dared to bring fights to us more than once. But you were pretty fast off the mark. Where did you find that stick?"

"It was there when I needed it. I lived on the street before Vaitkus found me. I didn't see any girls in Tomas's group, but there were a lot of us back then, after the war."

"I thought you didn't remember much."

"I don't, but there were others like me. Sometimes we helped one another and sometimes we stole each other's food. We had a common enemy and learned to hide away so the police wouldn't take us to orphanages."

On their way into the city, they passed through a small park where once a tall building had stood, and Kostas had hunkered down to await the siege of Vilnius in 1944. Now that building was gone, levelled by the war. In its place lay the park, not much more than a dusty space and a bench, public toilets, as well as a sapling struggling to survive. In this old city, they were always walking upon the ghosts of buildings and the dead who once inhabited them.

They went through the passage under the archway, Kristina holding his arm as if they were a much older couple. The archway had a shrine to the Virgin above it on the city side of the wall, a place where pious old aunties prayed on their knees before a window that revealed the miraculous painting of the Virgin. Hammered onto the walls beside the painting were many silver hearts with names on them in thanks for miracles in the past. Few miracles seemed to happen anymore.

The street led into the medieval part of the city, with its thick-walled houses and red-tiled roofs, its closed shutters and barred ground-floor windows. But for all the protection bars and thick walls afforded, nothing had saved many of those who had tried to hide there at the end of the war. The ones who did survive came out, blinking in the sunlight upon red liberation. Then the scattered survivors of the occupying German army were rounded up, their shoes taken away. The soldiers were forced to walk past the neoclassical city hall in bare feet, to demonstrate their humiliation to the people who had not fled or died during the war.

The old city of Vilnius lay in a broad river valley over which clouds flew by close and often. The city had made Napoleon uneasy even before his defeat, when he was still on his way to Moscow. Vilnius was easy to be fired upon from the surrounding hills. It was the kind of place that invited disasters.

"Do you miss your village?" Kristina asked.

"I do and I don't. I wanted to get out. My childhood had sweet moments, but it was a poor place, so my parents struggled to make ends meet, anxious that we wouldn't go hungry. My mother is still in the gulag. I send her a little something when I can. The irony is that my father was deported as bourgeois because he had twenty hectares of land, but the land was so poor it could barely feed us. I had an older brother, but he died during the war. I don't have any close family there anymore. I have no need to see the place without them. There were informers in the village and they're probably still there. The Soviets taught us to betray one another. Then came the Nazis who did the same. When the Soviets came back, we were already specialists in treachery. If I went back to my village, I'd look into the eyes of some neighbour, not knowing whether I should hate him or love him."

"Are those the only two options?"

"Back home they would be."

"And do you think this city is any better?"

"Of course not. There are no innocents. Only people who haven't been tempted or tortured believe in innocence. Maybe children are innocent, and not even all of them, depending on what they've seen. Everyone is potentially guilty, even if he isn't guilty at the moment."

"Very Catholic of you — very original sin. But some are more guilty than others?"

"Oh yes."

"It makes me shudder to think like that."

"Then let's not think about it. What about love? I have you on my arm and you're an antidote to the madness of the world."

She looked down as they walked and did not answer for a while. Martin began to feel uneasy.

"I wasn't sure I could love you," she finally said.

"No? why not?"

"I didn't think I could love anyone. The only man I ever loved before was taken away from me."

"He was your step-father. That's different. I'm your lover and nobody is taking me away."

"Not for now, no. But the world can be so cruel. Let's talk of other things. History weighs heavily on us. Is there no place without history? I'm not from the countryside like you, I guess, but even I want to forget and live in the moment. I like to hear birds sing. They sing just as beautifully to everyone."

They walked down through the old city, past the crumbling baroque churches which were like old Italians lost in the wrong country, all the way to the ancient park of the Bernardine Monastery, now rechristened "New Generation Park." It was one of the first places rebuilt after the war with walkways among symmetrical French gardens and a fountain in which three miniature concrete elephants shot water up from their trunks.

Like a saint offering his benediction, a large statue of Stalin stood above it all with his arm outstretched, unaware that he had fallen out of favour in Moscow and would have to come down eventually. But not yet. The local leader of the communist party had been installed by Stalin, and he was in no rush to remove the traces of his benefactor.

"Come and sit on a bench. I wanted to talk to you about something," said Martin. He could feel the stillness come over her, for what could there be to talk about that she didn't already know if it wasn't bad news?

"I have some unfinished business here in Vilnius. I'll need to take care of it sooner or later."

"What sort of business?"

He told her about Kostas, how Martin had stumbled across the poet when he first arrived in Vilnius. She listened, impassive, as he spoke. When he was done, they walked among the flowers in the garden and what he had been saying sounded very remote, like a folk tale told to children at night.

"It's a terrible story," she said. "Maybe you should put that behind you."

"I've tried, but I can't seem to do that."

"I've done it."

"By forgetting what happened to you. You didn't choose to forget, did you?"

"No, but it's been a kind of blessing." She shuddered. "I don't like anything of what I'm hearing. I had nothing in Vilnius and you had nothing either. It was good luck to fall into our work and good luck to find each other. I was beginning to think we might make something here."

"What makes you think we can't? I've told you I'm in love with you."

"Love, yes, now that things are easy. Please put this story of Kostas behind you. I just want to live. I want to forget the past."

"But the past won't forget us. Maybe I shouldn't have told you."

"That's right."

"Isn't it better to know the truth?"

"The truth is unbearable sometimes."

She was going to say more, but she stopped. "I think I need a drink. There's a place near here where we can get some beer."

She knew Vilnius far better than he did. They left the garden and walked along the side of the Vilnia River, not much bigger than a stream, and then over a small bridge into the Užupis district, a neighbourhood filled with prostitutes and drunkards living in the empty houses once owned by the Jews. Kristina led him along a filthy alley and down three steps to a cellar door which she pulled open. The room was low and dark and stank of mould, but there were tables and chairs where some men and a few women sat behind glasses of beer. The bartender seemed to know her. He poured them each a small glass of vodka as well as a litre of beer, and Kristina waited as Martin assembled enough money to pay for their drinks.

They settled into chairs at a table.

"Now we won't have money for bread," said Martin.

"I don't care."

She drank half the vodka, followed with a swallow of beer. He then felt her soften as she relaxed into her chair. She had stopped drinking daily for a while, but she still had bouts like this when she badly needed drinks. Martin could drink, and he did drink and alcohol was part of his culture, but his pay was poor and he would rather eat well than drink. He had been hungry too often in the gulag. He had given up smoking because of the cost, and he missed the reflective moments it had given him, but no cigarette was worth more than a thick slice of buttered bread.

Each of them was wounded, but she was worse off than he was. "So do you want me to help you?" Kristina asked, as if reading his mind and turning the tables on him.

"You don't need to assist me so much as to understand me and leave it to me."

"But we're in love, remember? And lovers help one another."

⁊

AFTER MARTIN LEFT KRISTINA at her room, he began to make his way home but found the evening still too early to spend in his basement flat. He rambled toward the train station with the idea of examining the place where the explosion had happened in 1945. The swallows were out, swooping above the square in front of the station, making their strangulated cries. Above the intermittent clouds, always low in Vilnius, almost touchable, showed hints of fading gold.

The nighthawk habitués of the train station had begun to gather as well. Three men stood talking beside their parked cars, one of them a taxi that did not seem to be taking fares. They measured Martin between puffs of cigarette smoke as he walked by.

The station exterior showed none of its explosive history, having been entirely rebuilt on the old foundations by German prisoners of war. It had a white neoclassical front with columns, and wings on each side, of a size suitable to one of the smaller Soviet republics. The open-air platforms lay behind. The station bustled by day with travellers and country folk coming in to sell flowers or vegetables and then it busied itself more guardedly by night.

Other small groups of men stood smoking and talking by the steps that led up to the interior. A little farther off were a few lone women, the older ones with small bouquets of flowers in their hands. It occurred to Martin that the quick delivery of one such small bouquet might brighten Kristina's evening, but then he remembered he was broke and didn't have money to spare.

As he stood on the sidewalk before the station steps, unsure what to do next, a woman in a green dress with a black handbag walked up to him. She was about to say something, but changed her mind, turning suddenly on her heels. For a moment, Martin thought nothing of it, but then something about her roused his curiosity. He felt compelled to follow her as she turned a corner off to the side of the station building. A man from behind put his hand on Martin's shoulder as if to dissuade him.

"Don't waste your money," he said.

But Martin shook him off and went around the corner of the station only to find she was gone.

He walked along until he came to a staircase that led down to a passageway under the tracks, which took passengers to one of several platforms above. There were three corridors and various doors in the passages, some with frosted glass and darkness on the other side, and some lit, but in all cases locked. There was a public toilet with a dour-faced attendant sitting in front of a table with a saucer on it holding small change. Martin asked if she had seen a woman in a green dress and she smirked at him and gestured down the far passage.

Martin followed her direction and saw nothing but three stairways leading up to the various train platforms. He walked up the first staircase and looked down the length of the platform. At first, he did not see her because she was on the far side of a baggage wagon. This attempt to avoid him and hide from him spurred his curiosity. He walked out and came close.

"Who are you and why are you avoiding me?" he asked.

She stared at him with a mixture of fear and aggression. Unlike most of the women in Vilnius, she wore makeup and it made her look like a movie star, all bright and vivid. Her hair was down to her shoulders, she had bangles on one wrist — like a gypsy — and she had her other hand in the bag she was holding.

"Leave me alone. I have a knife in here and I'm not afraid to use it."

That voice. How was it that she had recognized him after all the changes in his life, the loss of his hair, and yet he had not recognized her?

"Raminta? Is that you? What are you doing here?" he asked.

She laughed. "I'm waiting for a train, but I must have missed it."

He looked up and down the rails. He could see no train in either direction.

"I'm so glad to see you," he blurted out. "It's Martin. I've thought of you often over the years. How did you end up here?"

She didn't acknowledge his name. "Oh, you know. I had some ups and downs. Why should it matter to you?"

"Don't be so cold. When I was a boy, I was practically in love with you."

"Love, oh yes. A lot of good love did me. Love is what got me here in the first place."

Martin looked along the platform, but there was no one else there to hear them. "I gave you a pistol to protect yourself. Do you remember?"

"That was a long, long time ago. Besides, a pistol to defend me against the might of the whole Soviet Union. A lot of good that would have done. The teacher took it away when he came to warn me." She began to walk back toward the stair as if she were about to depart.

"Wait. Don't go. I want to know what happened."

"What does it matter? What would it change?"

"I was good to you within my means when I was a boy. Why can't you be good enough to talk to me now? No one can hear us."

She stopped and considered. "All right. We can talk, but not here and not for long. I'm busy. Nobody can hear us, but they can see us from the station. Follow me, but keep some distance between us and if anyone approaches, we don't know each other."

She led him back down the stairs and through one passageway and then another not far from the smirking toilet attendant. Raminta looked around, put a key in a door, opened it, and gestured for him to hurry. He stepped inside a small vestibule, and then she opened a second, heavy door into a small, windowless room with a cot, a table, and a chair.

"Sit down" she said. He saw she meant the bed while she took the chair. She put her bag on the table. "We can't be here for very long or someone will notice I'm gone."

"Who will notice?"

"Never mind. What do you want to know?"

"Well, how it was for you after they took you away?"

"They lied to me from beginning to end. Why should I have gotten a sentence when I'm the one who brought in Pretty Boy? They'd told me he would get a jail term somewhere in the north and I thought I could find one of those villages where the locals lived and do some kind of job to be near him, to help him if I could."

"You can't make deals with them."

"No. They brought me in to his trial but wouldn't let me speak. He was battered and bruised and was so frightened, like a little boy. He looked at me across the room as if it was all my fault, but I learned there what he'd done. The father of my girl was a killer."

"I know. I saw the bodies. He said it was an accident."

"He would say anything to get off. He asked for mercy."

"He didn't get it?"

"No. I still don't know why I had to pay as well."

"You said you had a daughter."

"Monika. I gave birth in transport."

"She survived?"

"She did, but there was a price. I couldn't bear to leave her in the care of the prison nursery. I needed to see her every day, and for that right, I had to do some favours."

"Favours?"

"Don't make me say it."

"And now?"

"I'm still doing favours. The need for favours never ends, and I need to get by."

"What kind of place is this?" There didn't seem to be enough air in that windowless room. Martin could barely breathe.

"There's a whole warren of rooms under the station. Most of

them are soundproof too, which is a good thing. It's not just howls of joy that come out of here."

"Do you ever get home?"

"No. I don't want to see my brother the way I am now, and I don't want to see anyone else from that time. Including you."

"But Raminta, I loved you then. I remember you from then. I still love you in memory of that time."

"If you want to love me now, you'll have to pay a going rate."

"That's not what I mean."

"That's all I'm good for."

"It's not true. Your Monika, did she survive?"

"Yes, but they won't let me see her."

"Where is she?"

"In an orphanage."

He asked her many more questions and, for all her hurt and disappointment, she talked to him a little less reluctantly the more time went on. Martin would have liked to ask her more questions, but there came a noise outside the door and then a turn in the lock. A burly man with a very short haircut appeared before them.

"Are you all right?" he asked Raminta.

"Yes. He is too. We're just talking."

"Does he have money?"

"No."

"Then stop talking and get back out there. You don't talk during working hours."

22

LYN LAKE, 1948

BADGER THREW OPEN THE lid of the bunker to look at the winter stars, faint glimmers compared to their confident summer selves. Inside the bunker he had the radio on and the accordion music playing out of Warsaw was romantic and French, and the sound of it carried over the night-time fields of snow. He should not have taken a chance like this, but sitting in the bunker alone for any length of time made him restless and the music in the open air was liberating.

Pike was out delivering the latest underground newspaper, and so Badger was alone and subject to melancholy thoughts. It was important not to think too much when he could not play a game of cards with a companion to pass the time. All the worse that snow had fallen recently and any step outside would give away the hiding place. A bunker was like a prison — it sucked the health right out of his body. When he was alone, he also fell into dull apathy. He felt helpless and wanted to do nothing to change that emotion. He was capable of doing nothing, and yet, he knew he had to fight this lack of emotion and rouse himself, so he played the music across the fields where nothing moved in the stillness of the night. The bite of the cold on his nose and ears was welcome, like a splash of water on his face in the morning.

It was already 1948. He was going into his fifth year in the underground. How quickly the time passed! The world he had lived in before seemed so far away, a time when he dreamed of a normal life after the war, a life with a career and a family. But now he could only have one thought — how best to resist the reds without getting killed. Regardless of the cost. For all he knew, the diplomats in London and Washington, in Moscow and elsewhere, were dividing up the world into their spheres of influence. His resistance and that of his men were nothing more than futile pinpricks against the beast that was devouring them. And the other beasts, such as the British imperial lion, must not be allowed to grow too thin!

It was important to keep his spirits up. But how was it possible? He had put his own mother in danger by joining the underground. For all the talk of code names, the reds knew who he was. Likely they were watching his mother in case he decided to visit her, but how could he could afford the risk? He needed to stay alive and free in order that they leave her alone. As soon as he died or was, God forbid, taken prisoner, she would be deported to the north. A woman her age would not have much of a chance there.

He had to believe the country's future depended on him and men like him. It was the one idea that sustained him. And it was all the harder to keep this one motivating idea in his mind when he thought about men like Pretty Boy, who stained their reputation by terrorizing the locals. It was bad enough that the reds planted false partisans to terrify the farmers. Some of his own had their weaknesses too, primarily drink, which he tried to forbid, but every grateful farmer in his region offered his men a bottle of *naminė*, and it was hard to turn down a warming gift like that if you were cold or frightened or bored.

The welcome sting of the cold on his ears and fingertips sharpened to numbness and pain as the minutes passed. He bore it as long as he could, and then shut the lid of the bunker again, wondering at the foolish desire of Skylark to join him there.

❧

"THIS MUST BE WHAT you'd call a 'deluxe bunker,' practically a four-star bunker," said Skylark.

"We don't use it very often because all bunkers get found eventually by some shepherd or wandering beggar, and the next thing you know, word gets out. The reds pay for this kind of information. If I want to print the underground press, I need some space, and this is one of the bigger bunkers. But I never use it unguarded. Pike is out there keeping watch and he'll give a whistle if there's any danger."

The bunker was deeper than most and therefore with a higher ceiling. A stencil copier stood on a table and beside it, a typewriter and stencil masters as well as a stack of precious paper. An oil lamp illuminated the earthen floor, wooden walls and ceiling, and its small flame and their body heat warmed the place to the point it was bearable to work without gloves. Martin lay on the lower straw mattress of a bunk bed, waiting to distribute the newspaper as soon as the men were done printing it.

"I never thought of myself as a journalist," said Skylark, "let alone a printer."

"Adversity teaches us to do whatever we need to do."

This was the public Badger, Martin could see, the man who treated his men as his brothers and Martin himself as a younger one. Martin did not like to see the other, doubtful Badger, a sensitive character who filled him with misgiving. The one that Skylark sometimes brought out.

"I have an idea," said Skylark. "I have a whole swathe of new poems. Why don't you type the stencils, and I'll read them aloud to you?"

"Are you avoiding menial labour?"

"I am offering you entertainment."

Skylark's words were charming, a mixture of patriotic poetry and children's poetry arranged in such a fashion that his ninety minutes of reading were like a story itself, with moments of light and darkness.

"Was I right or was I wrong?" asked Skylark as Badger finished up his typing and prepared to insert the stencil on the drum.

"You were right, my friend. But as I was listening to you, enjoying the talk, I wondered why we didn't have more like you among us."

"Oh, there were plenty like me, though probably not as talented. You know, when you and I were children in school, they taught us patriotism and sacrifice. But, when I thought about it recently, I realized that all the teachers who did that have immigrated to the west. They taught us to fight, but they didn't do it themselves. The intellectuals all ran away."

"I suppose they suffered the most the first time the reds came. Can intellectuals even be fighters? You're not much of a fighter, are you? Didn't you say you don't even know how to fire a pistol?"

"I'm sure I could if I had to, but that's not the point. I am a poet, you understand? I have to stay true to my own calling. It's a form of patriotism."

"Here we go again. You mean your poetry is more important than your country?"

"I'm not saying you put these things on a scale and weigh them. But listen, I stayed behind in this country for the sake of my poetry. Too bad for me, eh? Music and art can travel, but literature doesn't. Not really. My poetry made me into a patriot. I have to be where my language is, or else I'd wither like an uprooted flower."

"You're lucky, you know. You have a room and bed, food, and a few roubles to spare each month, and then you can write all you want."

"But I don't really have an audience, do I?"

"You miss that?"

"Of course I do. That's why I'm in with you. How else will I ever get an audience unless you manage to evict the reds?"

"What a curious man. Are all writers as egotistical as you?"

"What do you mean, *egotistical*? Every performer wants an audience. It's normal. You wouldn't tell an opera singer she should perform her arias in the forest."

"So would you write a poem to the glory of collectivization if it gave you an audience?"

"Don't tempt me. I just might let my standards slip."

"And anyway, you have an audience. This newspaper will get passed from hand to hand among a lot of people. Hundreds of them. And your poetry will be in there."

"Anonymously. Some good that does me."

"You are impossible!' said Badger, but he said it as one might say it of a charming ne'er-do-well brother, judging him but loving him at the same time.

"Will The Hawk read this newspaper?"

"I'm sure he will. He reads everything."

"I'd like to meet him. Does he ever come around here?"

Badger's face froze. "You have no business with him. But if you want, I'll ask him what he thinks of your verses the next time I see him."

"Don't be so suspicious. Listen, I have your interests and my interests in mind. The Hawk travels around the country trying to keep the partisan bands united. Everybody knows that. The man is famous among the peasants, and I'm sure he's famous among the reds too. His interests and mine coincide. I could be the poet of the united underground press instead of a local poet, you understand? I'd like to make my case to him."

"Your case? Have you gone out of your mind? You want him to be concerned about the poet laureate of the resistance?"

"You need someone who can talk and get your message out. You can't be setting off ambushes and blowing up trains without explaining yourselves. You need to move your audience. You need to rally them. Churchill could talk. Look what he achieved."

"Churchill was the leader of the United Kingdom."

"Yes, but there have been others. Think of *La Passionara* in Spain."

"I don't know about him."

"She was a woman. She spoke passionately to the defenders of Madrid during the Spanish Civil War. She coined the phrase, *They Shall Not Pass* that stiffened the backs of the army."

"And what became of this woman and this army?"

"Well, in the long run she lost, but that's not the point. The point is what she did while she could."

"Not so fast. They lost? You mean you are holding up a communist as a model to me?"

"Yes, I am. You don't reject the tactics of your enemy just because she's your enemy. You need a voice of the people here. I can be that voice. I am working for you now, but if The Hawk could centralize the partisan press, I could rally the nation."

"Or the children of the nation with your poetry about birds and flowers."

"Always ready to mock me. But yes, the children, if necessary, and their parents will be the happier for it. I can make this case to The Hawk. I just need a chance to speak to him."

"You ask for too much."

"Every idea seems unlikely. Every form of resistance is unlikely. The Germans tossed some loudmouth into Russia, and the next thing you knew you had Lenin leading a revolution."

"Again, communist examples."

"All right then. The Germans did the same with a socialist bandit called Pilsudski, and when he took over the reins of Poland, he led the army beating back the reds so deep into Russia they signed a document that gave up huge chunks of Europe. Every idea needs to be tried. This idea needs to be tried. Give me a chance."

"I don't even know when The Hawk will come through the district again. He hasn't been here for months."

"But he will come back. Promise me you'll at least tell him of my idea."

Badger laughed. "You are ridiculous but convincing. I will mention it to him."

"But not as an aside, you understand? Be an advocate for me. And if you can't be one, let me try to speak to him on my own behalf."

"You want too much. You artists are megalomaniacs. But I will think about it."

ↄ�

A LATE WINTER THAW had melted most of the snow before the winter winds regrouped, and thus it was so much easier to walk home to the village on the hardened ground, still taking a circuitous route, not needing to concern themselves with leaving telltale footprints. But if the ground was pleasantly firm underfoot, the mischievous winds insinuated themselves around the flaps on their hats, under the cuffs of their sleeves, and under the hems of their coats. Man and boy walked fast to warm themselves, but the wind stung their faces and made the bare branches of the trees rattle like the bones of the long-dead now rising again. Yet what would these skeletons find if they did rise again? No second coming, or if it was a second coming that included the reds, then God had a sense of irony.

"How old are you, Martin?" asked Mr. Kostas, who could not be thought of as Skylark when he was outside the realm of the partisans.

"I'll be fifteen on my name day."

"And remind me when that is."

"April thirteenth."

"So young still, and yet not surprising how you've turned out, given the name your parents gave you."

"I don't understand."

"Martin — based on Mars, the God of War and Saint Martin of Tours, a patron saint of war. How long have you been fighting with the partisans?"

"I don't fight. I just carry messages and bring them supplies. I post the newspapers."

"And what about The Hawk? Have you met him?"

"Oh no, but I wish I had."

"Why's that?"

"He's done so many great things. He and his partisans seized the town of Merkine for a day. Some say he was in the battle of Kalniškės, when the partisans held off a whole battalion of Red Army soldiers. And he never gets caught! People see him everywhere, in Kaunas and Vilnius and Klaipėda and Šiauliai. Some of the little kids say he has secret powers and some of the older ones say he must have body doubles."

"And what do you say?"

"I say he is a great man."

"Yes, I am sure he is. I should write some poems about him, or maybe some lyrics that could be turned into songs. And now tell me this, how are your studies going?"

Mr. Kostas went on to ask him about each subject in great detail, stressing the importance of studying hard in mathematics if Martin intended to be an engineer. It was not enough to be handy with motors and good with his hands. Any adept villager or self-taught mechanic had those qualities, but if Martin wanted to achieve something in his life, to climb higher, he would need to master the abstract subjects as well as the practical ones.

As to the humanities, Mr. Kostas was surprisingly dismissive of them. He blamed his life predicament on his addiction to poetry and admitted he would have done far better in life if he had not been afflicted with a love of words and gone on instead, as Martin would do, into a life of concrete and practical pursuits. These would have won him a good income and the respect of the government, which treated poets and writers if they were tiresome bards to be brought out on the occasions of weddings, christenings, and funerals, but otherwise placed in positions of low esteem and low income.

Martin listened closely to all that Mr. Kostas said. After all, Martin knew no else who had lived in the capital or had belonged to the Writers' Union. Mr. Kostas opened up the world to him, as if lifting Martin high above the surrounding forests until he could see Vilnius in the distance. Farther away lay the great metropolises of the world.

Even his high school teachers were all from the provincial capital of Varėna, which had always seemed so fine to him in the past, but now his ambitions had been enlarged. Now he knew what he wanted, and not much of it lay in his home. He loved his home and his family, but realized he would need to give them up if he sought to achieve greater things.

23

LYN LAKE, 1948

THE WINTER GAVE WAY to spring, first in a terrible, sudden thaw that mired wagons to their axles and horses to their knees, also stealing the boots of children who dashed home half-shod, looking for help. No cars or trucks could venture out. The run-off turned low-lying fields into lakes, over which the eternally patient farmers waited and watched, hoping for the best but inured to the worst. With any luck, the first buds on trees and the first shoots of winter wheat would not be bitten off by wicked frost or malicious wind. The storks swooped back to last year's nests and then loped out to look for frogs in the streams and ponds.

The partisans in the southern region including Lyn Lake began to make themselves known again, yet not as they had in the past. They were seen, of course, as they came for food because the farmers supported them. The partisans looked for boots to replace their sodden winter wear and thread to repair their torn clothes. They needed fresh ammunition, but they did not attack munitions dumps as they had in past, at least not around Lyn Lake or, indeed, anywhere in the province.

The strange passivity of the local partisans was a little disheartening to the farmers, villagers, and provincial townspeople as the red bureaucrats crept out of their offices to count chickens and eggs and to hand over pre-emptive fall requisitions for amounts of grain that exceeded what the farmers had ever grown before. The local collaborators seemed not as frightened as they had been in the past, and walked about in pairs rather than in the larger groups as in the years before.

Why then this sudden passivity in the region to which Lyn Lake belonged?

Martin felt restless and apathetic at the same time that spring. He wanted something, but he did not know the object of his wanting. Why was the partisan activity so very light that season? He missed Badger. Had they been beaten down, or was this simply the calm before a great storm? Maybe one that would herald the long-anticipated arrival of the Americans to save the day?

When Mr. Kostas asked if there was any word from Badger, Martin could only shrug. Mr. Kostas took the cup of tea Martin's mother had made for him and went into his room. As for Martin, he sat at the kitchen table with his books in front of him, but he kept looking out the window at the yard as his mother unwrapped fresh cheese behind him. His grandmother sat in the corner clicking along through the beads of her rosary.

He had celebrated his fifteenth birthday in April and the event concentrated his mind on his future. In a year he would be sixteen years old, a legal adult, and then he would have to consider which path to take. On the one hand, he dreamed of life in the city of Vilnius and the study of engineering. His high school teacher in Rudnia, having noticed Martin's interest, had shown him a slide rule from Germany, and Martin was fascinated by the device that seemed so much more sophisticated than the abacus used by the cashier in the government store where his father sent him to buy lamp oil.

He imagined himself in an office behind a desk while wielding such a device and then stepping out to some sort of massive machine shop that the communist press described in detail and praised as the best of its kind. He would walk about the whirring lathes to diagnose their problems as if he were a doctor of machines. He was very good with machines and he was turning out to be good in math as well, which Mr. Kostas had told him to devote himself to if he wanted to succeed.

While this dream of life as an engineer was vivid, it was also remote, involving places he had never seen and things he had never done. He did not even really know how to use the functions on a slide rule.

The smell of the raspberry cane tea that his mother had made now filled the room. She brought over a cup as well as a bowl of honey with a spoon and set them on the table beside him. She returned with a plate upon which lay a thick slice of heavy rye bread and a piece of the white farmer's cheese they made whenever there was milk to spare. Martin spooned the honey into his cup and then held the spoon above the cheese so a thin ribbon laced its way over the surface.

On the one hand, it would be exciting to leave, and on the other hand, it would take him far away from home and everything he knew. He was just becoming aware of the place he lived in; how strange that was when he had lived his entire life in Lyn Lake and had always taken it for granted. He now saw his father, as if for the first time, looking at the sky to judge the weather and then studying the land to determine when it would be ready for the plough. His father seemed older than Martin remembered, more susceptible to sore muscles and sprains. For the first time, Martin felt a touch of tenderness for him.

As the only surviving son, Martin should have been doing much more in the fields for his father, but he began to see the man indulged him because Martin had some talent for education. As to his mother, standing in the kitchen behind him with her own rosary wrapped around her left wrist, he began to wonder if the loss of her eldest son might be sharper for her than his own loss of a brother, and he imagined she must be praying for the lost one whenever she fingered her rosary in the free moments between the baking of bread and helping in the fields.

If he joined the partisans at sixteen, he would have the comfort of being close to home and he would be nearby to help his parents when he could. Badger had complained more than once that fewer and fewer young men came to the partisan ranks, but, at the same time, Badger had tried to talk him out of doing it because he was an only son. Badger said he wanted men who had no other choice because the risk in partisan life lay somewhere between very dangerous and suicidal.

Martin would have liked to be similar to Badger, the leader of men, the patriot fighting for his country.

The honeyed cheese was sweet on his tongue; it crumbled easily, and he wet the tip of his finger to lift the crumbs from the plate.

He would need to do something. He could not stay still in the current of time.

Martin opened his notebook to a blank page to work out an assignment of trigonometry. He found the page was not blank. There was a note to him to meet a messenger the next day at a spot just inside the forest on the far side of Lyn Lake and to be prepared to be away for a few hours, as well as an instruction to rub out the message and overwrite his mathematics problem on it. He looked up, but his mother was distracted and Mr. Kostas was in his own room.

Someone else in his class must also be a courier for the partisans, but he could not guess who it might be. He did as the message instructed and on the appointed day at the appointed time, rather than walk around the lake, he took his dugout canoe and brought along a long willow rod with a line on it in case he needed to explain what he was doing. He paddled across the lake. At ten metres into the forest on the other side, Pike came out from a stand of bushes and motioned for him to follow.

"What's going on?" asked Martin, but Pike was the least talkative man of anyone he knew and said only what needed to be said.

"Listen to me. You're going to be called *Mole*, all right?"

"What do you mean?"

"It's your name from now on."

"What, a code name? I don't like that name. Couldn't I be a falcon or something? A wolf? A tiger?"

Pike declined to get into conversation. Instead, he took the newly christened Mole deep into the forest. When they had been walking for thirty minutes, a whistle sounded from somewhere ahead. Pike whistled back. Further on, a voice called for a password. Pike called it back. The two approached a sentry, a red-haired partisan Martin had never seen before. As they walked on, they passed yet another pair of sentries, these two with a machine gun mounted on a rise in the land, and then beyond these two lay an encampment.

At the centre of the large clearing a whole complex of rough furniture had been set up, with log tables and rows of benches and thick, short logs set on their ends to act as stools. Beyond them, stood an outdoor kitchen where a pair of men oversaw the roasting of an entire pig and another pair stood stirring a gigantic pot of buckwheat porridge. Among these things were many partisans, at least three dozen of them, talking in groups and going about tasks. To judge by the sentries they had passed, another dozen were out in the forest around them. Nearby were half a dozen women and a girl called Ona from his high school class, a particularly shy one who hardly ever said a word. She must have been the one who wrote the note in his book. Aside from Ona, Martin knew only Pike and Badger and a handful of men from neighbouring villages whom he used to see at church.

"Sit down here and wait," said Pike. Martin found himself with Ona and the women. They were talking among themselves, but the girl was silent. She glanced up at him, but looked away when he smiled at her to give her to understand she must have written the note.

"Thank you, Ona," he said, and she shook her head when he used her name.

"They call me *Sparrow* whenever we're in the forest," she said. "And you?"

He didn't like his code name, but he admitted he was to be called Mole.

"I never knew you were involved," said Martin, and then he added her code name, Sparrow, for the feel of the word in his mouth.

"I can keep a secret. Better than you. I could tell right away you'd be the type, *Mole*." She said his code name as if it were a joke.

"What's going on?" Martin asked her.

"It's an award ceremony. The Hawk has brought everyone together to honour the couriers and helpers, those of us who live legally but pass on the partisan letters or provide them with news."

There were four women sitting together. They must have been the ones Sparrow was talking about.

The Hawk himself was going to be there. Martin was pleased. He studied the various groups of men to see if The Hawk stood out in some way. There was no one who looked as imposing as Martin imagined such a man must be, but when one man stood up from a circle of others on the grass, Martin could see that he commanded the attention of the rest. The whole clearing seemed to react as if to a magnetic pull to this leader of men. Yes, he was shorter than many and his hair was receding, so the impression he made came from some kind of inner magnetism rather than his looks.

And then things began to happen very quickly. The men moved as one, putting on hats and straightening out uniforms, all with the tricolour on their shoulders. Two women took their places at a rough table and removed papers from a leather briefcase. Everyone stood, including Sparrow and the women, and Badger stood beside The Hawk and began the national anthem, which had been banned by the communists since 1944.

Martin remembered ceremonies such as this before the war.

Those formalities were important for some reason to the adults, but boring to the children and adolescents. It was different now. Out here in the forest, he was with a gang of beloved outlaws. What the reds wouldn't give to swoop down on them and send them away to prisons where they could be interrogated at will. Failing that, killing them would clean up the "banditry" problem for a large part of the region.

How astonishing it was to have so many of them together in one place at a time. This meeting must have been the reason the partisans had taken no military action that spring, all for the sake of letting the reds be more active elsewhere. Martin would have loved to be one of the men standing at attention, ready to take orders from The Hawk.

After others had received their honours, the moment came when the names Sparrow and Mole were called and girl and boy stepped forward. The secretary recorded their code names in her log book and they each received a curious cloth gift, a kind of rolled tube of yellow woollen yarn with a green stripe through the middle of it, a talisman that did not give away its meaning. And when the words of gratitude were spoken by The Hawk, the men applauded and Sparrow looked at Mole, flushed and happy, and he kissed her impulsively, to the laughter of the onlookers.

When the ceremony was over, Martin received many claps on the back from men he knew and those he did not. The Hawk came and shook his hand and looked him in the eye and thanked him again for his service to the partisans. Some of the men went out to relieve the sentries. Then it came time to eat. The cook heaped buttered buckwheat into wooden bowls and topped it with pieces of roast pork. To drink, that spring the partisans had filled barrels full of birch sap, a beverage barely sweet, as if haunted by sweetness, and tasting of the freshness of the forest. Drinking it was like breathing air that had been flavoured by the woods.

Martin had never known such air of freedom. For all of his short life the country had been ruled by the Soviets and, before that, the

Germans. One always had to be careful not to excite their interest, not to make the wrong move, not to get caught. He was only a child when all of this began, and the concerns belonged mostly to the parents, but still, everyone who lived in the country lived with a sense of caution, of sleeping with one eye open, of watching what one said. But the partisans had made a circle of freedom, a magic circle, a zone where tensed muscles could be relaxed, where words could be spoken without fearing their consequences.

Sparrow, formerly Ona, must have felt this too because the silent girl, the one who had never spoken to him before, talked about her own dreams for the future, about loving railways because they took people to exotic locations. Martin told her about his dreams of engineering, knowing that he was lying as he spoke because the well-being he felt at the moment tipped his preference toward life with the partisans.

Badger came along and sat down beside her.

"Congratulations, you two," he said, and they glowed under his words.

"I don't see Skylark here," said Martin. "This is the kind of thing he would have liked."

Badger asked Sparrow to give them a moment, and she lifted her bowl and cup and went to another place.

"I've talked about him to The Hawk, but he says we need to move slowly. He's right, of course, but Skylark would be very useful to us and I'd hate to let him slip away."

Badger spoke to him as if he were a man, and Martin assumed an appropriate air of gravity.

"Will you introduce him to The Hawk?"

"Eventually. I love Skylark's talk and I think he has great talent, but he's an egotist like most artists of one kind or another. Most men don't think enough, but he thinks too much. They should meet. Definitely."

"The village loves him."

"I know that. Listen. The Hawk may hesitate, but I want you to bring Skylark to me, to a new place, a new bunker. It is going to be very hard for anyone to find. Even you. So listen carefully and I'll tell you how to get there. Later on, I'll take him to The Hawk from there."

Martin listened as he was told, and then he lingered as long as he could in that wonderful place. Later that night there would be a bonfire and singing and he wished that he could stay, but Pike came along and told him it was time for him to go so no one missed him from the village. Martin started to leave reluctantly, and then realized he had not said goodbye to Sparrow. He returned to take her hand and to say he would see her at school.

"But don't talk to me too much when you see me there," she said. "It will look too suspicious. We'll be better off if you ignore me."

"I can't ignore you, but I promise I won't give you away."

Ona seemed pleased with this, and she squeezed his hands, which prompted him to kiss her once more on the cheek. She did not seem displeased with this.

24

VILNIUS, 1957

THE FOUR *KIBINAI* SNACKS Martin found in the market across the street were beautifully browned, and the dough was delicately laced across the top. These baked Karaite meat dumplings would be enough for dinner alongside the beet soup Kristina had promised him. When he stepped out of the yellow brick building, an old woman thrust a handful of tiny blue wildflowers at him. He bought them and was about to walk off when Tomas presented himself, as always, in a coat too big.

"Flowers for Kristina?"

"Isn't it time someone bought you a new coat?"

"It's part of my uniform. Well, what about those flowers?"

"Yes, that's right, for Kristina. How are you?"

"I'm great. I'm fine, and you'll be happy to know I've come across some good luck for both of us."

"By that I guess you have something to sell."

"Right. A case of vermouth fell off the back of a truck, and I can sell you a bottle of it very cheaply."

"*Triple 7* brand?"

"Right."

"Cat piss."

"True, but it gets the job done."

"We're trying to cut down on our drinking."

"But you're carrying flowers. That's not enough. Do you have chocolates?"

"No."

"You can't give a girl just flowers alone. You need something along with them, and if you don't have chocolates, you need to bring wine. Come with me. My warehouse is just around the corner."

"Didn't you say you were twelve years old? Aren't you a little young to be giving advice on dating?"

"Actually, I'm fourteen and a bit more, but I'm small for my age, and I lie about it to keep myself employed for a couple more years. And keep in mind I've been around, so I know how certain things are done."

Martin couldn't resist the boy and followed his lead.

"Any more trouble from rival gangs?"

"Not for us. Some for them. We're doing just fine. You know, our boys all like Kristina. They've made her an honorary member of our group."

"Wonderful! But what does that even mean?"

"It means we do favours. When you need us, we'll be there."

Tomas led him up an alley and to a barred window. He tapped on the glass; the window opened, Tomas passed Martin's coins inside, and then a bottle came out between the bars.

"Are you going to marry Kristina?" Tomas asked.

"What a strange question. Very bold."

"You and I have fought together. We're brothers now. We help each other, and we share secrets. Weren't you ever in a gang when you were young?"

"Something like that."

"Then you understand the rules. You'll help me too. When you get married, you'll buy your reception wine and liquor from me."

"So — brotherhood means business?"

"It does. I trust you too. And if you don't have the money all at once, I know my boss can sell to you on time."

"Tomas, you are unbelievable. Where did you learn all of this?"

"On the street. It's a very good teacher if you can avoid the beatings.

AT KRISTINA'S HOUSE, MARTIN found her young neighbour, Diana, smoking a cigarette on the stoop out front. Her makeup was smeared, and it looked as if she had not slept all night.

"You'd better go in and see to your girlfriend," she said.

"Is something wrong?"

"She's sick, and she'll need your help."

The room was half dark as usual, and it smelled bad. He could see a bucket at her bedside.

"Hello," she said quietly. He sat down upon the rumpled blanket on the bed and put his hand on her forehead. It was cool to the touch, for all her being covered up. He straightened a strand of her hair over her ear, then rested his hand on her cheek.

"Let me take the bucket and rinse it out. Do you think you'll need it for a few minutes?"

"Not just now."

"I'll be right back."

There was a hand pump in the back yard, and he rinsed out the bucket and poured its contents behind a bush at the end of the yard. Diana had moved to a chair at an old wooden table out there.

"How's she feeling?" asked Diana. She was dark-haired and beautiful in her way, sure of herself, probably coming from many generations in the city. There were strong women in the countryside and he had met some very resilient ones in the gulag, but they were women who hardened under difficult field work. The tough women of Vilnius had a particularly sharp edge to them as well as deep irony. They made him feel unsophisticated. But for all of her bite, Diana was all right. She borrowed money but always paid it back, and sometimes she brought small gifts she had earned after a night's work — a slice of cake or a piece of decent cheese. Martin felt a moment's tenderness toward her.

"I was bringing her some wine," he said, showing Diana the bottle of Vermouth he took from his coat pocket, "but it doesn't look like she's going to want any for a while. Would you like it?"

"Save it for after she sees the doctor. She'll want it then."

"She didn't say anything about going to a doctor."

"She will. That drink is awful, but it will take the edge off the pain. Believe me."

Bewildered, Martin thanked her without asking for an explanation and walked back into Kristina's room. "Are you feeling any better?" he asked.

"You've only been gone a few minutes."

"I was talking to Diana outside and she said some of the strangest things. I hear you're planning on going to a doctor. Are you that sick?"

"What are you talking about? I have no intention of going to see a doctor, not yet."

He looked at her dumbly

"I'm not sick that way, you idiot. I'm pregnant, and if she thinks I'm going to let some hack abortionist at the hospital anywhere near me, she's mistaken."

LATER, WHEN MARTIN CAME out of the room, Diana took one look at his face, shook her head, and then turned to Auntie, who had come out to sit with her face in the sun by the ruined picket fence.

"Do you have any cotton balls Auntie?" asked Diana.

"Oh dear," said the old woman, shaking her head and adjusting her scarf. "No, but at least I have my ears covered by my scarf. You'll have to find rags to stuff into your own ears, or buy a second pillow to put on your head when the baby starts to squeal."

The two were laughing, and Martin felt the secret lines of communication that women seemed to have. If the resistance had consisted only of women and the KGB only of men, they never would have uncovered any secrets at all.

"Do you drink?" asked Auntie.

"Not much. Why?"

"Keep it under control. A young mother needs a caring man, not some lout who spends his time boozing with other oafs or presses her to let him put something in too soon after something's come out."

"How did you know she's going to keep the child?" asked Martin.

"By the stupid glow on your face after you came out. Give me that terrible bottle of wine and come inside. I'll give you something better to celebrate with."

Diana came along as well.

Auntie's room contained a bed, a table, and three chairs, as well as many photographs on the walls — most of them relatives, he guessed. There were men in czarist uniforms and moustaches, on horseback and sitting in groups during picnics in the past. Many of the items in the room were covered by knitted cozies of one kind or another, from the decorative pillow covers to the placemats on the table to even the frames in which the photos were found. What was this need of old women to knit miniature sweaters, as if not only their bodies but their belongings needed to be protected from drafts?

"Sit down," she said, and she shuffled to a cupboard from which she took a bottle and three glasses.

"I just decanted this yesterday, and I need someone to help me try it out. Black currant wine is the simplest drink to make because all you need to remember is the number one. You fill one of any kind of jar with black currants. Remember to pick off the leaves or the drink will be bitter. That's the first *one*. Then you fill all the gaps among the berries with sugar until the jar is full. That's the second *one*. Next you fill the jar with overproof spirits, the third *one*. Don't use regular spirits or the outcome won't be as good. Finally, you stopper the bottle and wait *one* year before you decant it. That makes four ones."

"It's not really wine then, is it? More like flavoured spirits."

"Country people call it wine, and who am I to argue with its name? There is some powerful mystery in black currant wine. I don't know if the charm lies in the berries or in the mixture, but the drink has amazing properties."

"Like all liquor, it makes you happy, and then makes you drunk. Isn't that it?"

"Oh, you young people don't believe in anything. Black currant wine is used as medicine, to heal you. But only if you are worthy. If you are unworthy, it makes you stupid. Didn't your parents use it on you when you were sick?"

"Sugar was expensive. We didn't have many sweet things, but yes. I remember my grandmother gave me a little once when I'd been bitten by an adder."

"And you survived. See? Now I know I said you should wait a year to drink it, but I am an old woman, and I am feeling the passage of time more and more. And so I'm opening this after ten months rather than twelve, breaking the rule of ones. Who knows if I'll be alive two months from now? It would be a waste to let my heirs drink it untested at my funeral."

"I didn't know you had heirs."

"What? Did you think I was always an old hag the way you find me now? I was a beauty, and I had children and grandchildren. Some are dead and some are living, but they are far away, scattered. I expect one or another of them to come and visit me one day. But maybe they'll only come to visit once they find out I am gone, even if only be to see if I had anything of value." She said it sardonically, but he could see her eyes were wet. "At least they'll have something to drink."

"How many of these bottles do you have?"

"One or two a year for the last ten years."

"Are you expecting a lot of guests at your funeral?"

"Who knows? People have come and gone throughout my life. Sometimes there were many, and sometimes I've been alone. But things never stay the same. For all I know, as we're speaking, my missing son might open the gate and walk in here with a girl he will introduce as my granddaughter. Sit down."

Martin and Diana did as she asked.

She poured the black currant wine until each glass was almost full. She clicked their glasses with hers and raised her own to drink half of it in one swallow, as if it were nothing stronger than fruit juice.

Martin followed her example and the flavour of the wine brought him back to his childhood, when his grandmother sent him out to the currant bushes in high summer to pick the tiny, sour fruit. If they had any sugar, she would make jam, but during the war years there was none and he made do with tasting infrequent single berries, astringent yet pleasant. Now the addition of sugar and alcohol brought out the full flavour of the currants and with it, the memory of Lyn Lake, where he had been happy as a boy without even knowing he was happy. His ignorance was bliss, marred by the war and what came after it. Especially what came after it.

Martin asked for a plate and a knife and he took out the four *kibinai* and laid them on a plate and cut them into smaller pieces.

"I gather Kristina's not hungry?" asked Auntie.

"No."

"Well, the food and drink are both delicious," said Diana. "This is my lucky day."

"Lucky today, unlucky tomorrow. The world is full of unlikely tragedies and of unlikely luck. The very first thing you need to do is be ready to seize it if luck should come your way."

"So will you marry her?" asked Diana.

"I will, if she'll take me."

"She could do worse, I suppose. I'll tell you what. Auntie sews and I used to sew, and if I can find any decent material, we'll make her a dress."

"You don't sew anymore?"

"Too busy."

Auntie laughed. "There's more money in what she does now."

"And what's that?"

She gave him a piercing look. "I work in the left luggage room at the train station."

"I know someone there. Have you ever met Raminta?"

Auntie and Diana seemed to have an understanding Martin did not share. They exchanged significant looks.

"I have, but if you're going to get married, you should probably drop that relationship."

"It's not a relationship. She came from my village, and she had a very sad story."

"There's no lack of those in this country."

"Drink up," said Auntie.

"You're very kind, both of you."

"The world we live in is a terrible place," said Auntie. "We need to help each other when we can. I've helped Diana and Kristina in the past, and they have helped me. Now you're part of the circle. Don't let us down."

Auntie finished her half tumbler of wine and refilled her glass. She encouraged them to finish theirs and then refilled their glasses too.

"I also managed to land some Arabica coffee. I couldn't believe it! They were selling two-kilo bags. I sold half of mine on the street and made back more than I paid in the first place!"

She lit a gas ring and put a kettle of water on it. She added heaping spoons of ground coffee right into three chipped china cups and poured boiling water on top. They waited until the grounds settled and then sipped from the coffee alternating with the wine.

They sat and they talked a long time in this manner in that

room filled with knitted items and old photographs. The light in the yard turned golden as the sun began its descent toward the horizon.

Auntie boiled more water for coffee and poured out more wine in increasingly smaller amounts. She searched among her reserves to find a piece of chocolate that she shared with them, and later three slices of rye bread spread with butter and honey. In this long, long conversation, they had some silences while one took time to consider the arguments of the other. And it was during such a silence, while Auntie was looking at a photograph on the wall of a young man in a uniform, that Martin saw her face take on a certain glow.

Martin had no idea who the man was, but he was clearly important to her. A loved one? By his age and dress, perhaps a son or grandson, a nephew, or a close friend of one of her children. It did not matter. Was this man alive? He did not know, and he did not want to ask. The smile on Auntie's face was very faint, and he did not want it to go away.

Maybe it was just the alcohol speaking, filling him with such a glow of well-being. He was among friends, and any dangers the world presented seemed far, far away.

25

PAŽAISLIS MONASTERY ASYLUM, 1959

BY THE TIME KOSTAS had drunk his fourth shot of vodka, he was an entirely different man from the hallucinating invalid Martin had met upon opening the barred window of his cell. He had become like a man singing for his supper, one eye always on the bottle on the table and one eye on his host, whom he imagined he needed to charm to keep the liquor flowing.

As to Martin, he drank very little, sipping from his glass after the initial shot, but even he could feel some of the alcohol flowing through his body, urging him to move more quickly, to state his purpose, to lay out his plan before Kostas.

But that would not do. He wanted to find out a great deal and for that he needed to move slowly, to let the alcohol take effect.

Kostas nudged Martin's pack on the floor and heard a clink of glass on glass.

"Yes?"

"Why so slow?"

"To draw out the enjoyment of the moment. I've heard it said that in France one can spend an hour over a single glass of wine in a café, and more hours over a meal."

"In France? Aren't you the child of peasants? How would you know such a thing?"

"In the gulag, I met a Frenchman who told stories of his homeland."

"A Frenchman? What was he doing there?"

"He'd been there for over twenty years, arrested in Spain during the civil war. He expected to be shot, but he never was. He hoped to be returned to his homeland eventually, but he was afraid to draw attention to himself and because he still might get shot. Anyway, that was what he thought."

"And how was it for you up there?"

"You want to know?"

"I am asking, aren't I?"

"What I remember most about it was the hunger. I was so hungry I thought I could kill a man and eat him if I could get away with it."

"And did you?"

"No. I made myself useful instead. Out in the forest I could produce, so they assigned me better rations as a working man. Then somebody noticed I was handier than others, and I began to work in the wood shop and then the garage."

"Is that where you lost your hair?"

"In a fever, yes. It was good, in a way, because it made me look older."

"I would like to know more about it."

"But I'm not here to tell my story. I'm here to hear your story."

"I've told you a writer doesn't have much to say about his own life. It all has to do with sitting at a desk and making up things. I have no biography. I exist in the imagination."

"I want you to talk. Start talking."

Kostas paused and looked carefully at Martin's face. "By all means. You're my host and I'd be glad to do as you say. But let me ask you this. You seem a little perturbed. A little irritated. Is something wrong?"

"Oh yes, things are very wrong."

"And is your intention to do me harm?"

"You'll have to guess for the moment."

"Well then, if I am in danger, maybe you could pour me another drink to help me meet it."

26

VILNIUS, 1957

THE LONG LUNCHEON BOARD was an uneven landscape as the assembled tables were of different heights, taken from different offices, alcoves, and corridors at the Book Depository. Coloured sashes lay across the tables at intervals, and flowers stood bunched in small vases every few feet with a bouquet of hothouse roses in a proper vase at the head of the table. There, on a broad, linen tablecloth lay a vast loaf of country rye bread as well as a tray with a tiny dish of salt and two small glasses of brandy, the traditional welcoming food for newlyweds. Glasses of various sizes and shapes and many bottles of cheap fortified wine provided by Tomas and four of vodka stood along with two large ceramic pitchers of fruit compote.

And at every setting at the table stood the Depository workers awaiting the entrance of the newlyweds: old men with bent backs and ancient suits smelling of naphthalene, women who had once been nuns now forced out of their habits, younger women who had needed refuge for one reason or another and with them children who were too young to be left at home alone. But none of these mothers had men — they were dead or in prison in the north.

Who knew there were so many employees in the vast rooms and grounds of the former monastery turned book depository?

They were normally hidden away in their pursuits like church mice, but came out now for the promise of a banquet.

The number of guests exceeded the places at the long table, so benches lined the refectory walls. Before them stood Peter the driver, the plumber, the doorman, and many cleaning women, who would each be given their turn to sit at the long table and eat some of the bread and cheese and butter and cake, to take a wrapped candy for themselves and perhaps another one or two in their pockets for grandchildren.

The young couple waited to enter at the doorway with the stacks of books behind them and the whirring of wings as birds fluttered about.

IT HAD NOT BEEN easy to get married. Complications with the application form at the marriage registry had made them travel through a myriad of offices down cigarette-smelling hallways in two different mouldering government buildings. There was some kind of smell beneath that of cigarettes, and it was worse — something like a drain that had stood too long uncleared. They finally found themselves in front of a man at a desk with bound portfolios stacked high behind him and no chairs for visitors in front of the desk. He didn't seem the type to work in an office. He had broad shoulders and thick hair combed back. Wire-rimmed eyeglasses lay on the desk before him. He did not look up from the document he was reading.

He finally leaned back in his chair and eyed them coolly, but with the hint of a smile around the edges of his lips. "Yes?"

"I'm Martin Averka and this is Kristina Minta," said Martin. "The marriage registry sent us here." He set down the document he had been given to take along.

The man sighed.

"So it's come to this. I see. My name is Jonas Simon. Do you know the name of this office?"

"No."

"It is the Office of Disorderly Applications." He smiled. "Ridiculous, I know, but there you have it."

"What does that even mean?"

"It means your request is a headache for me and a headache for you. There is something wrong with it. Luckily, I might be able to do something about it."

"But we just want to get married," said Kristina.

"Wonderful. Congratulations. Young love is admirable. But you need to be registered in the proper office for the act to be permitted. Mr. Averka, you have only registered recently to be permitted to live in Vilnius. Is that correct?"

Jonas Simon had not even looked down at the paper Martin had set before him.

"Yes."

"And your place of residence before that?"

"Krasnoyarsk."

"I see." He shook his head slightly like a teacher regretting a student's incorrect answer.

He seemed to think about it for a very long time.

"And you, Miss Kristina, your last name is Minta, but your father's last name was different."

"He was my stepfather."

"I see. There is a letter missing from the name you gave us on the application as compared to the name he was registered under."

"I'm sorry. I can fix that. Is that a problem?"

"Maybe. Maybe not. Details are very important, but we will see what we can do. I assure you I'll try my very best. But I should say part of the function of this office is to correct errors of those kinds and to prevent future errors."

He leaned back in his chair.

"I serve as a sort of counsellor to young people intending to get married, and in this case, my counsel is directed at you, Miss

Kristina. The man you intend to marry was convicted as a bandit. I'm sure it was all in the past. Look, he seems fine to me — an upstanding young man — and his actions were probably youthful foolishness. But my superiors believe it's hard to change one's character. I'm supposed to counsel you to reconsider your intention to marry him."

Kristina and Martin looked at one another.

"I know this sounds a bit harsh," he went on, "but sober second thought is always useful, and you, Miss Kristina, have no family to advise you. As to you, Mr. Averka, your mother is still in prison, sadly, but if she were here, she might ask you not to tarnish the reputation of the young woman you love. And I should add, since she is still in prison, she hasn't been pardoned. That casts a shadow too."

"This is outrageous," said Martin.

"I know it seems that way. Believe me, I wish we lived in a better world, and one day we will. We're aiming toward that. But for now, it's the hand of the state trying to help you at a time in your lives when you might not be capable of helping yourselves. It is friendly advice. Please think about it. If you want to call off the wedding, just let the main office know. I'll be in touch sooner or later. There are a few odds and ends I'll need to tie up."

"I'm pregnant," said Kristina.

"Congratulations! And is Mr. Averka the father?"

Martin did not permit himself to be provoked. Still, he seethed. Jonas Simon looked back down to his desk.

"And the documents I brought to you?" Martin asked.

"I'll make sure they go through the correct channels," he answered, without looking up.

WHAT HAPPENED NEXT? IT was hard to tell what, if anything, occurred to documents within the maw of the machine. Here, Director Stonkus went to work in his quiet way, contacting revolutionaries he had known before the war and making a miracle happen through the back channels, the only ones that worked. Then suddenly their completed marriage form came in the mail.

How did a man like Stonkus, this former revolutionary, this cog in the machinery of destruction of Lithuanian independence, ever become this protector of his flock? Had he seen the error of his ways and was trying to mitigate in some fashion the crimes of his past? Or was he a realist who accepted, perhaps even believed, in Soviet domination and simultaneously believed in helping those who had suffered from it? Motivations and contradictions were locked up tightly in most minds and sometimes even the owners of them did not have insight into themselves. It was dangerous to reveal too much of oneself to anyone and the less one understood of oneself, the less there was to reveal.

There was no easy way to get decent wedding clothes, but Diana was good to her word and found a dress, and Auntie had taken it all apart and resewn it into a pretty loose, green shift that barely showed Kristina's bulge. It was hanging up in her room when Tomas appeared along with another boy to bring a bag containing bottles of vermouth for the wedding reception.

"What a pretty dress!" he said to Martin.

"Yes, I suppose it is. But I don't usually notice dresses much."

"It's the colour I like. Nice and bright. I've seen that colour before."

Amused, Martin looked at his young friend.

"Maybe you should be a reporter or a policeman. You seem to notice things."

"Not a policeman," said Tomas disgustedly. "I don't trust anyone in uniform after what I've seen them do to me and others."

DIANA AND AUNTIE WERE the only guests from outside the Depository.

The youngest pair of co-working women held a sash up above the entranceway and Martin and Kristina walked under it. Stonkus and his beaming wife stood two small slices of bread and salt and the glasses of Armenian brandy on a tray from which the newlywed couple ate and drank. No one needed to remind them that the salt represented the bitterness of life. Better to focus on the uplift of the brandy.

The guests applauded and Martin reached into his pocket for a handful of candies and threw them about the room. Immediately the children squealed and charged after them. The adults knew they were lucky to be there and every moment deserved to be squeezed for all possible joy, so it was very fine indeed to be at the wedding of co-workers.

Once they had settled back into their places, Stonkus stood at the head of the table and proposed the first of the toasts to the men and women who loved books, who adored the printed words of the heroes of their country and put them up on the shelves in the church where they worked. The place, Stonkus said, might be thought of as a cemetery because so many of the writers of these books were no longer living, but on the other hand, it was a place like heaven, where the dead lived on and on and could speak of things they had known in the past. Their knowledge was a store-house of wealth for future generations.

He did not say, could not say, that the literary wealth of the country, its ancient books and manuscripts, its historical documents, had all been sacked repeatedly in the past; first the war, and then the Soviet sifting of the nation's valuables had left few fragments behind. But at least there were fragments. Stonkus's people were archaeologists reconstructing a civilization based on its cultural shards. So many of those who could assemble the shards into a meaningful picture were dead or in prison or had run for their lives to the west, but as long as the fragments were kept in one place, a new generation would rise up and find them.

This mission statement told Martin more than he had known in the past, but he was not entirely paying attention. Beside him he

had a pregnant wife, and back home they had a decent room —
he had moved in with her — and soon they would have a child. So
many blessings, the things he had wondered if he would ever have in
the cold, cold days in the north.

Kristina had drunk the brandy at the door, but she drank no
more after that — she had lost her taste for liquor with her pregnancy, and this loss of craving was a kind of gift in a country where
the consolation of liquor went on to ruin so many lives. As the
reception went on, some of the wittier wedding guests rose to tell
anecdotes that ended with toasts. No politics ever made it into the
tales, just stock characters — a jealous husband, a yokel, a greedy
speculator, an innocent maiden.

They ate bread and butter, country cheese, and smoked meat that
someone had brought in from a farm relative. They sang and one of
the men strapped on an accordion, and Martin and Kristina danced.
The children played games and had their own dances and then it
was time to boil the water for tea and await the cutting of the
modest cake one of the women had managed to bake on her own.

Martin's face glowed with drink and happiness. Kristina was
adjusting Martin's tie, which had come askew, when the music
suddenly stopped. She looked to the door, where two men were
standing, surveying the party.

Stonkus immediately stood up.

"Everyone, please welcome our poet and the former head of the
Writers' Union as well as minister of education, Comrade Vincentas, and the renowned children's poet, Comrade Kostas."

Those who were sitting rose, and those who held glasses or forks
set them down. Even the children stopped their play. A sense of
unease ran through the room. Although the wedding reception
was taking place after working hours, who knew how this former
minister might react? In this country, everything not explicitly permitted was forbidden, and so the revellers could be guilty of some
crime without knowingly having committed one.

But Vincentas was all smiles and kindness, a hand raised to prevent Stonkus from apologizing. He was stout and had a thick head of hair and wore eyeglasses, this leftist poet and once lean youthful advocate of Stalin now a much older and established man. Beside him, Kostas was a contrast of pale face against dark hair, back stooped a little, a tall man with his mind elsewhere.

Martin studied Kostas. Funny that the man should appear now. Kristina squeezed his hand.

"I'm so sorry to interrupt you," said Vincentas, "but I knew you often worked after hours and I thought you might have a copy of a rather rare children's book I was looking for," and he named a title.

"No bother," said Stonkus. "We don't have a proper full index, but I know where we might look."

"I don't want to take you away from your party," said Vincentas.

"No trouble."

"Come, Friend Kostas," said Vincentas as Stonkus was about to lead them into the stacks in the church nave.

"I'll wait here. I'm a little tired."

"The book we're looking for is for you," said Vincentas.

"I understand. And I appreciate it. I'll wait here with these people."

"Please join the festivities," said Stonkus. "My wife will be pleased to find you a place. Perhaps a drink?"

"Why not?"

Vincentas shook his head, but Kostas was already making his way into the room and Mrs. Stonkus came forward to find him a place as the other two went into the Book Depository for their search. She sat him not four metres from the newlyweds.

Mrs. Stonkus passed him a small glass.

"A toast to the bride!" said Kostas. Everyone who had sat down now stood for the toast, expecting Kostas to say more, but he did not even look at the bride and then just drank up. He grimaced. "Was that fortified wine?" he asked.

"Yes."

"Nothing stronger?" One of the old men brought a bottle of vodka, of which a half remained.

"Does the groom not want to drink to the bride?" asked Kostas.

"I do," said Martin, and he stepped forward to pour a shot for himself and Kostas. The poet had been unfocused, perhaps he had been drinking before he arrived, but now he looked up at Martin.

"I know you," said Kostas, and he held out the glass Martin had filled while looking him in the eye and awaiting his words.

Martin filled his own shot glass, held it up, and returned Kostas's look. So much was happening at once, the past colliding with the present.

"I propose a toast to the woman who has saved my life," said Martin, without breaking eyes with Kostas. "She has given me new purpose. She has consoled my troubled, young soul. Every moment with her has outweighed any of my past wounds. She has been a balm on my heart. I invite you to drink to her."

Kostas was quick to throw back the shot, and then he immediately held out his glass for another drink. This sort of abrupt demand for a second drink was rude by local custom, where the drinkers' rate was determined by the host, but Kostas was a serious drinker. He knew what he needed, and he was going to get it.

Martin poured another for Kostas and waited.

"Well, won't you join me?" asked Kostas. Drunkards preferred not to drink alone.

Martin poured himself a shot and then set the bottle down on the table, but did not let go of the neck of the bottle. Kostas was swaying a little. Yes, he had been drunk already when he came in. Vincentas was probably walking around with him to dry him out before they stumbled on the wedding party. Kostas had steered them here somehow; a drunk could smell alcohol from a long distance away.

Kostas was now far from the engaging young teacher Martin

had met nine years earlier, but he still had the remains of some kind of charisma. It was sodden charisma, to be sure, but somehow all the more human because of it — the whiff of past charisma.

"You said you know me?" asked Martin.

"Drink first."

They each threw back the shots, and Kostas held his glass out again to have it refilled. This time Martin was in no hurry. He waited for the answer.

"Yes, I do know you. Young men, all filled with hope and dreams. I know you and your kind well. Hold on to your dreams, but remember the salt they gave you at the door! The bitterness will come soon enough, unbidden."

"I need to get back to my bride."

"Leave what's left of the bottle."

The cake was brought in and cut to great applause, and water put on to boil for tea, but the exuberance of the party never returned. There was one important man among them and another out walking the stacks. These men represented danger, even if they meant no harm. Kostas finished the remains of the bottle unasked and accepted a half bottle of wine after the vodka was gone. He sat at the table with a slice of cake that he did not touch. Soon the mothers with children began to excuse themselves. Two had left by the time Stonkus and Vincentas returned. By then, Kostas had his head on the table and was deeply asleep.

Vincentas threw up his hands. "The man is incorrigible," he said, but he said it fondly, as if it were the mild eccentricity of a beloved nephew. "I know him well enough. He won't cause you any trouble, Comrade Stonkus. Leave him where he is and leave half a cup of liquor beside him for when he wakes up and he'll find his own way home. He's terribly talented or he wouldn't get away with all this. We have to permit our geniuses some leeway." He seemed to reconsider his own words. "Within limits, of course."

The party was effectively over, the mood of conviviality before the arrival of Vincentas now turning into memory. The women wanted to leave the leftovers for the newlyweds, but Kristina insisted the pieces of bread and cake, cheese and candies be divided up among the guests. For some it would be all they would have to eat for the rest of the day.

"Every wedding has a crasher," said Diana sardonically before taking Auntie by the arm to start the long walk home. The old woman was weak on her legs and there would be frequent resting on park benches and low stone fences before they made it back to their house.

IN THE END, THERE were only Mr. and Mrs. Stonkus and Martin and Kristina as well as the sleeping Kostas.

"Why don't the rest of you go ahead?" said Martin. "I'll catch up later. I'll stick around to take our poet home."

"I wouldn't dream of it," said Stonkus. "You're newlyweds. You are supposed to leave first."

"We've already fulfilled the obligations of newlyweds," said Martin, and he patted Kristina's belly.

She sensed something wrong and took his hands in hers. "Please, you have to come back to our house with me."

"You know the way."

"I am legally your wife for the first time. You need to show me the honour I deserve."

Stonkus and his wife looked on in astonishment. Kristina asked them to leave and they did so, clearly glad to escape an embarrassing domestic moment of some kind or another. Man and wife waited until the sounds of footsteps faded.

Martin looked to his new wife. "Look, fate has delivered him to me. Here he is, asleep at my table."

"So what, you would do something to a sleeping man on your wedding day?"

"I've put it off too long. I've been too happy, and there's unfinished business."

"Do something stupid now and you'll be lost to me forever. Is that what you want?"

"I can't do nothing."

"I understand that. We're married now. Let me help you." She leaned over the half bottle of wine that was left at Kostas's side and spat into it. "Now you do it too," she said.

He couldn't refuse her. Martin gathered up his phlegm and spat into the bottle as Kristina had.

"Good," she said, and she took him by the hand. "For now, you have a responsibility to your new wife. Forget the past. Pregnant or not, we have to go and do what newlyweds do. Let's go home."

27

LYN LAKE, 1948

MARTIN COULD HEAR THE barn door creak open right in the midst of his dream about the city of Vilnius, which he had never visited, but it resembled something like a palace in his dreamscape. Even at this time, an hour before first light, and even in his half-sleeping mind, Martin wondered at the sound because his father, for all of his farmer's work ethic, did not like to rise before the sun came up, especially in May when the night was so short there was never enough time for decent rest. Could it be someone coming to steal eggs? But then he heard the roar of the motorcycle and that made him wonder because there was hardly any gasoline in the tank.

The whole house rose up with banging of doors and shouts from his father and by the time Martin made it outside, his father had a lantern lit and his mother and grandmother were standing in their nightshirts by the open barn doors. They were bewildered and talking all at once, and his father told him to knock on Mr. Kostas's door to find out if he had heard or seen anything.

But the schoolteacher was gone.

Martin's father told him to help harness up the horse and wagon. His mother wailed at them to wait until dawn, but his father, angry and flustered, said that would be too late to catch the thief. The road the motorcycle had taken led in only one direction and that was to Marcinkonys, ten kilometres away.

His father extinguished the lantern when they got on the wagon. He did not want the thief to see them coming, and so they rode out along the ruts, the world much darker in the forest, neither of them speaking above the sound of the horse's hooves and the creak of the wagon's boards as they shifted on the rough and bumpy road. Soon the morning light came up and they were not half a dozen kilometres out of Lyn Lake when they came upon the abandoned motorcycle on the road.

"Hah!" said his father. "The fool ran out of gas and took off. Help me hitch the motorcycle to the wagon, and we'll tow it home before the thief gets back with gasoline."

"I could go after him. I could report the theft to the militia in Marcinkonys."

"Do nothing of the kind. The thief might be armed and, anyway, the militia are thieves themselves. If they remembered I had a motorcycle, they might confiscate it. Come on. I'll take the wagon and you can sit on the motorcycle to steer as I pull it back."

. His father imagined he was doing Martin a favour, but Martin seethed under the instruction, both because he was desperate to search out Badger and because his father was treating him like a child, one who might find it amusing to sit on a motorcycle being towed home.

Together they stowed the motorcycle under a tarp in the barn and then covered it with hay, although no one could drive it now that it had no gasoline.

After sitting with his parents over breakfast as they crowed about outsmarting the thief, Martin slipped away, following the long and complicated path to the bunker where he had taken Skylark the day before, all so the poet could get taken to meet The Hawk.

Wetlands lay throughout the forest, swamps and bogs and places where the water ran under layers of moss only strong enough to hold up a willowy youth. A heavier man might wet a pant leg and an unlucky one might leave nothing behind of his life but his hat on the patch of water: a joke performed by mischievous nature, which behaved in this part of the world more like a stepmother than a mother. These sorts of accidents befell reds and city folk who crashed through the forest, scattering birds and rabbits, and forewarning anyone who wanted to stay hidden.

The locals knew each rivulet and knoll, as well as the ways to the islands within the bogs. Martin was careful to step on springy moss or stumps so as not to leave footprints. He took off his shoes and walked through a deep, fast stream, feeling for familiar rocks, so his bare legs did not get wet above his calves. Then up he went to the other bank, part of an isthmus inside a big oxbow, with barberry bushes at the narrow part as well as whole fields of wild raspberries, which were called *ass rippers* for their long canes with unforgiving thorns. The only way onto the isthmus was across water.

A meadow lay among the trees ahead of him. The place was on a bare hillock within the forest, and Martin approached boldly, stepping on branches to announce his presence to a sentry and so not come upon him by surprise.

But there was no sentry.

Martin intended to observe the bunker from a distance for a while first, but he could see that the entranceway was not masked at all. The lid was thrown partway down the hillock, leaving the entrance-way open. He did not want to take anyone by surprise, so he sang out a country song. But his voice failed him. He whistled instead to announce his presence.

Any partisans who had been there were gone, melted into the countryside as if they had never existed.

Inside the bunker, down half a dozen ladder steps, he could see the bunk bed with a man on each level and before them a table and three chairs. He stepped gingerly down the ladder facing forward, as if he were on stairs, because he was afraid to turn his back on the men.

The man on the top bunk lay turned away on his side and two rivulets of dried blood trailed down the back of his head onto the pillow. Martin was afraid of what the exit wounds would look like on his face, but he nonetheless pulled on the man's shoulder until body rolled back. Pike's half-closed eyes were terrible enough, but not as bad as he had feared. Strange, but there were no exit wounds. Then he crouched down to see Badger looking straight at him, the white streak of hair on his head spattered with blood and another wound at his throat.

As Martin leaned forward, the dead man reached for this wrist and seized it, and Martin shrieked and pulled back in horror and Badger's hand fell away.

"What's happened to you?" Martin asked.

Badger did not speak. He was weak, and he pointed to his throat.

"Tell me who did this," said Martin.

But Badger could not speak, yet he was anxious about something and tapped Martin's hand and then pointed to the table. Upon it lay two grenades.

"Is that what you want?" asked Martin.

Badger made a practically imperceptible nod. But Martin hesitated. He wanted to know more. Badger blinked, then seemed to be present no longer. Martin looked around the bunker, half afraid that he would find The Hawk slumped somewhere. But there was no one else in the place. And then there, at the side of the bunk bed on the earthen floor he saw a pistol, one that he knew well. He had reloaded the bullets for the pistol himself.

He picked it up and studied it and wondered how it had travelled from Raminta's house to here. He tried to remove the magazine, but it was jammed. Whoever had used it to kill Pike and Badger had had a faulty weapon, one whose bullets had been hand-loaded by an amateur, bullets so weak that they would not go through the skull of a man and thus produce no exit wound. Whoever had done this had fired twice at the sleeping man on the upper bunk and then twice at the man sleeping on the lower bunk before the pistol jammed. Then he threw down the faulty pistol in a panic and ran.

Things never turned out quite the way one hoped. Martin had fixed the pistol, but it never worked properly. The killer had not finished his job before fleeing, and even the motorcycle he fled upon did not have enough gasoline to get him safely all the way he was going.

"Who did this?" asked Martin.

But Badger was too close to death to care about anything more than one last gesture more important to him than anything else. Again, he pointed toward the table.

"I understand. But did he get The Hawk as well?"

Badger could not respond to this, and Martin realized he would have to do the one favour Badger was asking for. First, he looked about the bunker and found Badger's Sturmgewehr 44, the German automatic weapon Martin had found and given to Badger. He picked it up as well as a spare clip of bullets. He stepped outside the bunker and lay them on the earth some distance away.

When he returned, he could see that Badger was agitated.

"Don't worry. I haven't forgotten."

Martin looked around the bunker, but could see nothing else he would need. Then he crouched beside Badger.

"Is there nothing else you can tell me? Was it him? Tell me it's true and tell me what happened to The Hawk."

But what Martin wanted was beyond Badger's ability to deliver. He simply looked at the younger man with his beseeching eyes.

"Badger, listen to me. I promise you this. I'll find him, and I will kill him." He wanted to say more, but he was weeping. Badger tapped on his wrist again.

Martin nodded and held Badger's hand for a moment before setting it down.

He went to the table and took the two grenades. He was doing the favour for Badger and whatever family he might have that would suffer deportation if he was known to have died. But the silent Pike might have had family too, so Martin decided to do him the same favour. Martin pulled the pin first from one grenade, and set it by Badger's head, and then he did the same for Pike.

As fast as he could, he climbed out of the bunker and ran toward the place he had set down the rifle. He lifted it and ran. When the twin explosions sounded behind him, he did not turn around. Their faces would be obliterated and the bodies unrecognizable when the reds found them.

As for Martin, he was going to Marcinkonys as fast as he could. With any luck, Skylark would still be there, and Martin could keep his promise.

28

LYN LAKE, 1948

MARTIN MOVED THROUGH THE forest as quickly and stealthily as he could, tucking the spare clip under his belt and jacket and first carrying the rifle as if he might need to fire it at any moment. Eventually, he slung the weapon across his back to make it easier to move. Any official who saw him now would assume he was a partisan, and so he was transformed in that moment from a farm youth to an enemy of the state.

The first warm days of May had awakened the mosquitos which swarmed upon him hungrily as they had the year before when he last ran through this forest with Dovas. Martin was obscurely grateful in some way for their bites to distract and at the same time to help him feed his rage at the man who had betrayed him and Badger. To kill Skylark would not be enough. He would need to kill him and to kill all the others who had lorded over his parents and his people from the Soviets this second time around, to the Germans before them and the Soviets again before them, and the Czar's henchmen in the time of his grandfather.

His people had survived decades upon decades, fearful, pulling on their forelocks in deference to whoever came to take away a share of their meagre produce. They had learned the languages of the various overseers, and they had lost their young men to conscriptions to armies that had ended up fighting one another. Other places in the world managed to free themselves from servitude, why not here? And if it was not possible to free themselves, then better to hurt the overseers as much as he could, to make them fearful, if not in the service of any victory but out of sheer spite for the suffering of the people on the land.

In his wrath, Martin misjudged his direction and stumbled into an unfamiliar part of the forest. Unlike the earth underfoot thus far, the ground was unstable and strangely pockmarked with low grasses but no trees except for a few low saplings. The earth was thickly covered with false morels, mushrooms called Hag's Ears, the first mushrooms of spring and nearly poisonous unless boiled three times, yet valuable too because they were the first mushrooms of spring and could be sold in the markets.

He was too much a boy of the land to rush through a valuable crop that might help some neighbour earn enough money to buy grain, and so he stepped among the patches of mushrooms to avoid damaging them, although these bare places seemed to contain stones or holes like gopher holes. He was picking among them when the earth beneath his right foot collapsed and he went down halfway up his calf. He stopped for a moment and considered himself lucky that nothing hurt and he had not broken or twisted any bone or muscle. But his foot was jammed into something, and he only pulled it up with difficulty to find that a jawbone was attached to the toe of his shoe.

This must have been the place where the Germans had buried the many dozens of Jews they had shot in 1942, when the captives tried to escape transport near the train station. Martin wanted to weep with renewed anger at the death all around him, but he did not wish to give up his own blood lust. He stood in a boneyard, a death field. Let the damned reds join the dead underfoot. He pushed forward.

Martin came to the edge of the forest and paused, surveying the place where he stood. There was a road between him and the small train station. He was only a few kilometres away from the place where the partisans had attacked the train the year before, but how much the times had changed since then, so many more had died.

Martin stopped and breathed deeply. His anger had driven him here, and he would use it as fuel for what he needed to do. But he must not get caught before he found Skylark, who was probably in the town, perhaps closer to the centre where there was a red outpost not far from the yellow wooden church on a hill.

He saw no one nearby, but he stepped back into the woods and searched for a place to hide the rifle, which he placed under a bush and covered with rotted leaves. Then he went out to the road and looked left and right and, when he saw no one, he walked toward the train station, not more than two rooms at the side of the platform. Skylark might be there, waiting for a train to speed him away to Vilnius. Martin stepped onto the empty platform and then looked through the window into the waiting room. There were a pair of red army soldiers there, and they beckoned to him when they saw him, but he pretended not to understand and began to walk away.

The door opened behind him, and he heard a soldier call out to him in Russian.

"What's your hurry? Come here, lad."

"The forest floor out there is full of mushrooms. I was looking for a basket to borrow. I want to get there before someone else takes them. Do you want to see?"

"In a moment. Come here."

"Someone will get to the mushrooms ahead of me."

"I said come here. I just want to give you a piece of advice. The forest is dangerous today."

"Dangerous?" Martin approached the soldier because he had no other choice, but he played the role of stupid peasant. Everyone expected the country folk to be ignorant, and usually this was irritating, but sometimes it could be useful because a long display of stupidity amused officials at first but bored them in the long run and he could get away.

"Where are you from, lad?"

"Lyn Lake."

"You've come a long way."

"Mushrooms are thin on the ground everywhere but here."

"Do you have your identity papers with you?"

"I didn't bring anything with me."

"Nothing in your pocket?" The soldier tapped a bulge under Martin's jacket at his waist, and he felt the spare magazine that Martin had taken from the bunker.

There was no lying his way out of this one. He would have to run, and with any luck he could be in the forest before the soldier unholstered his sidearm.

A blow to his head knocked him to the ground and a quick kick to his side knocked the wind out of him. He heard the soldier call to his companion saying they found the lad everyone was looking for.

29

LITHUANIAN SSR, RUSSIA,
KRASNOYARSK, 1948–1956

THEY BEAT HIM IN Marcinkonys, and then they moved him to the provincial capital of Varėna, where they beat him again. And when he still did not tell them anything, they moved him to the MGB prison in Vilnius, a city he had always wanted to see, but which he entered with eyelids swollen shut on the way to his basement prison.

There, for good measure, they beat him again, but this punishment was not the worst of it. Between beatings and interrogations, he was made to wait in a prisoners' box, a room so small his shoulders touched each wall as he sat on the concrete chair, and the tightness of the place frightened him more than he could have imagined. He had always been comfortable enough in the partisan bunkers, but here the cold stone walls seemed to get tighter every time he was put in to wait until a red bureaucrat was ready to photograph him, or make him fill in forms.

His rage withered to sullenness.

He thought about the pistol.

Skylark was to meet with The Hawk. Did that ever happen? And if Pike and Badger were dead, was The Hawk's body lying in a field somewhere too?

He thought of his family. Repeatedly his interrogators had said that things could end up badly for his mother and father and the thought preyed on him.

The pressure of the walls upon him in the small room was compounded by his fatigue. They did not let him sleep. By night they put him into a cell with a low metal pedestal upon which he had to stand barefoot and in his underwear. The room was flooded with water to just below the level of the pedestal. When he fell asleep, much closer to fainting than sleep, he fell into the water and had to get back up on the pedestal, cold and dripping until he passed out again.

He confessed everything after a while, convincing himself that he did it for the sake of his parents. What good would it have been to resist any more? Badger and Pike were dead. The other partisans had come from elsewhere, there was no way he could betray them. To salvage his pride, he kept only two things secret, the name of his fellow high school student, Ona, code name Sparrow, and his knowledge of Raminta. He did this as much for his own pride as for their safety.

He was reconciled to his fate when the interrogator made him sign the document that convicted him to ten years in the gulag. His interrogator had smiled at him benignly, and congratulated him on this *child's* sentence when most others were either executed or sentenced to twenty-five years.

MARTIN CONSIDERED HIMSELF LUCKY when he received a package from his parents while awaiting further deportation in a transit prison in Moscow in 1948. Thirty men were in a tight "temporary" cell, and they had been in there for three days, waiting for a train. In the end, the delay meant he was present to receive the parcel.

It had taken a long time to arrive, and he was glad because the reds had shipped him off with nothing besides the summer clothes he wore. His mother sent him a coat, a hat, and a change of underclothes. All of that was welcome, but most satisfying, for the moment: the package contained a slab of smoked meat, a bag of dried bread, and a brick of dried apples. There had never been quite enough food in the prisons he'd been through and there likely wouldn't be much on the train to the north either. The big brown paper parcel had arrived just in time.

A buzz came over some of the men in the holding cell. They were looking at him. Martin was among men of a kind he had never seen before, with tattoos visible above their shirt collars and below the cuffs of their shirts. Something was going on, but Martin was too pleased by the treasures he had received to pay close attention.

"My name is Povilas, and you need to know you're in danger," said a short, stocky man in Lithuanian. They were herded out of the cell, across a train yard and into a boxcar. The stranger pulled Martin onto an upper bunk within the car before the young man could understand what was going on.

Martin gaped at the man beside him on the upper tier of the wooden bunk and then looked to see two of the tattooed men coming at him. One reached for Martin's bundle of food as if intending to inspect it.

Povilas shouted something in Russian, but the tattooed man paid no attention. The Lithuanian slipped his boot off and struck the man across the face with the iron cleat of the hobnailed heel. Blood poured out of the man's mouth as he fell aside. Martin kicked the second man in the face.

Some kind of leader of the tattooed men pointed to another two to continue after Martin's package, but they were beaten back as well. An Estonian joined them on the upper bunk — he had a package of his own, and the three of them defended themselves well enough that the bloodied thieves gave up their attack after two sorties.

"What was that all about?" Martin asked when the car settled down into a kind of sullen truce.

"They're criminals, my friend. They tattoo themselves to demonstrate their exploits. Up to this point you've probably been in jail with the politicals — a whole different breed. Sheep, really, compared to these men. Wait. At some point they'll take off their shirts to reveal the rest of their tattoos. They tell the stories all over their bodies about people they have murdered and heists they have accomplished. They're dangerous to a point, but once we establish our place in the hierarchy, they'll leave us alone. I think I can even put my boot back on."

"Thank you for protecting me."

"Everything comes at a cost in prison and the same is true of this, so now you owe me a little something to eat. Not too much. It's going to be a long journey. I do have a couple of dried cheeses with me, so we can pool our food." The Estonian had a package of bread and cheese as well, so they were a little better provisioned than the others for the four-week trip across Russia.

Povilas had been a partisan from near Kaunas. He was short, but broad in the chest, and had a peasant's directness. He was a little shy about his survival because he had not had the heart to shoot himself once their bunker was betrayed. To compensate for this failure of nerve, Povilas tried to delay his confession as long as he could so the other partisans he knew about could flee their bunkers and move on before he revealed their hiding places. No one held up under torture. Povilas was sentenced to death, but death sentences were newly outlawed so his sentence was reduced to twenty-five years of prison, followed by ten years of exile.

"Lucky me," he said ironically. His whole demeanour was ironic. Whereas the other prisoners were morose or angry, depressed or sullen, Povilas could be counted on to tell a joke or give good counsel except at those times when he spoke of his wife and children. Thinking about them made him moody.

"How many years did they give you?" asked Povilas one day.

"I was sentenced to ten years," said Martin.

"Lucky you. Not much more than a slap on the wrist. But how old are you?"

"Fifteen."

"Ahh. It's illegal to deport you unless they're sending you off with your whole family. Where are they?"

"Back home."

"Well then, you can console yourself in the knowledge that Stalin's regime has sentenced you unjustly."

"They sentenced you unjustly too."

"Yes, but somehow within their rules. You, on the other hand, have been sentenced unjustly within their framework."

"What good will that do me?"

"None at all. They break their own rules whenever it suits them."

Later, Martin would learn not to talk too much about his past. Almost no place was private and every place had informers, but in the weeks on the upper bunk with Povilas he could tell the story of his life because no one else spoke Lithuanian in that rail car.

The clickety-clack of the wheels sometimes sounded for a day or more at a time, to be punctuated by hours of silence and then every couple of days a stop at a country station where the doors were thrown open so they could empty the toilet buckets and bring in some water or food. Too often it was herring, the saltiness of which tortured those who ate it when the water ran out.

"And what would you have chosen to do when you turned six-teen?" asked Povilas one night as the train was held up for a second day in an unidentified yard beyond the Urals.

"I wanted to be a partisan. I admired Badger. I wanted to be like him."

"Well, even a person you admire can be a bad model. Listen, the resistance is doomed now. Some of us kept with it because we had no way back to civilian life and we hoped we were making some kind of moral point. But to be a partisan is to be on death row. That poet gave you better advice."

"But the poet was a traitor. I'm here because of him."

"Even bad people sometimes give good advice. Every partisan will be killed or taken prisoner in the long run. You were convicted young, so it's not as bad for you as it is for me."

Over the long hours as the train moved slowly northeast, or sat still in rail yards, Martin pieced together the story of what had happened along with Povilas's help.

"The pistol was the giveaway," said Povilas. "There was no way Kostas could have got his hands on it without the cooperation of the reds. He must have been there when they took the pregnant girl, Raminta. But listen, all this may be true but all of it is meaningless to your life now. Forget about him."

"How can I forget about him? I'm here on this train because of him."

"The past is a dangerous place. If you don't put him behind yourself, you'll dwell on him. He'll poison your future. You'll still be young when you get out of prison. Do you want to devote your life to revenge?"

"The man killed my friend. He betrayed me too. I just want to bring him to justice."

Povilas waved his hand dismissively. "Justice takes a long time. You're better off letting it go."

Even with careful rationing, their supplementary food ran out after two weeks. Thoughts of the past evolved into memories of meals he had eaten and ones he hoped to eat in the future. He dedicated what mental space he had left to thoughts of his parents, whom he imagined he had somehow saved by being sent away, while hoping all the while they would send packages to him again to take the edge off his terrible hunger.

Then one day after yet another long stop, the boxcar doors clanged open to a clearing in the forest. They had arrived. Now they would have to build their own prison camp.

BY VIRTUE OF HIS youthful strength, Martin was eventually put on a heavy work brigade that went out to cut wood in the forests. The work in the snow was brutal. Accidents felled men as well as trees. The rations were better — as long as his team could keep up with the production quota. He even had a little time to himself before sleep in the evening; then he sharpened a skill he had started to work on back in his Moscow cell.

Holding back a piece of his precious bread, he chewed it and shaped it and then sculpted it into a single chess piece: a knight, a figure most likely to catch a chess fancier's eye. He managed to let it be seen by an assistant to the commandant, and over time he was permitted to create a whole set. They gave him enough bread that he had more left over to eat, and then because they wanted the pieces to be more vivid, he was allowed into the carpentry shop where there was a little paint. He took it upon himself to make a chessboard as well, out of scraps in the workshop.

Martin was good with his hands, and the chess set and the board pleased the assistant commandant so he had the good fortune to be given a spot in the carpentry shop when his predecessor died of tuberculosis. Martin had made furniture for his family, and so he used these skills to repair the desks and tables of some of the higher officials in the camp.

Then he was moved to another camp where he made a chess set for the boss of the garage, and so he ended up learning about engines and even how to weld. These various skills stood him in good stead through his years in prison because the bosses had quotas to meet and problems of their own and a man who could solve problems was useful to them. So much so that when he became very ill and lost all his hair, the commandant had him treated by the best doctor in the area and had him fed so he could get well enough to make another chess set for the commandant's brother-in-law.

The prisoners were moved around the camps like pawns, put where they were needed most. In one of them, Martin met Povilas once again. Six years had passed. Stalin had died. Things were not quite as bad as they had been before. Martin first noticed Povilas in the shop because he was whistling; it was unlucky to whistle indoors and generally frowned upon by the prisoners because it made them think anyone happy enough to whistle must be an informer. The guards generally did not like it either because it made it seem as if the prisoner was having a reasonably good time and the prisoners should feel punishment on their backs.

But Povilas was barely aware that he whistled, and if rebuked, would look startled and be quiet for a while until he unconsciously began to hum and, if not rebuked again, would eventually start to whistle once more.

Povilas did not recognize him after all the years that had passed. "What happened to your hair?" he asked.

"It escaped."

Povilas laughed. "You know, these are new times. I just might find a way to get out of here myself."

"You're planning to escape?"

"Impossible in the normal sense. We're thousands of kilometres away from Moscow, never mind Vilnius. Where could we possibly go? No, that's not it. I was born in America, you know."

"Come on."

"No. Really. My parents came back to Lithuania when I was small because they'd saved up some money and bought a farm."

"Take that bit of news to the commandant and see what it gets you."

"Well, not much, most likely. But if I could get word to the American embassy, they might help me."

"How will you do that?"

"I'm working on it. And I remember you were sentenced underage."

"Again, who cares?"

"I've heard there are commissions going around, willing to

study cases and adjust sentences. They don't exactly advertise themselves all that much, and they might not do what they say they will, but if you hear of something, don't pass up your opportunity."

Povilas turned out to be right. The man had saved him on the way into the gulag, and his advice had helped to get him out of the gulag. How was it possible that men like this existed in the worst of places?

Martin was lucky.

LUCK WAS A RELATIVE matter in Eastern Europe, where survival of any kind was in itself the best of luck, but the god of irony ruled in that region and in Martin's case, he was granted special dispensation by being tried and convicted on May 14, 1948, when he was only fifteen.

A week after Martin's arrest, massive deportations had begun as the reds decided the only way to rid the country of partisans was to annihilate their base of support. The farmers were chased off their lands and collectivization began in earnest. Those who were exiled later in the month were sent off to Siberia with wives and children, without any age restrictions at all. Mothers, fathers, and children all the way down to babies were declared guilty and sent away. No one cared about their ages. Those who survived had their own painful struggles to return from the gulag.

But Martin, convicted of aiding the partisans at the age of fifteen, was tried technically underage for that particular crime. And so his fate, awful as it was, turned out to be exactly what his interrogator had claimed — a child's sentence compared to the sentences of others. After all, what were eight years to a young man? So many more had suffered worse, and so many more would suffer worse in the future.

And the god of irony did not overlook the fate of his parents and grandmother. Although Martin had confessed in order to save them, they had been swept up with the other farmers and sent off to longer terms in another part of Krasnoyarsk. He did not expect to see them again. His grandmother died during transport. Later, he received piteous letters from his mother about the suffering and the death of his father.

And so the grand Soviet plan played itself out in the east, with remaining former farmers tied to collective farms as their grand-parent-serfs had been tied to the land of the nobles in Czarist times. The remaining partisans fought on in their hopeless battle until the last of them was killed or caught. Except for the few who managed to hide out in woodpiles and forests, hermits from the medieval past, some cross between relics and rumours when they were finally found decades later.

In the west, the young watched Superman and Disneyland on their new televisions, and the chrome on their fathers' cars flashed expensively in sunlight. Iceboxes ended up in the ash heap of history, making way for refrigerators in which skim milk and cottage cheese could be held to be poured onto cereal or spooned into bowls to keep down the weight put on by potato chips and onion dips.

There was much for the god of irony to laugh about.

30

VILNIUS, 1958

THE SCENT OF THE linden blossoms on one side of the chaotic yard competed with the perfume from the overgrown rose bush at the other end, while meticulous small beds of potatoes, carrots, cucumbers, and cabbages lay planted between.

"You never know when there's going to be another war," said Auntie. "And when there is, you'll be glad to have something to feed yourself and your loved ones."

"Do you think there will be another war soon?" asked Martin, rocking the baby in his arms. She was not entirely happy there, restless, puckering her lips from time to time as if searching for a nipple. He would need to bring her in to Kristina soon, but he wanted his wife to sleep as much as she could.

"Who can tell? I've seen five occupations of Vilnius in my lifetime, but none of them lasted. The armies come and go, and you just need to keep your head low and be able to feed yourself to survive for one more day."

"What about this occupation?"

She looked away and did not answer, an old, kind-hearted woman whom he had known for well over a year, the woman who had helped sew his wife's wedding dress, and yet she dared not call the current Soviet system an occupation, not even to him, not even out in the garden where no one could hear them except for the bees gathering nectar from the many blooming flowers.

And why even talk of such things now with the warmth of late spring, while they sat in the shade of an apple tree? The terrible past was behind them, and with a child in his arms, he did not wish to go back there. What good would it do? The apple tree had bloomed with great promise earlier in the season, but who could tell how many apples would survive disease or pests or the hands of impatient boys.

Auntie herself spoke Lithuanian with an accent, so she must not have been raised in the language, but she did not call herself a Pole or a Byelorussian. She was fiercely Lithuanian, what she described as the "best kind," namely a generations-long local, but she spoke Polish to some of her friends and Russian or Byelorussian to others. Wasn't a Scot still a Scot if he spoke English and an Irishman was still an Irishman if he, too, spoke English? She reminded him that Lithuania's greatest poet, Adam Mickiewicz, had written in Polish. She and her kind had always been in Vilnius, placed by God at the beginning of things and learning the languages that evolved as time went by while they stayed planted where they were. Their children went to wars or wars came to the residents of Vilnius and tried to annihilate them. But not everyone lasted in this place forever. The wars had taken very close to all of the Jews. Maybe the next war would take the rest of Auntie and her kind. Or not. How was it possible to think of these things in the beauty of spring?

The neighbourhood was a ruin of nineteenth century peeling brick and stucco houses, miniature plaster wedding-cake buildings compared to the bigger ones downtown. These houses once held the medium well-to-do. Some of the former inhabitants still lived in the single rooms after their houses had been expropriated and subdivided once, and then subdivided again, by the Soviet authorities, filled with families who shared a kitchen inside and a toilet in the yard. Some of these remnants of the pre-war gentry still had gilded mirrors or ancient beds with massive headboards that took up most of their rooms, and sometimes handmade ballroom slippers tucked under the beds as reminders of better times. The men were dead or gone, and among the old ladies of reduced circumstances were those who still lived by selling the occasional gold rouble coin from the time of the czar, or a deceased husband's shoes, last worn before *liberation*.

Auntie had no past that Martin knew of, and she made a living from her sewing, a modest pension, and whatever she raised in the garden. She cut some of the roses into bunches and sold them on the street for a few kopeks with which she bought sugar or bread. Her only relic wasn't worth any money at all — a basket of notes that the neighbourhood girls had collected back in the forties when the many trains that ran along the nearby tracks carried tens of thousands of deportees off to the gulag. Those unfortunates wrote notes and threw them out the air holes of the cattle cars. The notes were often last letters to relatives whose names and addresses were on the papers, but just as frequently, they were simply statements of farewell or of anguish, but with no forwarding addresses upon them. Those that could be sent were forwarded, but the dead letters sat in the basket. Auntie didn't have the heart to throw them away.

They heard laughter coming through the open door of Diana's room. Over the winter, she had rediscovered a lively mix of men and women she called cousins because she had no family of her own. They appeared and disappeared without warning, sometimes four or five of them at a time, carrying various antique silver place services to sell on the black market in Vilnius.

It had never occurred to Martin that there could be a market for those sorts of goods. He did not know anyone who owned silver or wanted silver because how could one show it? It seemed strange that a communist country would have trade in this sort of commodity.

There were worlds within worlds about which he had no knowledge, secrets within secrets.

As for the bearers of such fine goods, they were a boisterous lot,
not drinkers but jokers, lively card-players who did not set their cards
on the table but laid them down with a slap. Good-humoured and
generous, they offered him slices of bread or sausage or pickled
cucumber, whatever they might have on the table, and Martin did
his best to reciprocate whenever he could. Diana thrived in their
company. She grew moody if she was alone for too long; the past
lay heavily on her mind, and in those times, she went back to work
at the train station.

"Where did you get the green dress for the wedding?" Martin
had asked her.

"From a friend. Why do you ask?"

"When Tomas came here with the wine, he said he knew that
dress."

"Really? A street boy and man both remembering a dress? It
sounds unlikely to me."

"Not even the dress. Just its colour. He said there was no other
dress in Vilnius that shade of green. Whatever became of that
dress?"

"I gave it back to my friend. It was just on loan. It had to be
taken apart again."

"What is your friend's name?"

"What business is it of yours?"

"I knew a woman with a dress that colour. Her name was
Raminta."

Diana shook her head slowly and sadly. "And here I thought
you were different from the rest. But you're a man, and I suppose
all men are the same. Do you still see her?"

"I only saw her the once at the train station by accident. She
came from a village near mine, and I knew her when I was a boy."

"And what do you think of her now?"

"She's suffered."

"She's my friend. I have helped her, and she's helped me in the past. Do you have any objection to where the dress came from?"

"Kristina seemed to like the dress. If it made her happy, it made me happy too."

Diana nodded reluctantly, like a policeman who does not really believe the story but who can't prove otherwise.

KRISTINA SEEMED TO DO well as a new mother because the girl, whom they had named Alina, required so much attention and did not leave time for introspection. Kristina had been better after their marriage, but she still did not like bright light, or to be in a crowd, or to be called to from across the street. But she was not drinking, and that was good, and he did not drink either so liquor was not around.

Occasionally, Tomas would stop by to ask if Martin wanted a bottle, but the boy did not press him because Martin had given him the room he had lived in before the wedding. It was not official because the boy was not of legal age, but everything was possible with a little help from friends. It was not all that long ago that Martin had landed in the city without a job or a single friend, and now he had everything he needed, and most of what he had ever wanted. Kristina seemed happy too.

"Think of me as a mouse," she said. "Meek and quiet."

"But you aren't meek and quiet around me."

"No. I can be myself around you, and now with the baby too. She's good for me. Babies need fresh air and sunlight. Between the two of you, I feel as if I am almost human."

He found her in the room with the curtains partially closed, lying on the bed with her eyes open and wearing a faraway look. As soon as she saw him, she sat up and put a couple of pillows behind herself

and reached for the baby. "Did she give you any peace?" asked
Kristina.

"She likes the sound of Auntie's voice."

"Has Auntie been talking your ear off?"

"I don't mind."

The baby attached herself to Kristina's breast and the three of
them sat in the room, partially in the light coming in through the
open door and the gap in the curtains, and partially in shadow
where the fabric blocked the light.

THE ROSE BUSH HAD gone through its first flowering and the linden flowers had fallen. The apples on the tree were still green,
plump and tempting but bitterly sour in any impatient mouth.
Auntie brought in the letter as they were eating their sorrel soup.
She offered it to Kristina, who recoiled from it.

"What is it?" asked Kristina.

"A letter, of course. As plain as the nose on your face. And with
a beautiful foreign stamp on it too."

"I've never received a letter," she said.

"Of course, you have. I've seen the postman leave letters here."

"Notices, yes. But never a letter. Just put it down on the table,
would you?"

"It's care of your stepfather, actually, God rest his soul. But I
don't recognize the name. You're not going to open it?"

"Not now."

Auntie did a poor job of hiding her disappointment as she left
the room and closed the door. In Stalin's time such a letter was a
sign of foreign friends or family and a potential ticket to the gulag.
Times were better now, but still, surprises were not welcome. They
rarely brought good news.

Martin wiped his mouth with a napkin and picked up the letter.
"It has a French stamp. Do you know anyone in France?"

Kristina shook her head. "What name is on the return address?"

"Joana Melynė. Do you know her?"

"I don't." Kristina had set down her spoon and was looking at the letter in his hand. "Maybe we should return it."

"What are you so worried about? It might be something important."

He set the letter on the table, and they both looked at it. He tried to eat some soup, but stopped after a spoonful. "I really think you have to open it."

"You do it for me."

He rose, took a clean knife from the shelf, and then returned and carefully slit the envelope across the top. The letter was written on very thin paper, a type of onion skin he had never seen before, and it was written on both sides of the sheet, in careful, but spidery script. The lines of text on one side lay between the lines on the other to make the words stand out clearly against the pale blue of the paper.

"Read it for me," said Kristina.

Martin shifted his chair so the light from the open door illuminated the page. He glanced up first at Kristina, the baby at her breast and her brow furrowed with concern.

Dear Kristina,

I am writing to you after a very long time, much later than I should have. I am so sorry but the passage of years has not been easy for me, and there are loose ends I have been meaning to take care of, but I never found the time or I lost the thread of contacts. And I was often unwell and in institutions, not myself for months and sometimes for years at a time.

After many years I finally had the health and presence of mind to write to Auntie and she told me how to address this letter. Now I have found you again.

You may not remember me.

*I know a little bit of your story, and I will tell it to you,
but first I will need to tell you a little of my story to explain
myself.*

*I am a librarian, and I have been one my entire life. I
think I loved books more than people in my youth because
the books never did me any harm, unlike some of the
unfortunate human specimens I have met. But I was guilty
of loving books too much, I think, and I ignored my poor
mother who died young. I wish now that I had been better
to her while she was alive.*

*I only really became aware of people after the Soviets
came in 1940. So much changed then. I won't speak about
that trouble now. But then things went completely to hell
after the Germans came. I won't say I was particularly
aware of the suffering of people then either, at least not at
first. I was still deeply wrapped up in my books.*

*I was a librarian, and responsible for the books that
were outstanding, and in German times, many of them
were outstanding in the Jewish ghetto. I applied for and
received permission from the German authorities to go into
the ghetto and retrieve those books. There were so many of
them that I carried them out in sacks on my back.*

*But what I saw inside woke me up to the reality of the
world I was living in. And so, when I could, on my many
trips through the ghetto, I once carried a little girl out in my
sack, and met ones at a gap in the ghetto wall where I could
find them and where their mothers sent them for safety. The
guards knew me well by that time and they looked away.
But I couldn't do much for the girls when I got them out,
and so I appealed to my friend, Petras Vaitkus to find refuge
for them. I understand he hid them along with some adults
behind the Jewish books that were being stored in the old
Basilian monastery down from the Dawn Gate in Vilnius.*

There was some kind of secret room there behind a whole wall of books, from floor to ceiling.

Things fell apart in the end. I was betrayed by someone and sent to the Stutthof concentration camp. But I was lucky because it was very near the end of the war. There was not enough time to starve me, and I was not tortured as badly as some of the others, but there was still time to finish me off in other ways. They marched us out as the liberators approached, and I was lucky again because I was not yet as weak as many of the others who died on our march. Still, these difficulties took their toll. After the war, I moved to France, where I am working again as a librarian.

And I have finally begun to take care of some unfinished business much later than I should have. My past was scrambled and my memory returns to me in patches, when it returns at all.

I have begun to look for my girls. I need to know what happened to them and I think you are one of them. You are one of my girls.

Petras Vaitkus told me he'd found you again in the cemetery. The Germans were gone by then and neither of us knew how you got there. But you were not well, and when he tried to tell you of your past, you did not understand. I don't know why. That is what he said. As far as he knew, all of your family was dead. I was lost to myself and then poor Petras died, and it has taken years to put the pieces of your story together and track you down through old Auntie, who was ancient when I knew her, and must be immortal since I understand she is still alive.

I can tell you this. Your name was Esther, and of your family I know very little except for one thing. You have an older brother who tracked me down after looking for you for years. He lives in Warsaw for now, but I believe he intends to emigrate. He is married but has no children or family from the past except you, and he wants you and your family to come and join him ...

The letter continued with details of her brother and how to reach him.

Martin was struck by the news, unsure what to make of it, whether to believe it or not. When he looked up at Kristina, she was shaking her head slowly and then she began to weep. The baby sensed the change in them both and pulled away from her breast and began to wail. A little milk dripped from her bare breast.

31

VILNIUS, 1958

"YOU CAN'T IMAGINE THE number of forlorn children who wandered through here at the end of the war! Lost nestlings! Sometimes more than one a day and once a small gang that broke into my kitchen and took every scrap of food they could find. The train station down the way was a magnet for them and Vilnius became a transit point. Some were trying to board trains and some were jumping off them. Children, you understand? One boy came to my door and asked to be fed and spend the night because the next day he was going to walk the tracks east. His parents had been taken away by train and he was going to follow the tracks until he found them. I said it was thousands of kilometres to Siberia and no one could tell which part his parents were sent to or even if they were still alive. But I could not convince him. He walked out to the railway line and for all I know, he's still wandering out there somewhere, all grown up and still lost."

They were sitting in the shade of the apple tree now. It was far too warm to go in, and Auntie had made tea and brought out some bread and jam for them to share during their talk. Kristina neither ate nor drank and kept the baby on her lap the whole time. Martin watched her, unsure exactly how the news in the letter would change things now. Kristina did not look overjoyed.

"There were older ones too. One girl, close to being a young woman, came to my door barefoot and in a woollen coat. She was naked underneath. She couldn't tell me anything because she spoke nothing but German. I gave her a skirt and shirt so she could at least cover herself."

Kristina said nothing to this. Martin needed to let Auntie talk because no one ever listened to the old woman and once someone did, it was like a dam had broken open inside Auntie and the memories came spilling out in words.

"What happened to that naked woman?" asked Martin.

"She never left. It's Diana. She knew a little more of her history than some of the younger ones. Her parents were Prussians, and they were all killed when the red army crossed into Germany. This country is full of their children. They had nothing to eat and they fanned out this way looking for potato skins or herring heads to keep from starving. It was dangerous to be out and alone for a girl Diana's age, almost a woman. The Soviet soldiers wanted to have some fun. We called the little ones *wolf children*. Most of the girls got married as soon as they were old enough in order to get a legitimate last name."

"But not Diana."

"No. She's managed in other ways. I gave her my son's room until he gets back and she's stayed there ever since."

"Over a decade."

"Yes, over a decade."

"I didn't know you had a son."

"There's so much you don't know. And I don't know it either. When poor Petras brought Kristina here, he left for a while. I thought Kristina was German too because her language sounded like it, but Diana said she wasn't speaking German, so it must have been Yiddish."

"Why have you kept all this hidden from me?" Kristina asked sharply.

"I never hid anything. You've lived here the whole time, haven't you? Nobody ever asked and anyway, what good did it do to talk about all this? We spoke Lithuanian here, but it wasn't a native language to any one of us except Petras."

"Who am I then?" asked Kristina.

"You are Kristina. The girl who's lived here for a long time, and you're a mother and a wife. What more do you need?"

"I needed some kind of past. It was all a blank slate. Couldn't you have told me something about my past?"

"I don't know anything about your past. All I know is Petras brought you here, and he and I took care of you. Diana helped too, and you're beginning to make it sound like we kidnapped you."

"I have all these questions now."

"But I don't have any answers. All I know is you were the girl from the cemetery that Petras brought here."

"What about this Joana from France? She used your name. You must know her."

"I don't know her at all. Petras must have known her. Maybe he talked about me to her. Why are you blaming me for things I don't even know? You're the one who seems conveniently to have forgotten everything."

"Conveniently? My mind was blank. I've suffered, and now you're being cruel."

"I fed you, girl. I dressed you. I kept you when that Petras dropped you on me, a responsibility he couldn't handle any longer. I kept you after he died."

"And you lied to me with your silence."

Auntie clenched her fists and was going to say something but held back. Eventually, she said, "I'm going inside."

"Go then. I can't look at you."

The old woman raised herself with difficulty and went into the house without looking back.

"Why did you do that to her?" asked Martin. "You've hurt her for no good reason."

"You don't understand anything."

"She raised you like a daughter."

"I don't have a mother, and if I did, it wouldn't be her."

Kristina stood up with the baby and went inside as well, closing the door behind her. Martin was left in the garden with no place to go, half-drunk cups of tea in front of him and sandwich crumbs, all under the tree hung with bitter apples.

32

VILNIUS, 1958–1959

THEY SAT WITH STONKUS at the very place where the wedding had been celebrated not so very long before. But all the other assembled tables had long since been returned to their places and the trio now had only cups of tea and biscuits that Kristina had made, a small gesture for the man to whom they were appealing for help. Around them were stacks of books, some open, on shelves and side tables, but not on the floor. Stonkus would never put a book he had saved on the floor.

"The first thing you need to ask yourselves is what you are going to lose by going away. Is your life here so bad? You have important work, a home, and a child, and some security too. Once you get out there, you won't know how the world works. You'll have to start all over again."

Martin was silent.

"I appreciate everything we have here," she said, "and especially you and this place. You have stood for us and made a kind of family here, but it's not quite the same as a real family. I thought I had nothing, and now that I have found something, I need to reach out for it."

"I understand. But Martin has family too. His mother is still away, but people are coming back now. His mother might need his help. Most people who come back from there are not quite as resourceful as Martin was."

"We can help her from afar. We'll send her packages the way people in America send packages to people here."

"But your brother could help you from afar too, if you needed it."

"Don't you think Martin's mother would want him to get out if he could?"

Stonkus was silent. Any admission would be damning the world he had helped to create.

None of them articulated the knowledge that Martin would never see his mother again if he emigrated with Kristina. Stonkus did not say anything about Judaism or Israel, nor did Kristina, but each knew how crucial it was. Jews were not supposed to exist as a separate category. In the Soviet Union, according to official doctrine, there were only people. And yet.

Poland was under Soviet domination, but it was not inside the Soviet Union. There were many Jews in Poland, but there were many in America and more in Israel, and who knew what the intentions of this lost brother were? It was hard enough to get out of the Soviet Union and into Poland, but it might not be the final destination. This brother was not just a brother, although as such he was already a treasure, but he was also a doorway to one of many other places, other futures. Everyone knew the world was better outside than the place where they lived. Poland was freer because it wasn't one of the Soviet republics. They barely even had collectivization there. Western Europe and Israel were better still and, to most, America was best of all. Her brother was her lost brother, but he represented all these possibilities.

They had written to one another, but the words were stilted and he didn't say much in his letters, which he wrote in Polish. He had some kind of standing in the country, was some kind of important official in a hierarchy Kristina and Martin did not understand. The brother had let them know he could make things happen.

Yet he was more like the idea of a brother than a brother one knew. He would likely say more once they met in person, become a real brother, if that was possible at this stage of life. And indeed, he was a real brother because he had gone looking for her, hadn't he?

It would be gratifying to have the past filled in, that terrible black hole she had lived with for such a long time. Kristina also wanted a future lying in front of her, one open more broadly than the narrow roads of Vilnius. In any case, he had written nothing of a mother and father or of any other siblings — merely said the family was lost during the war. But why didn't he tell her about their parents? They were certainly dead, but who had they been? Why was he so circumspect? She didn't know. There were mysteries in the past.

"How do you even know this brother is really your brother?" asked Stonkus.

"Why would anyone lie about a thing like that? Who would go looking for some woman in Lithuania unless she was related to him? It's too unlikely to be a lie."

"And why did it take so long?" Stonkus persisted.

"I don't know."

"Is this place really so bad that you need to escape from it?"

Stonkus had been an ardent communist in his youth, once an underground activist and even now a party member. But things had not turned out quite as he had hoped. He was saddened by some of the steps the party had taken, yet part of him still hoped there was a future for socialism if only people like Kristina and her generation were patient and worked by increments to improve their lives. The regime in Moscow after Stalin's death was so much milder. Maybe the cruelty was coming to an end.

He was curious about Poland and even resented Kristina slightly for being able to go there, a country he had never visited and likely never would. It was very difficult to travel anywhere outside the Soviet Union, even to socialist nations. But his good nature beat down these feelings. He looked upon his employees as his charges, hurt people whom he felt he should shelter. It was not up to him to decide their ultimate fates. He had to permit them to make their own choices.

"If you are determined, I suppose I can help you. But don't expect miracles! Martin, you haven't said anything at all. Do you agree with this decision?"

"I want whatever is best for my wife," he said, but he tried not to think of his mother. She was a mother like all mothers, and would want what was best for him. But like all grandmothers, she would have liked to hold her granddaughter, and now that might never happen.

"All right then," said Stonkus, and he opened some files in front of him. "There is a lot of work to do, and it won't be easy."

AFTER THIS MEETING, IN which many complicated steps were enumerated, Kristina and Martin made their way home, walking back through the old city of Vilnius, past its ruins and its new blocks of concrete and stucco, past its beggars and thieves and ordinary people going about their business. Martin was aware of the city in a way he had not been since he had first arrived, because soon he was going to lose it.

Women were praying on their knees before the picture of the Virgin above the Dawn Gate and Martin had been in the habit of crossing himself when he passed the women and the shrine, but now he did not. He was unsure how Kristina would feel about her rediscovered Judaism, and she was not revealing very much about her feelings. He was unsure what to call her now that her Christian name felt so strange. Had her poet stepfather known her real name and changed it to mask her? Or was it some strange irony of history that had given a Jew an especially Christian name? She did not ask Martin to call her by her new name. But what would he call in her in Poland, if not Esther? Her brother would call her by that name and it would be the name on her passport.

Kristina was opaque to him now. He had thought he knew her well, but he did not know Esther. He did not know if Kristina knew Esther.

THE SYSTEM THAT WAS to take the grain of human nature and mill it into a Soviet product did indeed wear them down. It ground them not only with the politics of the land but also in day-to-day life, and thus they waited to buy tea and bread, and asked for permits at work to buy baby clothes and shoes.

That was the way of ordinary life, but now they had embarked on a riskier and more complicated enterprise. Papers needed to be signed and unsympathetic bureau masters needed to be appeased either with bribes or with the shakes of a stick from Stonkus or one of his men and women in the Soviet machine. But Stonkus could not do everything for them — he was already busy saving the literature of the country, the many wounded intellectuals who worked for him, and even himself, a long-time communist who, in the eyes of his comrades, had lost too much of his enthusiasm for the cause.

The synagogues of Vilnius had largely been destroyed along with most of the Jews of Lithuania, but the grand old chorale synagogue on Communist Youth Street still stood where it always had, although converted now into a metal-workers' shop and rundown, as with so many other places. Martin went to look at it to try to find something that might explain Kristina's past and, even more, her membership in it. But architecture did nothing to help him better explain her people. The place was simply empty once the work day was done. Martin walked away from the synagogue unenlightened.

Was it better to forget the past or to remember it? She was all for remembering now, it seemed, but his life in Vilnius had been one of forgetting his village childhood and the suffering in the north. What to do about Kostas? Was it better to forget him or to remember him? To forget him would mean to forget Badger and Pike and, as it was, he thought less and less often of them as he lived the sweet but busy life of a father and husband.

He walked in the yard with the little girl, who held one hand in his and the other in Kristina's as they made their way across the winter-matted grass outside Auntie's door. There had been a rupture since Kristina's accusations last summer, and although she had apologized and Martin had as well, Auntie remained hurt, as if some wounds could not heal. Kristina continued to secretly harbour a grudge, as if Auntie had been the source of her problems instead of someone who helped her deal with them.

They had called the girl Alina, but Kristina said it would be a provisional name, one they might change once they got out. Alina could not walk alone yet, but she disliked crawling and wanted her parents to hold her hands.

"I don't know who you are any more," he said to Kristina as the child stumbled forward between them.

"I am the mother of your child. I'm the woman you saved from the bottle. I am your wife."

"And what am I to you now?"

"Why are you so anxious? Nothing has changed. You're my husband. You're the father of my child."

"I didn't know how much I needed you until I found you, and now I'm afraid I'm losing you."

"Come on. You're not losing me. We're going off together to a new world. A better one, we hope."

"We hope, we hope. Yes. I hope too."

The machinery of the state had been at work and it recreated Esther Levinas and discarded the other names. But once Kristina had attracted the interest of the state, she could not un-attract it. The state noticed that this Jew wanted to emigrate, and it noticed the man she was married to had once been sentenced to prison, no matter the pardon he had subsequently received. Thus, they were enemies at worst and surely suspects at best and no further favours needed to be done for them.

Everyday life became much harder than before. It was bad enough that the various documents they needed in order to emigrate were taking so very long, but, worse, routine documents such as residency renewals were taking a long time too. Letters about electricity and water never appeared, and suddenly the water was turned off to their house. Was it possible they were being punished? But surely all the bad luck had to be a coincidence, aggravated by their unsureness about what was happening in the bureaucratic domain of passports and visas.

A Jew was not a special category for emigration, although it was an unspoken category in other ways, none of which helped them in their cause. Kristina had to be made Polish in order for the right papers to get created and so the machinery of state ground on in its monotonous, maddening way.

33

VILNIUS, 1959

MONTHS OF PAPERS SUBMITTED, refused, sent to wrong offices, furrowed bureaucratic brows, admonitions not to leave from friends who were probably working for the government; even threats from a group of three men one dark night on the road. All this dragged on and on and then all at once they received tickets to leave the country in ten days on a Tuesday evening train to Warsaw. Kristina's mythical brother must have pulled strings of some kind in Poland.

Together, the four adults and the toddler sat in Diana's room on a Saturday afternoon with a bottle of black currant wine that Auntie had donated to the going-away celebration.

The couple had few proper friends outside of work and what friends they had would have made their own lives hard by associating with traitors like Martin and Kristina. Little by little, these friends disappeared, fading back like ghosts towards dawn. Even their colleagues at the office had been slower to say hello, and no one greeted them on the sidewalks any longer.

"You know I wish you well and I would have liked to see you off, but some things are impossible, even for me," Stonkus had said. If they were to leave Vilnius, the city had to die to them and they to it. They were not gone yet, but they were already on their Vilnius deathbeds.

Outside, late spring snow was falling.

"I'll be like that snow," said Auntie, all bundled up in layers of sweaters and scarves. "Your memory of me will melt and fade away."

The old woman had tears in her eyes. And then there were tears in Kristina's eyes too. She had been so determined, so sure of herself, so hard, but now she put her arms around Auntie.

"I'm sorry I made you suffer. I shouldn't have blamed you."

"That's how I knew you were like a real daughter to me. Real children make you suffer, but knowing it doesn't make it any easier for me to lose you."

"I wish you would stop weeping, Auntie," said Diana. "Look how lucky these three are! It's like winning the lottery. Most of this city would go with them if they could. You're going to freedom, my friends, and maybe riches too. You're going to make a real life for this little girl instead of a pinched and miserable time here. So come on, let's have a little happiness for a change."

A knock came at the door. They looked at one another.

"Were you expecting someone?" Auntie asked Diana.

"No."

They looked to Martin who had been holding Alina on his lap. He passed her over to Kristina and went to the door.

A telegraph man stood there in his cap.

"Martin Averka?"

"Yes."

"Telegram. Sign here."

He did as he was told and returned to the room where the others still sat. Martin took a pocket knife and slit open the envelope.

He was to present himself to a certain office at the train station at ten in the morning the next day, and he was to go alone.

"Alone?" Kristina asked.

"That's what it says."

IT SNOWED HEAVILY AGAIN that day, but most of the flakes melted as soon as they hit the ground, leaving a kind of grey slurry running in the gutters by the sidewalks. It looked as if spring would never come. At the train station, Martin had a hard time finding the office, which no one seemed able to direct him to, but in the end, it was in the corridor next to the station buffet and had a large window that overlooked the main platform where the train to Warsaw would be waiting for them the next week.

"Thanks for coming in," said Jonas Simon, a wry smile on his face as if his expression had not changed since they met before the wedding at the Office of Disorderly Applications.

"What are you doing here?" asked Martin.

"It's my alternate office. I have a few places I work from. You'd be surprised how many problems have to be dealt with in many parts of town."

"Problems?"

"Glitches, really. Please sit down."

Martin did as he was asked, wary, but unwilling to seem confrontational when he would be leaving the country shortly.

Simon ran his hand over his thick, combed-back hair as if to make sure it was still there.

"I just need to straighten out something about your plans to leave." He shuffled through his papers, didn't find what he was looking for, and then began to search in the desk drawers. The wall behind him consisted mostly of a window looking onto the platform and tracks.

He took a long time, but finally pulled a document from the lowest drawer. "Do you have your marriage certificate with you by any chance?"

"No, of course not. I don't carry it with me. But I can get it from home if you want."

"No need. Can you confirm that this is what it says?"

Martin bent over and read the facts that gave his and Kristina's names on the day they were married.

"Yes, that's right."

"And this is the name of your wife?"

"Of course."

"But the name of the woman who intends to leave next week is not this name, is it?"

"It's the same person. She went under the name Kristina Minta until we were married and then she took on my last name."

"But the woman intending to leave is not Kristina Averka or Kristina Minta. Her name is Esther Levinas."

"I don't understand."

"You are not married to Esther Levinas, my friend. For the marriage certificate to be legal, you need to have married the woman under her real name."

"But nobody knew her real name then."

"I'm sure you're aware ignorance of the law is no excuse. Of course, you are free to marry the woman, and to legitimize the child, but she seems to be leaving the country soon. I wonder if you will have time."

Jonas Simon had a look on his face to make it seem as if he had just told a magnificent joke and was awaiting some kind of praise. Martin needed to understand what this meant.

"We can straighten that up once we emigrate."

"I don't think so."

Who went out of their way to create this sort of mischief? Miniature devils were once said to wander the fields of Lithuania, looking to deceive unwary country folk. But since the countryside was emptying because of urbanization, the imps must have moved into the government offices in the cites to carry on their work of entrapment.

"What should I do?" Martin asked. If he could understand what the man wanted, maybe he could give it to him.

"Well, that's up to you. But from my perspective, you have two choices. You can keep her here and get the matter straightened out. It could take a little time, of course, but getting married is not that difficult a task to achieve."

"But we don't have passports any more. They were taken away. And then we'd need to apply to emigrate again and we might not get permission a second time. It could take years, or it might never happen."

"Ah, well. There's not much I could do about that."

"What's the other choice?"

"Well, she is the one who received the permission to emigrate with her child and husband. Her documents are all in order and so are the child's. You could let them go ahead."

So here it was, then, the spirit of Stalin that lingered long after the tyrant's death. The humour of the situation was what made this man so genial, so smiling. He was having a good time.

"I don't have much of value, but I have a reasonably good watch."

"I have no need of a watch. Besides, you should hang on to yours because time seems to be running out. As a matter of fact, you'll need money soon. I think you have quit your job, right? So you'll have no income and you'll need to live somehow. I suggest you return the train tickets."

"What for?"

"Well, you're clearly not going to use them so you might as well get your money back. The only question is, should you exchange just your ticket or the ticket of your wife as well? I guess the two of you will have to decide that."

"My wife has a brother in Poland. We understand he is an important person. He can make things happen."

"Well, I must say, that sounds almost like a threat. But believe me, your so-called brother-in-law could be a superman in Poland, but all of his influence there will mean nothing inside the Soviet

Union. And from what I can see, you won't be leaving the Lithuanian Soviet Socialist Republic any time soon."

Martin had been leaning forward in his chair and now he sat back.

"What does all of this mean?" he asked.

"Meaning? There is no meaning. There are only the rules. And you will have to play by them."

He walked out of the office in a daze and stood for a while in the corridor. He was not sure which way to go. A woman gestured at him in the corridor.

"Come here," she whispered and pulled him around the corner into the train station buffet, empty now between meals.

"Raminta," he said.

"Yes, it's me. What's wrong with you?"

"You wouldn't understand."

"The man in that office is a monster. I might understand better than you think. I'd do anything to cause him pain."

"What's he done to you?"

"Nothing you need to know. He likes to see our type squirm. I'm sorry he's got his talons into you."

Martin was still too dazed to take in her words. She read him, and patted him on the shoulder to console him. She turned the corner, opened the office door and went inside. Martin could hear a jolly sort of greeting from Simon, but he could not hear how Raminta responded.

34

"WHAT HAPPENS IF YOU just get on the train?" asked Diana. "You have the tickets and you have the documents you need for transit. Who is going to stop you?"

Alina was whimpering, running a low fever and needing to be held. She was in Kristina's lap as her mother sat up in the bed, letting the others fill the three chairs she had in her room. Auntie had stepped out for a moment, but she came back with an Afghan she laid on the child.

"They never let you go, do they?" said Auntie. "All these invisible bureaucrats keep track of everything you do or have done and they put them into files, like miniature prosecuting lawyers, building their cases. And they never let you see the files until someone like this Simon appears. Honestly, this country has always been full of devils. They just keep changing their form to suit the times."

"If we just get on the train, they'll take us off. Did you think the police, or KGB, or whoever they are will issue their orders and then go away and assume we'll obey? They have their people at the train station," said Kristina.

"There is a way to do it," said Martin. "I'm the one they're holding back. The two of you can get on the train and then I'll follow as soon as I straighten matters out here."

Nobody said anything to that. There were stories of wives still waiting to rejoin husbands who had fled fifteen years earlier, at the end of the war.

"I won't go without you," said Kristina. "Why should Alina grow up without a father? I want her to have everything I didn't have. If you can't go, we don't go either."

Martin turned on her. "How can you be so selfish?"

"What?"

"I've come back from the gulag. Pardoned or not, I'm still a marked man. While we worked for Stonkus we were like mice inside our holes, but as soon as I came out, the cats came for me. And if I am under a shadow, poor Alina is going to grow up under a shadow too. At least you can get her out, to where she can have a decent life."

"And what about you?"

"I'll get by. I'll get out eventually. I'll never give up."

"No," said Kristina. "I don't care what you say. I won't do it."

Alina began to cry and Martin felt as if he was on the verge of tears too, but it wouldn't do to show them. He had to convince Kristina to let him stay behind.

"What about that Polish brother of yours?" asked Diana.

"I only know him from his letters. What about him?"

"Couldn't he pull some strings? I hear he's a big shot of some kind."

"I thought that too," said Martin. "Simon said he would be a nobody here in Lithuania. He could be the king of Poland, but his reach wouldn't extend beyond the border."

"But what if you made it into Poland somehow?" asked Diana. "Do you think you'd be safe there?"

"Poland isn't America," said Martin.

"No, but it's not the Soviet Union either."

"The border has been sealed tight for years."

"But if you got out there somehow. Do you think your brother-in-law would find a way to keep you there?"

"Do you have something in mind?" asked Martin.

"We have over a week. Maybe I can think of something."

DIANA HAD SOME IDEAS, but she needed to get some wheels to turn. She did not consult Martin about them and so he was in a purgatory of sorts, frozen in a time when there was nothing to do but wait, as if his life depended on a roulette wheel.

He tried again and again to convince Kristina to use the tickets and flee, and usually she fought him and sometimes she wept and sometimes she seemed on the verge of accepting his plan. He went out walking to burn off some of his anxiety, and while out walking he glanced at a newspaper in a kiosk window and saw this headline:

Last of the Forest Bandits Finally Brought to Justice

Martin took the newspaper from the woman in the kiosk without studying the article under the headline, paid for it, folded it, and put it in his pocket. He carried it with him to a bench. He sat down and unfolded the newspaper in front of him, peering at the words.

They had finally found The Hawk and executed him. Poor man. Or was he a lucky man? It meant Kostas had not killed him back in 1948 and The Hawk managed to survive for over ten years. That was some consolation to Martin. Survival in the underground for that long had to be some kind of miracle. All the other partisans were probably dead or somewhere in the north. Once there were many thousands of partisans, and many more like Martin had been helpers. Now that was all over.

The Hawk was dead. Of course he was dead, and the news eventually chased his melancholy and replaced it with anger. Martin had sworn he would not be broken by what had happened to him and the others he loved and admired. It was important to move forward, to forget some of the feelings of the past if not the facts, but then news like this arrived. How was it possible to bear all of this?

Martin went on to read the list of The Hawk's alleged crimes. The article listed the attack on the town of Merkine in 1945, but described it as a failure. Martin knew better. The partisans had seized the town and held it for a day to raise the morale of the locals. Two collective farm directors were named as victims, and that was true enough, but the men were collaborators who had been given a chance to change their ways and turned down the ultimatum. There were many of the usual lies: The Hawk was a Nazi collaborator and executioner; he had killed a whole family in Rudnia.

The last part was interesting. They were ascribing those civilian deaths to the wrong person. Pretty Boy was guilty of that killing, and Pretty Boy would have been executed by The Hawk if it had been possible to carry out the verdict. It was too bad they didn't get it done in time, because one error led to another and Raminta had ended up paying the price. She was still paying it.

The Hawk had got away from Kostas the night Badger and Pike were killed. What must it have been like to live these last few years in the knowledge that everything they had hoped for, a new war and the collapse of the Soviet Union, was never going to happen? What was it like to be Kostas and to know that he had done the sensible thing, accommodated himself, and gone on to be beloved among the children and their parents?

And the children did love him. Again and again, Martin had read in the paper about school visits and readings by the talented Comrade Kostas.

And then he asked himself how such a man — a liar, a murderer — could still have such talent. Wasn't the ability to write a gift that came from God, or, if not from God, then from the muses? Why was it that this horrible man should have such a gift when someone like The Hawk, so brave, should die by execution?

Death was not given easily to partisans who were taken alive. Martin had been beaten when caught, but he had not resisted; and he had little to confess and they saw he was very young. The rule of thumb for other partisans taken alive was to resist torture for as long as they could in order to give their comrades time to evacuate the bunkers they inhabited. How much beating could one take? How many ghoulish cuts with pins and scissors could one withstand if one had to, and for how long?

News of The Hawk reminded Martin of what he had sworn to do for love of Badger and Pike and others like them. He remembered for the first time in a long time, the code name they had given him in the forest. He was Mole, a name he had not appreciated, but prescient somehow for a young man buried so long in the gulag.

He had some unfinished business, and this was the time to complete it.

35

PAŽAISLIS MONASTERY ASYLUM, 1959

IN HIS CELL, KOSTAS behaved like a plant being watered after a long time, one that was now raising its wilted branches and fanning out its curled leaves. Could it be true that writers needed alcohol to flourish? And yet his terrible yellow colour was deepening even as the man sat cross-legged on the side of his bed as if he were talking with a friend on a bench in a park.

So little could be undone from the past, but some things could be reckoned with.

"You say you worked in the service of literature, not your country or the proletariat?"

"Please, let's leave the slogans for the Mayday parade. I did all I did for art, if you like. It's the only thing worth anything."

"But you worked for art by way of the secret police?"

"Who says I ever did?"

"I know it for a fact. You won't get another drink unless you admit it. For all you know, I'm a figment of your imagination, so saying anything to me won't make a difference."

"Poor reasoning, my boy. I know a thing or two about interrogations. You offer me a drink to confess, and you know I'd say anything for a drink. You're like the Spanish Inquisition. You'll torture me until I confess what you want me to confess. And as for being a figment of my imagination, we've already settled that. How could a figment bring real vodka?"

"Games. How do you know you're not real either?"

"Because I am suffering. I suffer, therefore I am."

Kostas looked at Martin to share the joke, but Martin had never heard of Descartes either in high school, or in the gulag, or in his adult life as a carpenter.

"Just give me the drink, will you?"

Martin poured an inch in the cup.

"Miserably cheap of you, but I'll accept it."

He drank and then looked at the bottom of the cup as if another shot might be hiding in there.

"It was my fate to be a writer. I'm good for nothing else. It was my fate to be born in this small country with a language that's good nowhere else. I couldn't flee anywhere because what would I be there, a gas station attendant in Brazil? An elevator operator in New York? It's not enough to write verses and put them in a drawer, is it? A poet is like a bird that sings, but it doesn't sing without an audience. I can't help it that I am what I am."

"What's that got to do with anything?"

"It means I need to write verses. I can't help it. And I have to make them public no matter what the public happens to be at the moment."

"You're a justified collaborator."

"What a dismissive word that is, an easy word. Whenever I hear the word 'collaborator' it means someone has cooperated with your enemy, as if everyone didn't need to adapt to new rulers. In those terrible years, you adapted or you resisted and died. I adapted under the independence regime. I adapted under the Germans, and I adapted under the Soviets. And as for the latter, so did the Americans and the Brits, who loved Stalin and hated Hitler. They could only permit themselves to hate Stalin after he wasn't useful any more. It's not like I'm one of those Lithuanians who killed Jews for the Germans."

"What did you do for the Germans?"

"I wrote poetry. I'm a satirist. I satirized Stalin and I satirized others."

"But not the Germans at the time."

"I wasn't a fool."

"And that's what got you into trouble when the Soviets came back."

"Oh, yes."

"And you agreed to kill for them."

"I agreed to no such thing! What a monstrous accusation. I'm not going to sit here and listen to that kind of slander. Pour me a drink. Not a tablespoon, you miser. A real drink. Ach, all right. I'll take it. But you still owe me."

Kostas wiped his lips. With every drink he became less and less like the recovering invalid and more and more like the teacher and performer he had been in the past, one accustomed to an attentive public. Was it possible that alcohol had made him a performer in the first place?

"I agreed simply to keep my eyes open in the village where they sent me to teach. What do you think would have happened to me if I hadn't agreed to that, eh? You saw what happened when the Soviets came the first time. How many of those they shipped off are still alive? And after the war, they continued their harvest — you saw the train yards full of sullen men, wailing women, and crying children. I could have been one of them, and what good would that have done anyone, eh? I could have died in the north, or been brutalized by the criminals, or my talent could have withered on the permafrost."

"I survived there."

"Yes, many do, one way or another, but you're from the countryside, if I recall correctly. You are tough and numb to pain from working outside in all kinds of weather. Insensitive, really. I'm not blaming you. You're just a product of your peasant upbringing. I was like that too, but I softened as I became educated. A superior mind is usually found in a tender body. Besides, my duty was to my talent."

"What a strange word. You make it sound like you're a soldier of some kind. I love my friends and family and they're no kind of duty. I love the place I live too. But what is duty to your talent?"

"Some people believe in God and some in country, some in the Party and some in their families. We're surrounded by those bores, the unimaginative ones, the dullards who plod on like workhorses. We do need them, because who else would haul loads, cut grass, or dig wells?

"But some of us are different. I believe in art in general and literature in particular. It's a living thing. It needs to be tended like a garden, and it rewards you the way a garden does with both food and flowers."

From outside the door came the wailing of a man in the throes of his withdrawal. But no one would come for him now, after curfew. He might even be in a strait jacket. Martin had not heard anything like those sounds since his interrogation in prison in Vilnius after he was arrested.

"What kind of art is it if you write rhymes for children?"

"Don't you be so dismissive, like one of those practical people who knows engineering and nothing else, or only history and philosophy, as if they were all that counted. More people have read *Grimms' Fairy Tales* than Emmanuel Kant's philosophy. Children will remember my rhymes their entire lives, long after the classics have evaporated from their brains."

"You believe in literature enough to kill for it, but not enough to die for it. You are a rhyming assassin, not a rhyming martyr."

"But I am indeed a martyr. I suffered!"

"Talk to me about Badger."

Kostas did not seem in the least surprised by the demand.

"A very fine man. A man doomed, like me, to suffer in terrible times. But he had such a great weakness, similar to mine, really. He believed in ideas, in philosophy and patriotism and God. Badger believed in the sentimental heart beating inside his body.

"He was hungry for someone to talk to. I could see right through him. He played the rough leader, but he longed for someone like me. If I hadn't arrived, he would have needed to create me. But he believed in a version of his country — independence and democracy — as if those qualities would arise like spring grass after Stalin and Hitler had mown down a quarter of the country — it was impossible to achieve what he wanted. He was doomed by his idea of freedom, and he was a romantic who was willing to die for this impossible dream. Everybody claims to love Cervantes, but imagine Don Quixote tilting at the Kremlin. The image is ridiculous. Badger should have learned to live in the world as he found it instead of trying to change the world in impossible ways.

"I have wanted to serve the world too, but in a better way. I always wanted to enrich the language and the culture, to give something that couldn't be locked up in a cell or bought and sold. Mine is a long-term project. Governments come and go, but culture is a living thing that keeps on growing."

"If you remember him so easily, how is it that you don't remember me, Martin, the boy who helped you and him? The boy you told could be an engineer one day?"

"I have no memory at all of such a boy. Help me to remember." Kostas tipped the cup toward Martin.

Was it possible Kostas did not remember him? He had been so quick to recall Badger. Was Martin a fly Kostas had swatted away?

"I was a village boy."

"Ah yes, a village intellectual, a bit like me, I guess. Village boys are dreamers if they're smart, but their dreams don't generally add up to much."

"You told me I could be an engineer. It gave me hope."

"So you should thank me for letting you dream for a while. Stalin loved to build things. Engineers were what he wanted after the war. If you'd played your cards right, you could have joined the Communist Youth and, who knows, studied in Moscow where engineers have plenty of opportunities. But I'm guessing things didn't work out quite that way for you?"

"You sent me to the gulag and you don't even remember me."

"I'm sure you deserved it. Were you mixed up with Badger?"

"You lived in my father's house and I am the one who found Badger's body after you put a pair of bullets in his head."

Kostas tapped his cup on the table and Martin refilled it.

"I'm not saying I did that. I'm not saying I ever knew him well."

"He called you Skylark because of your poetry. He said you sang well."

"And did you have a code name as well?"

"They called me Mole, but I didn't last long under that name."

"Very amusing. So now you've peeked out of your burrow. But as to calling me Skylark, well, at least Badger had good taste. But let me ask you this. What happened to all those freedom fighters in the woods, eh? Where are they now? All dead or in prison, and their families too. And what happened to the stubborn types taken alive? They suffered terribly under interrogation and they all eventually gave up their secrets anyway. And what about the crimes of the partisans? They shot people who were accommodating themselves to the new reality. There were some nasty fascists among them, weren't there, men who had shot Jews and didn't get away? I'm not saying I shot Badger, but whoever shot him did him a favour. Maybe he deserved it, but even if he didn't, at least his death was fast. Now pour me another."

Martin did as he asked, wondering if he could get Kostas to confess to anything. The man was firm in his belief in himself, in the rightness of his actions, in the necessity the world order imposed on him Where did this stubbornness come from?

"Why do you drink so much?" asked Martin.

"Always the same question, one without an answer. I drink because I drink. But I also drink because I have a hole in me that I keep trying to fill. Creative people are unhappy with the world the way it is. They want something more. They pour their talent into their art and need to take in some kind of sustenance to compensate for it."

"Tell me about the men who recruited you."

"Now there was an evil bunch. I was a tool for them. They were going to use me to infiltrate partisans again and again. Put my neck at risk without end. There were others who did that. But the work was damned dangerous. You got no respect from your handlers. And they were so stupid they might kill you while they were trying to encircle a bunker you'd revealed to them. The partisans could kill you or your handlers could kill you and there was no easy way out."

"You found a way out. You killed Badger to ingratiate yourself to them, but you made sure people found out what you did. You were revealed as an agent, so they couldn't use you again. It was perfect."

"Clever boy. Maybe you could have gone far after all."

"What did they call you?"

"Who?"

"Your handlers. Badger called you Skylark, but you had to have another alias with them."

"Oh yes. They called me Crow. Damned insulting of them. Now give me a drink and make it a good one."

"Have you no remorse? I think of poor Pike as well, who took two bullets to the head."

"In times of peace, the moralists spring up like weeds in order to denounce anyone who fought against them in the war, as if most of the fighters had any choice, and to denounce those of us who were caught in the crosshairs. And everything I've done in my life is supposed to be blotted out by some great sin. As if everyone is nothing more than the worst thing he ever did. Oh, you armchair moralists. Such noble comments! Such ethics! As if the moralist themselves would have been heroes. But no one wants to die. You'd do anything to avoid it."

"Some are willing to die."

"They are fools who die useless deaths."

"Do you know Badger didn't die as soon as you shot him? He was badly wounded and he couldn't talk. He begged me to finish him off. I had to look into the eyes of a man pleading for death. He died for the truth."

Kostas laughed. "The truth. What a joke. There is no truth. There are only stories of one kind or another."

Martin shook his head and poured Kostas a large measure, over half the cup.

"Oh, there is truth all right. I know it, because we all know we are living in a lie here in this monstrous regime, and if a big lie exists, truth must exist somewhere too."

"Sophistry, really."

"How is it you can drink so much without passing out? You've already had more than half a bottle."

"I can drink half a bottle before lunch. Liquor elates me. It makes ideas flow. It finds my rhymes for me."

"Then let's find some rhymes together. Do you think you can take another?"

"Take another? Young man, you're an amateur compared to me. There's not even very much left in the bottle."

"Oh, I have more than what you see. But before I open any more bottles, let me ask you this again. Do you feel any remorse?"

"Such a Catholic country. Why does everyone need to confess in this country?"

"To ease our consciences for the crimes we have committed and for the ones we intend to commit. To save our souls."

"I regret nothing but the weakness of my liver. Now pour me another."

"Very well then."

What little was left of his liver would never withstand much more of this. Martin poured out a full glass.

"I want to remind you that the alcohol can kill you," said Martin.

"I'm an adult. I know my limits."

"Look, we have pretty much finished a bottle of vodka. I have two more bottles with me. Should I leave them behind?"

"What a question! Of course you should. Very generous of you."

"They say your liver is in danger of giving out entirely."

"I'll be fine."

"Are you sure?"

"I swear it. And I am grateful you came by with these gifts and to have a chat about old times."

"Then I'll have one more drink with you," said Martin. "I propose a toast to the future."

"Whose future?"

"Why, yours and mine. May we each get what we deserve."

Even in his drunkenness, Kostas sensed the irony, but a drink was a drink and he would not refuse.

Martin drank with him and then took out the two other bottles and placed them on the table. He tied up the string on his bag, opened the window, swung away the bars and set the pack outside. He looked back at Kostas once before stepping out, and the poet saluted him merrily.

Once outside, Martin lingered for a while, and then looked back in the window. Kostas had already opened the second bottle and was pouring it into his glass. Time had passed and the sun was setting, and it was hard to tell if the awful colour of Kostas's skin came through liver failure alone, or from the orange light cast by the fading sun.

36

1959

THE TRAIN TO WARSAW arrived from Leningrad at eleven forty-five and departed from Vilnius fifteen minutes later. Jonas Simon stepped out of his office and walked along the platform as passengers loaded themselves into their carriages. Among them were men with billed caps and quilted jackets and women in headscarves. Some of their bundles were very large. One woman hung out of a window as her man passed a massive knotted sheet with its unknown contents up to the opening and then pushed from below as she pulled from above until the bag popped inside.

Travellers from Leningrad slipped out into the station to buy coffee and sandwiches, vodka and chocolate and biscuits, if available, for the ten-hour ride to Warsaw in a train without a dining car. The distance was not all that long, but the gauge of the tracks was narrower in Poland than it was in the Soviet Union, and so just inside the Polish border the train was raised and the so-called trucks, consisting of wheels and axles, were changed to accommodate the new size.

Martin Averka and his family had gone missing two days earlier. Simon suspected they naively intended to get on the train in Vilnius because they had not bothered to return the train tickets for refund. Or mother and child might show up to board the train and bid a tearful farewell to Martin. It would be amusing to see which choice the man had made. Through an unfortunate oversight, all the original permissions and border documents had not been confiscated from him. But there should be no problem as long as they did not board the train.

To be safe, in a few hours he would call the border crossing at Bruzgi, where the train left the Byelorussian SSR and paused inside Poland at Kuznica to change the trucks of wheels. One final check, just to be safe.

Simon had never been to Poland. Close neighbour though it might be, the country was hard to get into and the object of many dreams of Soviet citizens. If the Baltics, including Lithuania, were considered something like the west in the Soviet Union, so much more sophisticated, still smelling of interwar independence, Poland might as well be America itself. Not exactly America, of course, but the closest approximation one could conceivably reach under lucky circumstances; perhaps as a singer or dancer in a folk troupe on tour, or a farm drainage specialist attending a conference at the Grassland Reclamation Centre in Falenty, a hop, skip, and a jump from Warsaw. Simon sighed. KGB officers of his rank never received perks of international travel. Whenever he got to go anywhere, it was always some kind of conference on a subject like deviant psychology in what might as well be a warehouse on the outskirts of Smolensk.

Still, he wasn't complaining. The life was good enough as long as he got his job done, and he had every intention of getting his job done.

Simon had two soldiers with him, working their way through the railway carriages from front to back to make sure Averka's family had not slipped on by some sort of subterfuge. To be sure, after they were done, Simon had the men search the cars from back to front. Following standard procedure, a railway policeman had already walked a German shepherd along the wheels, sniffing for anyone tucked in the undercarriages somewhere precariously close to the rails.

Eventually, Simon received the all-clear from his operatives. He and his two soldiers, a pair of short-haired youths, stood on the platform to watch the train pull out of the station, and they saw it gain speed and grow smaller in the distance.

SENOVĖ WAS THE LAST train stop within the borders of the Lithuanian Soviet Socialist Republic. After that, the cars passed into the Byelorussian Republic, also Soviet, so there was no border control there. That came when the train reached the frontier with Poland seventy-five kilometres later. Senovė did not really have a railway station, just a platform with a bench and an overhanging roof. The train rarely picked up passengers there, but the place did supply goods to Poland from time to time so the train made a whistle stop.

"Not too many bags," Diana had suggested. "But not empty-handed either or you'll look like runaways. And nothing of value inside beyond clothing. Make sure Alina is dressed as beautifully as possible. Put a ribbon in her hair. A child is distracting to some people with a sentimental side."

"But how do we know our tickets will still be good there?"

"You didn't return the tickets, so your places will be empty, but expect the travellers to resent you because they'll have to move their bags off your seats."

"And the conductor?"

"That's the first tricky part. Not exactly dangerous unless you cause a fuss. The conductor's job is to make sure you have tickets, nothing more, not usually."

"Nothing more?"

"Well, yes, the conductor will report anything suspicious to the guard."

"Is there a guard on the train?"

"Maybe. Not always. There will be border police later, but some of the conductors work for the KGB as well."

"What if they ask why we didn't board the train in Vilnius?"

"None of their business, but if necessary, you could say you needed to deliver medication from Vilnius for your grandmother in a village nearby."

"My grandmother? Why didn't she just come to the station to get her medication?"

"She's so old she can barely walk. Have you no respect for your elders?"

"How can you know all these things?"

"Train stations and railways are a separate world from the one we live in here, with separate rules. You have to learn to operate in them."

The compartment consisted of two bunk beds facing one another across the space on the floor. Passengers slept on them by night and sat on the lower ones by day. As Diana had predicted, the other pair of passengers, a massive peasant woman and her daughter, sullenly gave up the space on the facing lower bunk by moving their bags above. Martin helped her and received no thanks.

With a giant white bow on her hair, Alina elicited no interest from the woman, but the teenage daughter smiled at the child and patted her shoulder, and said to her mother in Byelorussian that Alina was cute. Alina was fascinated by the train and stared out the window while holding on to the inside frame with both hands.

Kristina had her hair tied back in a scarf. She seemed serene. Martin hoped he projected the same sense of calm.

When the conductor finally showed up, she turned out to be a young woman, one who wore the frozen face of officialdom so accustomed to freeloaders, liars, and smugglers on trains. She took their tickets and examined them.

"Why didn't you board the train in Vilnius?" she asked in Russian.

Martin told her the story he had been told to tell, and as he finished speaking, he saw the conductor look at him hard. Was this going to be it, then? The plan had sounded too good to be true, and here they were undergoing scrutiny on the first juncture.

"I think you went to school in Rudnia, didn't you?" the conductor asked.

If she knew that, she knew a great deal more. He waited for her to step out into the corridor to summon help.

He hesitated and must have betrayed his unease.

"Didn't you used to have a nickname, Mole?" She said these words in Lithuanian.

He looked at her hard. For all her fierceness, she was pretty with a few strands of hair escaping from beneath her cap. Despite her impassive face, he felt a moment of warmth toward her but did his best not to show it.

"Sparrow."

She glanced knowingly at him for a moment, and then immediately became officious again, explaining there was no restaurant car on the train. The train would stop for half an hour at the train station in Grodno, but the passengers should not wander off too far because the train would not wait for them if they were late. The toilets would be locked shut for four hours just inside the Polish border as the wheels were changed at Kuznica. If they needed to do their business during that time they should disembark and find some bushes. Tea with lemon would be served to all passengers in an hour. There was no sugar.

Once she had finished this little speech, she turned to the mother and daughter on the lower bunk across the way and repeated the words in Russian before leaving without looking back.

"She recognized you from your childhood," whispered Kristina in Lithuanian.

"Yes."

"Is that a good or a bad thing?"

"Well, she knows what I was involved in then. But I know what she was involved in too."

He did not say that most people who had been caught by the

KGB eventually gave up their secrets. Sparrtow had been such a small part of his partisan past that he had said nothing about her under interrogation. But had she done the same when she was caught? Or was she not caught at all? Probably the latter or she never would have landed a job as a train conductor.

Still, Martin couldn't be sure of her intentions. He listened hard in case determined steps came down the corridor toward them.

JONAS SIMON HAD NO further use for the two soldiers who had been assigned to him that day, so he set them free, and they left the station to smoke cigarettes by a side door.

"Do you think we should report back now?" the one asked the other as they stood on the broken curb.

"What, and to be assigned to some other detail? We just wait around here as long as we can, maybe have a little lunch and report back too late in the afternoon to get anything new to do."

As they stood there, a boy on the verge of adolescence and wearing a filthy coat too long for him approached them.

"Hello friends," he said.

"Bugger off. We don't have any spare change, and your coat stinks. Or maybe it's you."

"I'm not after money," said the boy.

"What do you want?"

"My boss found a lost case of black currant wine and he is selling the bottles cheap."

"How much?"

"One rouble each."

The one soldier looked to the other. "Do you have any money?"

"Five roubles. We could buy five bottles and sell them for two roubles each."

"Or sell four bottles at three roubles each and still have one left over for ourselves."

"How many bottles did you say you had?"

As it turned out, he had only two, but they could still drink one and make a profit. They made the boy stay with them until they opened one of the bottles and sniffed it and the smell of black currants came up.

"This better not be just juice."

"Try it," said the boy.

One took a swallow and almost lost the mouthful for coughing due to its strength.

"That's not exactly wine. Very strong. Better than wine," he said, hacking and gasping for breath.

They let the boy go, intending to share one of the bottles after they went off duty that night. On the other hand, a bottle in hand was a very tempting thing and the buzz one soldier had from a single mouthful was so delightful that the second wanted a mouthful too. They were not intending to report back for some time, so they walked out to the cargo yard and found a place between a car undergoing renovation and a pile of scrap metal. By good fortune, there was a bench there, and they could drink unseen.

SIMON, FOR HIS PART, managed at the station buffet to buy a bowl of *solyanka* soup and a couple of meat pastries that he took back to his office to eat with a glass of tea on the side. He ate and drank and looked at the monstrous stack of documents in his inbox. The paperwork was endless. He would need to do it but had no enthusiasm for the task. When a knock came at his door, he was glad for the distraction, but put on his dour face to give the right impression of a serious man.

Raminta walked into the room and shut the door behind her.

"What are you doing here?"

He had use for her and summoned her from time to time, but did not like it that she should come looking for him. She probably wanted something, and he was in no mood to give it.

"It's my birthday today," said Raminta.

He laughed. "Congratulations. Good for you. Should I give you a rouble so you can buy yourself a box of chocolates?"

"Actually, I have a bottle of good black currant wine and a lemon cake. I was wondering if you might want to join me downstairs for a drink."

"It's a bit early, isn't it?" He reflected on the prospect. "You could bring the bottle up here."

"I could, but it's more private down there, as you know."

"I don't ordinarily drink sweet wine. It gives me a hangover."

"Not this one. It's barely sweet at all and very strong, and it goes well with the cake."

Something stirred in him. She was a terrible whore, but still young and attractive in her own way. He was mildly interested in her, less than she gave herself credit for, he was sure. And he had never tasted black currant wine but imagined he would not be terribly fond of it. On the other hand, a drink after lunch might help to pass the long afternoon. And then there was the stack of paperwork on his desk. In the end, it was not so much the attraction of Raminta and her drink so much as his aversion to the papers that led him to follow her down to her lair a few minutes later so they would not be seen by anyone going together.

THERE WERE MANY FORESTS in this part of Byelorussia and many level crossings where local guards stood with red sticks in hand to alert the empty country roads behind them that a train was passing. The forest reminded Martin of his childhood home in Lyn Lake. He always felt safe in forests because one could melt into them if necessary.

Here and there, modest wooden houses stood close to the tracks, often with garden plots for cabbages and carrots, onions and potatoes. Sometimes the train slowed to a crawl for no reason Martin could discern; when this happened, Kristina reached out to hold his hand. Alina was oblivious to their tension and babbled happily with the Byelorussian girl, although the child barely spoke any language yet.

And then the train pulled in to Grodno. A heated exchange took place between the girl and her mother about who had the right to get off the train to see what was available at the kiosk; in the end, the mother got off while her daughter settled in sullenly on her bunk with her arms crossed.

The corridor was full of movement as some passengers got off and others boarded. Occasionally men in various uniforms passed by and looked into the compartment without saying anything. Some seemed to be railway officials and a pair must have been soldiers because they carried side arms.

Martin looked back when they looked in, wearing at all times the slightly aggressive stance he had learned in the gulag, never seeming too friendly because friendliness betrayed weakness and awakened the bloodlust of predatory officialdom.

OUT IN THE VILNIUS train yard, the first bottle of black currant wine went down very well indeed, and wiped out all thoughts of profit on the second bottle. It would have been nice to have something to eat because the drink made them hungry, but it would have been risky for the soldiers to show themselves. After the second bottle, it seemed like a good idea to stretch out for a nap right where they were after a brief tussle over who got the right to lie on the bench and who had to lie down on the ground.

DOWN IN HER BASEMENT room, Raminta had not only a bottle of black currant wine, but also a bottle of mineral water and a lemon cake and a bowl of hazelnuts set on a narrow table across from the narrow bed.

Simon looked up at her in surprise after coming through the second of double doors.

"Quite a spread," he said. "But isn't this the place where you work? Didn't you want to celebrate your birthday somewhere at a table with your friends?"

"I still might, but I thought it would be nice to spend an hour here with you."

"I'm not sure I have an hour. It's cramped in here, isn't it? I mean, enough room to work in, but not really a pleasant place to eat cake and drink wine."

"It will be pleasant enough after the first drink."

She was right. The cake was surprisingly good too. After the second glass of wine, he remembered his time as a conscript in the army and how hungry he had been then and how a cake such as they had between them would have been an unimaginable treat.

For all the fact that Raminta was a whore, she seemed able to listen better than anyone else, certainly better than his wife, and he appreciated that. He warmed toward her, especially since she'd invited him to join her when he was sure she had other customers who would be happy for a drink.

And a little more. His appreciation warmed when she didn't seem opposed to doing for him what she usually did for money.

AT THE BRUZGI CROSSING into Poland, guards walked along the side of the train as their dog sniffed its way underneath. Footsteps sounded above as another pair walked the top.

Martin, Kristina, and Alina were made to stand outside the compartment as two border guards examined the documents of the woman and her daughter. She was invited to open her suitcases, which she did, and one of the guards went through it carefully, rubbing the seams of the dresses and trousers in case something had been sewn in there.

Then mother and daughter were told to leave the compartment and Martin and Kristina and Alina were invited to go back in as the guards sat across from them to examine their documents.

It was hard to tell exactly what kind of official the grey-haired

man was. Border guard? Customs official? He looked at the photos
on the documents and then looked at the faces of Martin, Kristina,
and Alina. He held an exit permit up to the light to see if any
changes had been made on it.

"Leaving the fatherland, are you?"

"We are reuniting with our family in Poland," said Kristina.

"Life's not good enough for you here?"

"It's a good life, but family is family."

"Any gold or jewelry you're taking out?"

"No."

He fell silent and looked at their papers again and again. He stood
up and began to walk away with them.

"Is everything all right?" asked Kristina. "We're going to need
those documents on the Polish side."

"I'm just going to check something in Vilnius."

IN VILNIUS IN JONAS Simon's office, the telephone rang again and
again. There was no one there to answer it. Down in Raminta's
lair, Simon was half asleep in a combination of postprandial tor-
por, post-coital relaxation, and serious intoxication. He was not
fully asleep, and indeed was beginning to wake up as the need
to urinate grew. He hoped Raminta would come back from the
bathroom quickly because soon he would need to take his turn
and she'd locked the door behind her.

THE POLISH CUSTOMS GUARD was much less obstreperous than the
Soviet one. He was used to seeing happy people leaving the Soviet
Union, and this happiness reflected upon his country and on him.
In his mind, his own life was shit, but it seemed to be so much worse
in the Soviet Union; his *schadenfreude* put him in a jolly mood.

Just after he left, the train was shunted onto to special tracks
where the wheels would be changed. Many passengers got out here
to walk around, after being cooped up, or to seek out bushes behind

which to urinate. They had a few hours and there was plenty of time to look around, although the setting was industrial, not really pretty at all. There was no kiosk with newspapers and candies, so some of the passengers wandered a little farther up a road to see if there was anything worth seeing.

Martin and Kristina, with Alina holding hands between both of them, walked out as well. They left their luggage on the train because, after all, they were just going out for a short stroll. Martin looked for the conductor he'd known as Sparrow, but she had not crossed into Poland. He blessed her in his mind.

They came to a side road, and they walked up it, holding on to Alina between them when she wanted to walk and carrying her when she did not. Large pieces of obscure industrial machinery lay in the scraggly yards on either side of the road, much of it rusted. There were no people around, the railway workers left far behind where the men worked on the wheels. They came to a garage for trucks, double width and tall, but with the doors closed. A driveway led around behind, and they followed this driveway to where a car was waiting. They got in the car.

"Hello, brother," Kristina said to the man at the wheel. He was considerably older, greying at the temples, and he did not look entirely happy.

"Hello, sister. We'll catch up later. All of you keep your heads down until I tell you to sit up. This is going to be very tricky. Just getting out of this place is going to be a challenge. Then it's going to get harder. I'm not even sure I'll be able to hang on to you once they find out you're in this country, so don't get your hopes up."

"Quite a welcome."

"Don't be ridiculous. I found you, and I'm happy to have you here. As to this man you have with you, his presence is giving us all a headache. I just hope he is worth the trouble."

37

RONCESVALLES AVENUE, TORONTO, CANADA, 1969

ALINA STUDIED THE WIDE bolts of cloth set upon rollers on a wall in the store. One of the rolls had a furry leopard design on it, like something she would see on a bedspread in an old lady's house. There were rolls of black, blue, and grey wool for men's and women's suits, as well as silk lining in two colours. Spools of thread and balls of yarn stood on the shelves, and over on the women's side, there were bolts of printed cotton, taffeta, velveteen, brocade, and rayon.

None of this was interesting to the girl and the place smelled bad, like the suits of old men.

Alina would not even be able to describe this store to anyone because it was not even a clothing store. Or not just one. There were large jars of instant coffee, coffee beans in five-pound bags, cocoa, but no sugar. Cooking oil in tins. Shoes, hats, galoshes. Old-lady Turkish scarves in many colours. Gigantic bottles of aspirin and twelve-pack boxes of yellow Wrigley's Juicy Fruit and white Spearmint chewing gum, but no individual packs a girl could beg her mother to buy.

When she became too bored for words, her mother let her walk out on the sidewalk as far down the block as the first set of traffic lights. This neighbourhood was so different from the suburb where they lived in a house with a picture window that gave onto a sunny yard. Here the houses she saw down the side streets were big and old with no driveways and broken up into apartments. On the main street itself, men and women walked about speaking in languages she did not understand, although her parents understood them. And the older ones looked like they did their clothes shopping in the store where she had left her mother.

The shops on the street down toward the stop light were kind of interesting but not that interesting. One of the windows showed children's books, but from what she could see, none of them were in English and none of them had Disney characters on their covers. One food store displayed a variety of cooked dishes — fried smelts stacked in a neat ring with their heads placed to face the outside of the plate. Hamburgers more like big meatballs, with chunks of onion visible from the sides. Fried schnitzels in a pyramid. And, at last, something she craved, a bowl of cream fudge candies, "cow candies" she called them for the picture on the package.

But her mother would buy none of these for her once she was done in the store. She made Alina get in the car and then immediately put on the sunglasses that she wore all the time.

"Why no candies?"

"Those packages I send cost a fortune. That old witch must make a healthy profit on top of the money she sends to Moscow."

"Why do you have to spend all our money there?"

"Because your grandmother is poor and she needs the help."

"Dad's mother."

"Right."

"What about your parents?"

"We've been through this a hundred times. My parents are dead."

"In Lithuania, I know, I know. Nobody in school even knows where that is. If you send packages to my grandmother, why don't you send packages to my uncle?"

"Because he lives in Sweden. He doesn't need our packages."

"You mean he's rich?"

"No. But he gets by. It was hard for him to start over again at his age after he left Poland."

"Because he's a Jew, right?"

"That's right. You keep going over all of this. You know this. We'll tell you more when you get older."

"I'm starving. Can we get something to eat?"

"There will be food when you get home."

She opened the glove compartment because sometimes her mother kept hard candies there. They were European hard candies with paper twists at either end. She didn't really like them if she had a choice, but she had no choice and anyway there was nothing in the glove compartment except a kind of funny ruler that she pulled out.

"What's this?"

"It's a slide rule. Your father uses it at work. He must have forgotten it here. Leave it out on the dashboard and we'll take it inside for him."

"What does a slide rule do that's different from a ruler?"

"It makes calculations."

"Like multiplying and dividing?"

"Right, and more. Engineers and scientists use them."

"It sounds boring."

That was the problem with life. They drove past High Park with its boring trees and its boring pond. It was all right in the winter when she could skate on the ice, but now it had not much to offer besides old men sitting around chess boards.

"Mom?"

"What is it?"

"Did you and dad ever do anything interesting, or were you always boring like this?"

AFTERWORD
AND ACKNOWLEDGEMENTS

ABOUT TEN YEARS AGO, a stranger from Lithuania began to write intriguing letters to me. The true stories he told were so vivid and extraordinary that I encouraged my correspondent, Eirimas Martūnas, to continue writing. He sent a few dozen more missives describing the life of his father's family in a remote Lithuanian village close to the Belarusian border. (At the time of the action in this novel, Belarus was known as Byelorussia.) Death or deportation came there frequently from the hands of German occupiers during the war, followed by varieties of Soviet violence. Anti-Soviet partisans tried to protect the locals, but these partisans could be violent against collaborators as well.

Villagers were terrorized again and again.

And the village schoolteacher, Kostas Kubilinskas, played a central role in the violence. He was sent to the village of Lyn Lake (*Lynežeris* in Lithuanian) to teach elementary school but also secretly as a KGB agent to infiltrate the local anti-Soviet partisan resistance. Kubilinskas eventually fulfilled the second part of his assignment by shooting one of the sleeping partisans in the head and betraying another four who died in their bunker while under attack by Soviet authorities.

Having murdered the partisan, Kubilinskas fled to Vilnius where he became the most celebrated children's writer of Lithuania, widely translated in the Soviet period. He was a Dr. Seuss of the Soviet Union, but with a troubling secret that may have contributed to the alcoholism that killed him in a rehabilitation facility near Moscow in 1962. I dubbed him The Rhyming Assassin and plunged into research concerning the period of the 1950s, intending to write a simple novel loosely based on Kubilinskas's crimes.

That was the idea that started a journey of ten years that took me through KGB archives and several other sources that led to an expansion of the novel far beyond the story of this murderous versifier.

Important sources included Vilnius KGB files which I researched for the official story of Kostas Kubilinskas with the help of Marija Čepaitytė (who also defended me when the archivist accused us of stealing files.) These Russian language sources were then translated into Lithuanian and explained to me by Erika Paliukaitė. Thanks to Rūta Melynė of the Lithuanian Cultural Centre for finding these two brilliant women.

I was further inspired by the work of some excellent nonfiction writers. Julia Šukys's biography of Ona Šimaitė, *Espistolophilia*, tells the story of this librarian's saving of Vilnius Jewish children during The Holocaust. Šukys's depiction of Ona Šimaitė and other characters inspired the construction of some of my fictional characters.

A very vivid picture of post-war Vilnius came out in Gražina Mareckaitė's *Šiapus ir anapus Vilniaus vartų* (*From Both Sides of the Vilnius Gates*). I placed my fictional characters in the neighbourhood Mareckaitė portrays in her memoir and imagined an alternative biography for one of the characters she describes.

Lionginas Baliukevičius, code-named Dzūkas, was a partisan whose posthumously published diary describes the betrayal of the partisans by Kostas Kubilinskas. Baliukevičius was an intellectual who longed for the company of like-minded friends, and Kubilinskas exploited Baliukevicius's need for intellectual nourishment.

Adolfas Ramanauskas, code-named "The Hawk" was a partisan leader who went into hiding after the movement failed in 1952. He was caught four years later and tortured and executed. His remains were buried secretly, but found in an unmarked grave in 2018. He was posthumously accused of many crimes, none of which were substantiated.

I often spend time in Vilnius in a very dusty used bookstore, Knygavisiems, a place with atrocious light and no chairs. My arthritic knees complain when I crouch down to look at lower shelves, but the pain is worth it because I come upon unlikely treasures. One such treasure consisted of the minutes of the meetings of the Lithuanian Writers' Union, covering the period from the late forties through to the early sixties. By going through this book carefully, I found the trajectory of the career of Kostas Kubilinskas, from promising young poet, to disgraced bourgeois nationalist, to misunderstood and underrated hero of children's literature. I used a modified version of this book to have my Martin trace the career of Skylark, my fictional double for Kostas Kubilinskas.

I came upon the story of the Vilnius book depository, that marvelous and mysterious former church with its enlightened director, in the popular Lithuanian press.

I returned to the late partisan, Povilas Pečiulaitis's, *Šitą paimkite gyva (Take This One Alive)*, for his depiction of his deportation and time in the gulag.

The Holocaust in Lithuania was particularly brutal and the murder by Germans and their Lithuanian accomplices has been explored in many memoirs, histories, and novels, most recently by Canadian novelist Gary Barwin in *Nothing the Same, Everything Haunted*. I was particularly moved by what happened to traumatized children who survived that horror.

Not only did Eirimas Martūnas spur the writing of this novel, thanks to his many letters, he also took me to Lyn Lake and the nearby town of Marcinkonys to introduce me to local people who described their post-war lives in that difficult and dangerous place. These included Antanas and Marija Akulavičius, Ona Mortūnienė and Stasys Avižnis. This latter man's memoir, *Gyvi jie mano atmintyje (They are Alive in my Memory)*, a history of his imprisonment by the Soviets, and his torture, and deportation to the gulag were useful inspirations for part of this novel.

The character Petras Vaitkus in this novel was inspired by the life of Kazys Jakubėnas, a poet who helped save Jewish children. He was stripped and beaten by the KGB and left to freeze to death outside Vilnius in 1950.

Many thanks to my readers who made so many contributions to this manuscript as it went through a dozen versions. These include my wife, Snaige Sileika and sons, Dainius and Gintaras. Also Joe Kertes and my agent, Anne McDermid. Generous help was offered to me by a variety of people, and in no special order here they are: Aušra Marija Sluckaitė, Jonas Jurašas, Silvija Sondeckienė, Mindaugas Šnipas, Danulė and Antanas Šipaila, Eglė Jurkevičienė, Stasys Baltakis, Laimonas Briedis, and others I may have forgotten over the ten-year span of writing, but to whom I remain indebted. Thank you to Marc Côté and his team at Cormorant Books for believing in this book.

I am grateful for generous funding from the Canada Council and the Ontario Arts Council, both of which permitted me to take several research trips. The Canadian Embassy Office in Vilnius has helped me again and again, in particular when I became stranded in Vilnius at the beginning of the world-wide Covid lockdowns. The office connected me with Global Affairs Canada, which arranged for strays like me to buy tickets on one of the rare planes flying out of that region.

Thanks for the refuge I found in the Toronto Writers' Centre, a good workplace for writers who would otherwise procrastinate their way through whole days at home.

The word *gulag* is used in this novel at least a decade before it was coined as a shorthand word for Soviet prison work camps. Those living in the time depicted in this novel, the forties and fifties, would have said *Siberia* or used a circumlocution, such as *the place where polar bears roam*. The latter two sound inappropriate to my contemporary ears, so I took the liberty of inserting a modern word into the past.

Although I keep intending to write about something else, I return again and again to the stories of Lithuania for the painful and grotesque suffering people went through in that small country, before, during, and after the Second World War. But I don't go there just to describe that time, place, and people. I go in order to find what the human heart is capable of under great pressure in terrible circumstances, and how it is possible to survive these horrors and prevail.

As I write these words late in 2022, I cannot know what the political and military situations will be like in Eastern Europe when this novel comes out in 2023. At the moment, the brutal, hot war of Russia's invasion of Ukraine and the subsequent flight of millions of refugees dominate the news and seem to echo some of the events in this novel. They remind me of Faulkner's frequently quoted statement: "The Past is not dead. It isn't even past." As a writer of historical novels, I aim to write not historical stories, but *forever* stories about the human condition, sad or joyful as it may sometimes be.

We acknowledge the sacred land on which Cormorant Books operates. It has been a site of human activity for 15,000 years. This land is the territory of the Huron-Wendat and Petun First Nations, the Seneca, and most recently, the Mississaugas of the Credit River. The territory was the subject of the Dish With One Spoon Wampum Belt Covenant, an agreement between the Iroquois Confederacy and Confederacy of the Anishinaabe and allied nations to peaceably share and steward the resources around the Great Lakes. Today, the meeting place of Toronto is still home to many Indigenous people from across Turtle Island. We are grateful to have the opportunity to work in the community, on this territory.

We are also mindful of broken covenants and the need to strive to make right with all our relations.